Endless PURSUIT

BETHANY ROSA

GALLATIN PUBLISHING

1

MCASSHOLE

Poppy

"Thanks for the ride, Matt." I lean in to hug him.

"No problem. I'll be right behind you on Saturday and leave the car here since I'll only be gone one night. Sorry I can't go with you," he says as he closes the trunk.

"Don't be. We'll be busy with the bachelorette party and rehearsal dinner anyway. I'm so excited to meet Cici's friends."

"Have fun and give her a big hug for me."

"I will. See you soon." With a final wave and smile, I head inside the airport.

Once I'm through the dreaded security checkpoint, I make it to the gate with fifteen minutes to spare and find a seat. I text another thank-you to Matt and message Cici that I'm here. I'm on my way to be a bridesmaid at her wedding. We met when she moved to Bozeman a few years ago and were at the same real estate company as new agents. It wasn't long until we became inseparable and have been besties ever since.

She was the friend I never knew I needed—someone wild and

carefree, who brought me out of my shell. She was the yin to my yang and pushed me while I reined her in.

Sadly, she recently moved back to her hometown of San Diego to marry Eli, somebody she'd dated before moving away. Super happy for her, but for me…? Not so much. I still have Matt, the third in our trio, but he's not as good a wingman as Cici. It's a little harder to pick up guys when you're with one.

I put my phone down and glance around. Bozeman is still a small town, and it's common to see a familiar face. However, these days, it's less and less likely with all the tourists coming in because of that *Yellowstone* show. It never fails to amuse me when new clients ask if anything like that really happens. My answer is always the same: a shrug with a quick "I hope not," leaving them to wonder.

I'm still perusing my surroundings when the hottest guy I've ever laid eyes on catches my attention. He's in a suit, which is the first thing to make him stand out. Bozeman's business attire is casual, and ties are rare.

His smooth, chiseled jaw contrasts with sideburns that should look that good on no one. His dark brown hair is perfectly trimmed and styled, like he's about to do a photo shoot, not sit on a cramped plane for hours. He reminds me of the lawyers on the show *Suits,* and I can't seem to drag my eyes away.

He catches me staring and raises one eyebrow. It's like I can read his mind, asking me if I like what I see. My cheeks heat as I divert my attention to my phone in embarrassment. I'm sure the guy knows he's hot, so I won't inflate his ego any more than it probably is. It's not as if someone like that would spare me the time of day anyway.

I'm not unattractive, but I tend to give off nerd vibes that turn men away. Could be the freckles that are basically unavoidable if your hair color rhymes with bed. Add in the glasses, since I'm too lazy most days to put in my contacts, and you're left with a pretty librarian. Notice I didn't say *sexy.* I'm just not the stereotypical idea of a hot date.

I'm twenty-five, single, have zero prospects, and expectations higher than a kite. I'm losing hope and I blame my parents. They met young, have been married for thirty years, and are still as in love, if not more so, than when they said, '*I do*'. They're the main reason I'm so picky, but after watching Cici sampling all the goods before her happily ever after, I'm rethinking my thought process.

Though that's hard to do with my brother's parting words before he left for the Navy. He said every male is out for one thing and one thing only, and if you give it to him, you might as well kiss them goodbye.

So I've decided that when the right man comes along, I'll know. At least, that's what I keep telling myself. Maybe my luck will turn, and a single hottie will be at the wedding. Sparks will fly, and we'll have an instant connection. That's how it works in the movies, anyway, so I'm praying it happens.

I chance another glance in Suits' direction, and this time I catch him staring at me. He's smirking, like he knew I'd look again. Jerk with an inflated ego, but then again, that's to be expected when the guy looks that good.

I'm saved from any more embarrassment when the gate agent announces boarding. Suits stands up and walks over to the line for zone one, which tells me he's blessed not only in the looks department but also the entitled one. Figures. He's definitely way out of my league. Not that it matters, since we won't be talking anyway, but sometimes it's nice to fantasize.

Waiting for my group to be called, which is probably the last, I contemplate what I'll need to do when I arrive. I won't have much time before the bachelorette party tonight, so I wore my going-out clothes, a skirt with a cute tank top and a jean jacket. I'll have to freshen up, though—apply some makeup, take my hair down, and replace my glasses with contacts. Other than that, I should be ready to go.

It'll work out perfectly, since not only did Cici book and pay for my room where the wedding is taking place, but she insisted on having her driver pick me up from the airport. Did I mention she's marrying a billionaire? She certainly chose well. But then again, do you really have a choice where love is concerned, or does fate choose for you? I'm going with fate.

When what feels like group eighty is called, I pop up, anxious to board, but when I scan my boarding pass, the machine makes a loud beeping sound that causes me to panic. Thankfully, it's short-lived since the gate agent grabs a small piece of paper that spits out, and hands it to me with a smile on her face.

"It's your lucky day, you've been upgraded to first class, seat 2A."

I take the slip of paper from her. "Wow, thank you!"

"Enjoy your flight."

I'm beaming as I walk away. This has never happened before—not that I fly a lot, but still, this is so cool. It could be a sign that good things *are* coming this weekend.

I'm giddy as I wait in the line of people on the jetway, excited to experience first class, already picturing the glass of champagne I'll be greeted with. At least I think they do that. They might even serve a meal, though the alcohol alone makes it worth it.

The flight attendant greets me warmly, and I beam back excitedly as I go by. My eyes are trained upward until I spot my row and letter, when I glance down in surprise at the person seated next to me. It's Suits. Quickly schooling myself to act natural, I sit to let the people behind me pass while my heart thunders in my chest.

He's busy with his phone and doesn't notice right away, giving me a minute to calm my nerves. But when he does, he starts at my lap and slowly makes his way up my body until the most stunning green eyes connect with mine. If we had children, would our kids have green eyes since we both do?

Oh my God, Poppy, shut up.

Some people appear attractive from a distance but are disappointing up close. Not this guy. He's even better looking front and center—the dazzling smile and suggestive stare cause my cheeks to heat while my heart continues to pound. I'm no match for a man like this.

At least, that's where my head is until he speaks. "That's a fine set of legs. What time do they open?"

My jaw drops. Before I form a response, the flight attendant unknowingly intervenes.

"Sorry to interrupt. Would either of you like a water or a champagne?" she asks while holding a tray of both.

She's pretty and not at all shy about checking out McAsshole, making me want to roll my eyes, but I refrain. Can I really blame her?

"I'll have champagne, please," I say enthusiastically, determined not to ruin my experience. After accepting the glass she holds out, I thank her with a huge smile, ready to enjoy my good fortune and ignore the jerk next to me.

"I'll join the lady," he says.

Not in this lifetime, buddy.

She hands one to him, and I swear she grazes his hand intentionally as he takes it. "Here you go. I'll be through with an assortment of snacks after takeoff. Until then, enjoy your drink and flag me down or push the call button if you need *anything*." She winks at him before moving on; this time, I don't withhold the eye roll.

Suits turns toward me and raises his glass, causing me to scowl. "Shall we toast our grapes to the carpet matching the drapes?" His eyes follow his statement, going from my lap to my hair, making my jaw drop yet again.

He did not...

"I'm not toasting to that, you pervert," I say, shaking my head in disgust.

"Oh, come on now, cut me some slack. I can't be the first person to give you that line with that delectable body."

"Lovely. There's more," I say under my breath, before facing him. "You actually *are* the first, and I hope the last, to ever say those words. Maybe that will educate you as to what a pig you are." I huff and turn away.

He shakes his head and chuckles. "Nah. I'm just a typical male, sweetheart. I may be the only one who's said it out loud, but I guarantee I'm not the first to think it. As for being a pervert, you're probably right about that."

God, this guy is so annoying. "Please stop talking," I mutter before taking a sip of champagne.

"I pegged you as a stuffy librarian. But since you felt the need to educate me, does that mean you're a teacher? Not sure why I gravitated to the librarian when teachers are equally uptight."

"Seriously? I'm neither, and I don't appreciate you calling me uptight or stuffy. You don't even know me."

"Sorry, you're right. How about we start over, and you tell me what it would take for you to let your hair down…" He leans toward me and whispers close to my ear, "Because there's nothing sexier than thinking about bending the teacher over her desk, or you could play the librarian up against the stacks. I could get behind either." He winks as he rises back up.

The shiver in response to his words comes unbidden, but I won't give him the satisfaction of seeing his effect on me.

"Can we be done talking now? You obviously have a one-track mind, and I'm *not* sorry to say you won't be reaching the finish line, so you might as well quit now."

"The word quit isn't in my vocabulary, sugar. But I'll give you some time to sit with the vision I planted and check in with you later. Enjoy your drink," I raise my glass in a mock toast.

The nerve…

Braden

The first thing I noticed was her smell. It was sweet and… cute. That's the only way to describe it. Initially, I thought it must have been a kid who sat down next to me, but when I saw the fine set of legs from the corner of my eye, it was apparent they certainly didn't belong to a child.

Working my way up the impeccable body, inch by inch, I decided it was my lucky day when I met the eyes of the little librarian who was checking me out while waiting to board. That's what I'm calling her anyway, with the bun, the glasses, and that air about her that screams prim and proper. Although if her fiery red hair is anything to go by, she must have a wild streak, which is my kind of woman.

Man, I'd love to know what she's like in the sack. Would she keep up this innocent act, or would she become a hellcat in the bedroom? I could be wrong about the wild streak. It might be a rumor, though I wouldn't know since I've never been with a redhead—something I'd love to check off my list, especially if it's the one next to me. Hell yeah.

I noticed her at the gate immediately and was hoping she'd end up sitting closer, but she took a seat near the boarding door instead. Luckily, she was in my line of sight, so I could at least check her out. She's understatedly gorgeous. All I could think about was unpinning that hair and wrapping it around my fist while directing her naturally plump lips wherever I wanted them.

Now that she's right in front of me, not only are those lips perfect, but everything else about her is too. She has beautiful green eyes, hidden behind her glasses, an adorable button nose with freckles lining it, and fuck, that neck. It's begging to be explored to find each and every spot that makes her whimper.

Unfortunately, she doesn't appear to be on the same page as she aims a deadly scowl at me before turning her attention away. She's definitely feistier than she looks.

With my parting statement, I refocus and pick up where I left off with Warren, whose five unanswered texts have become increasingly impatient.

> Me: Dude, I've got a hottie sitting next to me. I'm hoping for a BJ in the bathroom.
>
> Warren: You get laid more than a bitch in heat. We need this deposition filed, quit fucking around.
>
> Me: You know the case inside and out. Do what you do best and finish the damn thing.
>
> Warren: Remind me why I work for you.
>
> Me: Because you love my acquisitions.

Warren: You're an ass.

Me: I know. And I'm busy trying to get some ass, so leave me alone. This one's being difficult.

Warren: Oh boy, I almost feel sorry for her. Going up against the BUTCHER? She doesn't stand a chance.

Me: Damn right she doesn't. Now back to work.

Warren: Fucker

Me: Hopefully…

Warren and I have an interesting relationship. Yes, he's my assistant, and a damn good one at that, but he's also a partner of sorts. We make a great team in the courtroom and an even better one in the bedroom.

We've shared quite a few women over the past couple of years, in addition to passing on the best of the best when we can't enjoy them together. We're not attracted to each other in the slightest, nor do we ever cross swords, but we sure know how to please a woman with four hands and two dicks.

However, this chick doesn't seem the type to play outside the box. Usually when a woman shuts me down, I don't give a fuck. I'd walk away and not think twice, knowing the next one to grab my attention *won't* say no. This girl, though, is appealing to my competitive nature, and *no* isn't an answer I'm ready to take.

Partly because I sense there's more to her than meets the eye and because she's too tempting to resist. She's like a timid little mouse, and I'd like to unleash whatever's holding her back since her body is certainly speaking a different language than her mouth.

She could be in a relationship, I suppose. Some vanilla guy who only fucks missionary. She probably has no clue what she's missing. Or, given her reaction to the scene I described, she might. This girl needs someone who can give her what she wants—what she's been craving.

An hour after takeoff and two refills of champagne later, I turn, unable to refrain.

"Do you have a boyfriend? Is that the problem here?"

She lowers the device she's been reading and faces me with a dropped jaw.

"Oh my God, seriously? You honestly assume the only reason I'm not falling at your feet is because I have a boyfriend and not because you're an absolute ass?"

"That's a no then. So what will it take to loosen up? I'd offer you a drink, but you've had two. You need a name? We should introduce ourselves. I'm—"

She covers my mouth with her hand.

Man, would I like that hand to be somewhere else.

"Stop," she says, removing it as quickly as she placed it, embarrassed. "I'd rather not do names." When I raise an eyebrow in question, she adds, "Seriously."

"All right, how about this? Ask me anything you want to know, and I'll ask you something in return. We'll go back and forth until you're comfortable enough to slip into the bathroom with me so I can see about that carpet myself. You might even enjoy it."

"Un-fricking believable. You don't quit." She shakes her head and sighs. "Listen, I appreciate your tenacity, but this is a no-win situation. I'm not interested in guys like you. You may be good-looking, which I'm sure you know, but you are *not* my type in the slightest, I can assure you."

"What *is* your type then?"

She appears exasperated, like she can't believe I'm still talking. Which, in a way, I can't either, because *what the fuck*? I never work this hard for a chick. Hell, if I were smart, I would've taken the flight attendant up on her blatant offer and gone behind the curtain for a quick blow job. I could've at least imagined it was my little mouse with her pouty lips around my cock.

The problem in taking the easy route with the stewardess is that it's been a while since I've been challenged, and the thrill of the chase is egging me on. The poor girl next to me has no idea what she's in for.

She finally answers after pondering the question. "Nice. Kind.

Considerate. Not condescending or sexist. And interested in more than just sex."

"Hm. Sounds boring."

"Not that you would know."

"I know that I'm anything but boring," I smirk and wiggle my brows.

"You're obnoxious, is what you are."

"Obnoxiously handsome?"

She scoffs in reply, quickly returning her attention to her device.

Curious, I glance down without angling my head to take a peek, and it doesn't take me long to figure out it's a romance. The explicit sex scene gives it away because I'm only one page in, and holy shit, it's basically porn on pages. No wonder she was annoyed by the interruption.

I'm literally getting hard from reading over her shoulder, and don't notice her staring at me as I'm impatiently waiting for the page to turn. When it doesn't, I look up to find her smirking.

"Enjoying yourself, are you?" She casts her eyes toward the bulge in my pants and back up with raised brows.

"Well, shit, can you blame me? You're practically waving porn in my face."

"No. I'm reading, and *you're* snooping."

"It started that way, but now I'm reading along with you, so could you hurry and flip the page?"

She scowls before tilting her head in contemplation. "Let's make a deal. I'll let you read over my shoulder the rest of the flight if you stop talking or trying to hit on me."

I lean close and whisper, "There was no *trying* about it—I *was* hitting on you."

"Fine, no deal." She passes the tablet to the hand closest to me and angles it away. But not before I caught her telltale shudder.

"Okay, okay, I'll behave." I give in, holding my hands up in defeat.

"No more talking?"

Without another word, I make the motion of zipping my lips, and she smiles in triumph. Damn. She's something else.

I'm fully entrenched in the story by the time the wheels touch down at LAX, so I'm not happy when Mouse exits the book to make a grab for her phone.

"Hey, I was reading that," I protest.

"I need to send a text. You won't have time to finish it anyway," she says while typing.

I'm tempted to ask the name of the book so I can download it myself. I'll have plenty of time between the layover and one more flight.

The quick visit to Bozeman was to meet with a potential client at his second home in Big Sky. We're talking big money. But I'm used to it. I'd say 95% of my clients are the ten percenters, and about 50% are the one percenters. I'm a sought-after divorce attorney who's not called the Butcher simply because it's my last name.

I'm as fierce in the courtroom as out of it, cutting my opponents to shreds. Hence the nickname and the reason I became the youngest partner in the law firm I've been at since college. Starting as an intern, I was offered a full-time position after passing my bar exam four years ago, and have worked my ass off since, proving myself tenfold with the amount of money I've brought in.

It's why clients like Jim Marlow call me specifically. They only *attain* me, however, if I believe them worthy. In this instance, Jim's wife decided she was ready for a younger version. The proof was undeniable in the pictures he provided from a private investigator, and was all I needed to accept his case. With the contract signed, it'll be weeks of gathering records and data, which I gratefully have Warren for.

"Is this your destination, then?" I ask, assuming she's informing someone she landed.

She never did answer whether she had a boyfriend or tell me her name.

"No. I'm here long enough to grab food before the next flight," she says dismissively, not even glancing from her phone.

"Where are you headed?"

She hesitates, causing me to laugh.

"What? It's not like I can stalk you or anything. I don't even know your name."

She huffs but ends up answering. "Thank God for that. I'm on my way to San Diego."

My eyes widen. "No shit. That's where I'm going. I live there. Do you?" It's like fate put her in my lap, or at least that's where she'll be later if I'm lucky.

"No," she quickly states. "Just visiting."

"Ah, so Bozeman's home then."

"I'm not giving you that information. Then you *could* stalk me."

I laugh again. "No name, remember? Although you could fix that and introduce yourself. And since you'll be around," I lean in and lower my voice. "I'd be happy to add you to my list of things to do tonight so we can bring those fantasies I mentioned to life." I inhale her scent once more, then sit back, wiggling my brows.

Her lips purse as she takes a deep breath. "I'll be too busy, and if I weren't, you would be the last *thing* I'd be doing."

"That's unfortunate."

"For you maybe."

"I promise it's just as unfortunate for you."

She rolls her eyes and shakes her head.

We're coming up to the gate, but I'm not finished with her yet. "Well, hopefully we'll be next to each other again so we can read some more."

She shrugs. "We won't be. I was randomly upgraded, so I'll be with the commoners."

The plane stops, and when the ding signals it's safe to rise, she quickly stands to grab her bags, ready to bolt. I can't let her escape so easily, especially knowing she'll be in my city. Fuck, I need *something* to go on. I'm not about to throw in the towel so soon.

"How about I buy you a meal on the way to the next gate, and we can get to know each other. Maybe you'll reconsider seeing me while you're in town." I suggest, hoping she'll take the bait so I can keep working her.

"I'll pass. I meant it earlier when I said you weren't my type. Plus, I need to make a call. Sorry."

The '*Not sorry*' comes out loud and clear with the tight-lipped smile she delivers. Damn, this girl is a hard nut to crack. It's a good thing that's my specialty.

"Well, my sexy librarian, it was nice to meet you. Hopefully, I'll see you on the next flight."

"Doubtful," she delivers with a sardonic smile and walks away.

I wouldn't be so sure about that.

2

LAST KING STANDING

Poppy

KNOWING MY ZONE IS PROBABLY DEAD LAST AND THE CHANCES of being upgraded again are zero, I wander aimlessly after I eat to avoid getting to the gate early. I'd rather not have another encounter with Suits. I'll have to pass him on the way to my seat, but I can handle that much.

What I can't handle is him making constant passes at me. What's his deal, anyway? He had a flight attendant practically begging for attention, yet he chose to waste his efforts on me instead. He's smug, completely inappropriate, and utterly exhausting. Do women actually go for that sort of thing?

I mean, fine, he is the epitome of Adonis, and I guess if that's all you're looking for, so be it. But come on, every woman can't be that shallow, can they?

The one positive thing I'll say is that it was cute when he read with me. At first, I thought he was only interested in the sex scene I happened to be on, but then he kept going and even became impatient when I took longer, making him wait for the page to turn.

Three chapters were left by the time we touched down, and I could tell he was pretty invested at that point. I almost felt bad cutting him off, but once he opened his mouth again, the weight was lifted. His crassness is next level. I might use some of the scenarios he mentioned as material later, but I'd never give in to someone so... crude.

I've already texted Cici that I'll have a fun story for everyone and that my connection is on schedule. I'm so excited to see her that it overrides my irritation from earlier. This flight is only an hour, so it'll go quickly while I read. It's too bad I won't have any champagne, but that's okay since I'll be drinking again tonight.

When I arrive at the gate, hardly anyone is left to board, which means I timed it perfectly. Passing first class, I can't help but discreetly scan the seats in search of him. Oddly enough, he's nowhere to be found. Hmm, there could be more than one flight to San Diego.

It is a big city after all, which I'm looking forward to, coming from small-town Bozeman. I've never been to San Diego and am excited to stay at the Hotel del Coronado right on the beach. I love the mountains of Montana, but I'm eager to be near the ocean. Just thinking about it puts a smile on my face.

Seconds later, that smile disappears when I make it to my row and see a familiar face. Suits? I double-check the numbers above to confirm that it's correct and that he is, in fact, next to *my* seat.

When I stop, he stands, donning a devastating grin. "Let me help you," he says, taking the carry-on and lifting it into the overhead bin.

"Why are you back here?" I whisper aggressively.

He wraps his arm around me and leans in, his lips dangerously close to my ear, causing goose bumps to break out everywhere.

"Is that any way to greet your fiancé?"

I extract myself forcefully. "What are you talking about?"

"How else could I convince the person next to you to change seats with me?" He smiles again, almost making me forget to be annoyed.

When he sits, I have no choice but to do the same since the people behind me are anxious to move past.

"I would think the opportunity to be in first class would have been enough. Seriously, why would you do that, and how did you find out where I was sitting?"

"They looked you up from your seat on the last flight, and with a little persuasion, they paged the guy next to you so I could ask him to switch with me. And yes, first class probably would have convinced him, but this was way more fun. The gate agents were highly entertained." He smirks as if he's so clever, and I can't stop the eye roll.

One thing's for sure. He's persistent.

"I need to finish the book. Unless you were hoping I'd keep trying to get in your pants."

"Definitely not. If I hear one more cheesy pick-up line, I might throw up in your lap."

"Well, we certainly can't have that since I'd rather *you* be in my lap later." He wags his brows.

All I can do is groan and shake my head. This is going to be a long flight.

After making the same deal as last time, he shuts up, and we continue reading. It was going perfectly until we made it to a sex scene. Usually, when I read around other people, I zone out. Sometimes I catch myself panting, but I always rein it in.

Right now, that's impossible. When I try to flip past it, he brushes my hand away. "What are you doing?" we both ask at once.

I answer first. "It's not necessary to the story. We can skip to the next part."

"No way, it'll mess with the flow."

"Either we move on or stop altogether."

He lasers in, salaciously. "Are you afraid you might get aroused? Will it have you wet and aching? I'm right here, Little Mouse. I could help you out with that."

Oh my God. Of all that's holy. Who says those kinds of things? Men don't talk like that in real life—do they? And why, oh why, is my body responding to this creep?

Shaking the unwanted thoughts away, I reply, addressing the easier topic. "I am not a mouse. Don't be so condescending."

"Then don't act like one by skipping the good stuff. You know it's your favorite part. I could tell by how angry you were when I interrupted the last scene."

"That is not why I was angry." I deny his claim, despite knowing that that's exactly why I was irritated.

He lets my protest go. "Come on. I'd like to see how I stack up to these fictional men. Come on, baby. Don't leave us hanging," he begs.

Holy guacamole. He's killing me. I finally give in and bring the tablet up to resume reading, although my attention is certainly not on the words in front of me. How in the world am I so turned on? This guy has been spewing more innuendos than a confetti cannon at New Year's, making me gag at his forwardness, yet suddenly, my juices are flowing while my mind is going places it shouldn't.

Snapping out of it, I force myself to continue. Within seconds, I'm absorbed once more, naturally blocking everything around me. Only when I'm deep into the book, at the end of *the scene,* does something bring me back to the present—the real-life sex god beside me.

His lips are so close to my ear that his breath feels like velvet as he speaks, causing me to shiver. "He was good, but there's room for improvement. If I were him, I would have—"

"Don't. Please stop. I don't want to know." *I don't think my libido can take it.*

"Are you sure about that? I think your body disagrees. In fact, I think it wants a demonstration." In what seems like slow motion, his hand snakes over the armrest and lands on my leg, half on my skirt and half on my bare thigh. I watch but don't register it in time to stop him.

My core clenches automatically, the traitor. But before he makes it any farther, I grab his hand firmly, only to have him tighten his grip.

"Good thing my body isn't in charge and my mind is smart enough to steer clear of men like you," I say through gritted teeth while warring over my reaction to him.

He leans over, and his voice drips out like maple syrup, slow and rich. "Men like me, huh? You mean men who know what they're doing in the bedroom? Men who can please a woman and have her begging for more?"

My insides quiver, and I'm seriously torn between letting him roam higher or putting an end to this madness.

Sensing my hesitation, he continues. "Wouldn't you like to experience what you've only read about up until now?"

The awareness of his words jolts me from my stupor, and I shove him away. He couldn't know I've never done those things. He must be talking about the wild stuff they only put in books. The stuff that doesn't happen in real life. At least… I don't think it does.

"You're the last guy on earth I'd want to experience anything with," I say weakly.

He has the audacity to chuckle. "Keep telling yourself that, and your body might start to believe you."

Ignoring his comment, our conversation dies, and we continue reading. We're halfway through the final chapter when a jolt drags me back to reality. Pulling my phone out and turning it on, I text Cici that we've landed.

"How about we keep reading and be the last off," he suggests.

"Someone's waiting for me, so I can't." No use telling him it's a driver picking me up and not my friends. But even so, I only have so much time before meeting everyone and still need to freshen up.

"How about until it gets to us, then?" He sounds desperate, so I take pity.

"Fine, but you're getting my bag down."

His smile once again does me in. "Of course I am."

We finish the last page while we're still five rows away from our turn.

"What the fuck? You can't end a book like that. Is that legal?"

I can't help but laugh. "It's called a cliffhanger. It's no different than watching a TV series where they leave you guessing at the end of an episode."

"Which is why I don't watch anything until the whole series is out. So, what's the next book?"

"There isn't one yet. I think the release date is in January."

"That's bullshit. Not only do they make you buy the next book to finish this one, but you have to wait for it?"

I bite my lip from cracking a smile since he's currently behaving like a toddler who's being punished. It's sort of adorable.

"It keeps people hooked. Hence, a series. You're usually prepared going in. I was anyway." I shrug.

"Well I fucking wasn't. Now what?"

"Now you wait for the sequel."

He scowls and grabs his phone, opening his notes app. "What's the name then?"

"Wait, you really want to read the next one?"

"How else will I find out if she's dead or alive?"

"It's a romance—she'll live. Romance novels don't have bad endings."

He looks confused. "Never?"

"No, or it wouldn't be considered a romance."

"Not all relationships end well." He's so deadpan, I laugh.

"Most people don't want to read about shitty relationships and failed marriages. Romances are meant to make you happy and dream. I'd pick a different genre if I wanted reality."

He ponders for a minute. "Maybe that's true, but what if all it's doing is filling your head with delusional ideas of the opposite sex?"

"It is. But it's also giving you hope that you'll find what you're looking for someday with fantasies along the way."

"The only thing that gave me was a way to pass the time and a few new phrases for the bedroom." He says seductively.

"So you didn't take away anything on how to treat a woman out of it? Shocking. On that note, it's time to go." I jerk my head to the people exiting their seats in front of us.

He hands me his phone. "Here, type the name of the book while

I get your bag. And feel free to leave your number. I'd love to test those phrases out, and you seemed pretty into them when we were reading."

Asshole. He just had to go there again. I should be flattered that he won't give up, but guys like him are like this with anything on two legs.

I enter the author's name and book title, but instead of leaving my name or number, I add a short message. He sets my backpack on his vacated seat and reaches for his phone. I quickly close the notes app before handing it over with a smile. He can look at it later.

"You put the name in there?"

"Yep. If you follow the author online, you'll get an email when the sequel comes out."

"Cool, thanks."

I still can't believe he wants to read the next one. It's kind of cute. If he weren't such a douchebag, I'd be interested. But I can't get past those terrible pickup lines he started with. Only one type of guy behaves that way, and that's certainly not the type for me.

He stands where he is, letting me go in front of him. He's probably checking out my ass down the aisle. When we leave the jetway and enter the terminal, he stays with me while we walk toward the exit. I'm not sure how to lose him.

"All right, I've got it—if you're not a teacher or a librarian, you must be an astronaut because your ass is out of this world."

I groan, making him laugh. "I knew that's why you let me go ahead. You're too much."

"I'm growing on you, admit it, Mouse." His head cocks accompanied by a smile.

I shake my head with a huff. "The only thing you're growing on is my nerves."

"Listen, I know you're busy, but if you do have any time, I'd love to see you while you're here."

Hmmm. That's the most normal, nonsexual way he's asked. But too little, too late, so the joke's on him. Plus, it's a moot point, since I really am too busy.

"Like I said, I'm tied up this trip."

He releases a low growl. "Fuck, baby. You can't say things like that. I'm gonna have visions of you tied to my bed all night."

Unbelievable.

I stop in my tracks and face him right before we go through the doors to the baggage area. "Look, this was… interesting. I'm sure you'll survive being turned down for what must be the first time in your life and shift your efforts to the next girl. You might want to attempt an actual conversation with a woman someday. I'd wish you luck if I didn't feel sorry for whoever falls for your crap."

"Yeah, well, you'd probably be a boring fuck anyway, so really, it's your loss, not mine. Try a few things from those books you read, and you might just get laid more often."

I'm seething inside. How dare he? "You know what? Go fuck yourself."

"Gladly, I'm sure I'll do a better job than you."

I stomp off, fuming mad, but when I walk through the exit, I panic. Waiting in the crowd at arrivals is a man holding a sign with my name on it. The last thing I need is for this asshole to be able to look me up somehow. It sucks that he knows where I live.

Making a beeline for the bathroom, I quickly enter and grab my phone.

> Me: I just got to baggage and saw your driver. Can you tell him I'll meet him at the car and text me the location? Long story, which I'll tell you tonight, but I don't want this guy from the plane to find out my name, so I can't walk up to him with that sign.

> Cici: Texting him now. I'll ask where he parked and let you know. Are you safe?

> Me: Yeah, it's nothing like that. He's just a jerk with no boundaries whatsoever.

> Cici: Damn, can't wait to hear about it. Okay, he just texted me. I'll forward it to you.

> Me: Thank you!

Braden

What the actual hell just happened? I've never blown my chances with a girl that badly. Shit, come to think of it, I've never struck out. Nor have I had a woman push my buttons like her. Am I losing my touch? I contemplated waiting when I saw her go into the bathroom, but to what end? She won't change her mind at this point. And she's for sure not my type if she wasn't all over those attempts, so would I even want the meek little mouse?

Yes. Yes, I would, I admit as I make my way to the car. I'm lying to myself, trying to play it off. I don't remember the last time I was that attracted to someone and wanted in their pants that badly. Damn, it must be her resistance. It's not like she's the hottest chick I've seen, so what else could it be? The red hair? Those green eyes? Those fucking legs—that ass. Or was it simply the challenge factor? Fuck. Who am I kidding? It was all the above.

The stubborn girl wouldn't even give me her name, which means brooding about this will do nothing, so I might as well let it go. Thankfully, I've got the bachelor party tonight. The guys and whatever woman I pick up for the night will take my mind off the sexy little librarian who got away.

Hours later and three whiskeys in, I'm starting to think otherwise. Here we are at a bachelor party, where I'm the only bachelor, and considering how many women have offered themselves up, I should have already had a blow job by now. So why haven't I?

It's a good question, especially with the selection of fine ladies around. We're at the club Eli and his brother Sebastian own, because why have the hottest nightclub in San Diego and not take advantage of the VIP section at every opportunity?

Not that any of them care we're here. They're the most pussy-whipped men around. But hey, more power to them. Their wives, or soon-to-be wives, are bangin' hot and available to fuck whenever they want, so who am I to talk shit? I just hope it works out for them.

I was in love once—almost asked the girl to marry me, even. Four fucking years ago. I ended up dodging a bullet when I came home to find her screwing my roommate. I honestly should've sent them both a thank you. Because I, of all people, should have known better. Between my dad's infidelities and the amount of shit I see daily, what the fuck was I thinking? Love doesn't mean crap. If someone wants sex, they go for it, screw the consequences.

"Dude, what's up with you tonight? You look like somebody kicked your puppy. Was the Big Sky trip a bust?" Jackson, my best friend and one of the grooms, asks.

"Of course not. When have I ever failed to land a client?" True story.

"Then what's your deal?" Jackson persists.

"I got shot down by a woman today. Something else that never happens."

Jeers and chuckles break out.

"Ah, so you're pouting." Jackson derives.

While Eli, the other groom, adds, "Ego a bit bruised, buddy?"

And before you get the wrong idea, they're not marrying each other. Not that I'd care, but they're not. Jackson is marrying Mia, who he met through work, and Eli is marrying Jackson's sister, Cici. The timing simply worked in their favor to have a double wedding.

"Hardly. The girl was a prude. I had a hunch, but got distracted by the red hair and was dying to find out if she was red everywhere."

"You can't tell me you've never been with a ginger in your many pursuits." This comes from Justin, the final guy here and Sebastian's former security guard turned friend.

Yeah, Eli and Sebastian Dubree? Rich as fuck and have private security. Might have something to do with Sebastian's wife, Lily, being kidnapped while they were dating. That and the paparazzi who hound them daily. It's slowed down now that they're both off the market, but before, shit, they couldn't go anywhere without being harassed.

I was introduced to Justin through Eli and have subsequently used his PI and security firm for work. I'm always digging into people's shit and having them followed. Whatever it takes to win a settlement in my client's favor. Hey, it's not like I represent the asshole side of the divorce; people know better than to seek my services if they're the cheating spouse.

And nine times out of ten, a cheating spouse is involved, whether that's why they're divorcing or not. You'd be surprised by the amount of shit that surfaces while going through proceedings… things no one should hear about. Take it from me, people are fucked up.

"Have any of you? There aren't many around." I'm curious if anyone has the answer to my burning question. I could look up some redheaded porn, but A, they're always shaved, and B, can you even trust that shit?

Heads shake around the table except for Justin, who answers, "I was years ago, and yes, the carpet matches the drapes."

I full belly laugh. "That's exactly what I asked her. She wasn't too impressed, but fuck, why beat around the bush?" We all bust up laughing.

I hold my glass up, and they follow suit. "Fuck, that's some funny shit, and I didn't even plan it. Damn, now I wish I'd have hit the jackpot. Would've liked to add *that* to my spank bank."

"Most chicks are bare these days anyway. You probably wouldn't have seen the proof. Also, if that's how you talk to women, I'd say that may be your problem, man," Jackson says.

He and I have been friends since our freshman year of college and were each other's wingmen until he found Mia. Now they're about to be married, and I'll be the last man standing after this weekend. Fuck.

"Hey, douchebag, I don't remember you being any better little more than a year ago. Just because you're moving to the dark side doesn't mean you need to dim *my* lights."

"I'm just saying, you attract more bees with honey."

"That'd be great advice if I were looking to get stung."

"Touché," Jackson says with a sip of his drink.

"So I take it Red didn't give you her number?" Eli asks.

Eli and I became closer last year while Jackson was off searching for his bride. I saw Eli's relationship with Cici develop firsthand. May have even given them a nudge or two in the right direction. They'd been dancing around each other forever, so when they finally sealed the deal after nearly three years, we were all relieved.

However, I'm not excited to be the only single one in our circle. At least I've still got Warren, who's embracing his bachelorhood with me. He's a little gentler than I am when it comes to smooth-talking and... *other things*, but that's why we're a good team. Nothing like a little sweet *and* salty to make it just right for the ladies.

"She wouldn't even give me her name," I answer, earning jeers from the group.

"Dude, you bombed hard. No wonder you're such a downer. She must have done a number on you if you're not taking any women up on their offers so far. You could've had at least five already," Jackson says.

"Nah. Tonight's about you. Besides, I'm wiped, and since we're all headed to the hotel after this, it doesn't make sense to find a hookup. Your women better have some hot friends, though. Who's the chick I'm walking with? Is she available?"

Eli answers, "We paired you with Cici's friend Poppy, since you two are the only singles in the wedding party—other than Walker, who's giving Mia away. But speaking of redheads, Poppy happens to be one, but she's feisty. I'm not sure she's your type."

"What does that mean?" I ask suspiciously.

"Just means I don't think she'd fall for your shit." Eli chuckles, then adds, "Seems a little more conservative than you're into anyway."

"Fuck, as long as she's not as mousy as the gal today, I can handle her."

"Cici'll kill you if you screw around with her friend," Eli warns.

"You sure about that? Need I remind you she was into me before you?" I smirk as the rest of the guys shake their heads, having heard this story plenty of times.

"No, asshole, you don't, since you like to throw it in my face as much as possible."

"Well, I'm pretty sure bro code says what Cici doesn't know won't hurt her." I look around the table, seeking the others' agreement.

"Husband code says to fuck off," Eli quips in return.

Sebastian releases a cough that sounds like bullshit, grabbing Eli's attention.

"That was dire circumstances, and you know it," Eli tells Sebastian. "Plus, it ended fine. You can't keep holding that against me."

The rest of the table is clueless at this point, but that tends to happen with those two. Twins, business partners, neighbors, and now a pair of long-time best friends for wives. It doesn't get much cozier.

Sebastian ignores him, passing me advice instead. "I say go for it if she's hot. Banging a bridesmaid should be on everyone's bachelor list."

"Fuck, yeah." I give him knuckles. "I knew I liked you for a reason." Of all of us, Sebastian is usually the most reserved. Normally broody and quiet, he's slowly come out of his shell since he married Lily. It's been fascinating to witness the change.

Eli shakes his head, glaring at Sebastian, ready to go off, but Jackson pipes in first. "Cici wouldn't have paired them up if she were worried about her friend. She knows Braden as well as the rest of us. I'm sure this Poppy gal can hold her own, or not, if that's what she wants." Then he looks pointedly at me. "Just don't piss my sister off at her own wedding."

My hands go up in defense. "Listen, it's Justin's fault. I may have let my fascination go if he hadn't told me about the carpet."

"Don't make *me* your excuse to bang her tomorrow. If anything, it's Sebastian's fault," Justin accuses while cocking his thumb in Sebastian's direction.

"All I'm hearing is that you're a bunch of pussies," Sebastian says deadpan, causing us to crack up.

A couple of hours later, we load into the limo that will take us to the hotel, and I'm drunker than a skunk. Hell, we all are. Along the way, Justin tells us how he started dating Lucy the second time around, and it's some good shit. Didn't know the guy had a funny bone in his body, but man, can he tell a story.

I haven't laughed that much in a while. What a great fucking night, with no *fucking* involved—go figure. But I'm ready to fall over from exhaustion as we walk into the hotel. We're handed our keys on arrival, and thankfully, the bags have been brought to the rooms because I'm not sure I can handle *myself*, let alone a bag.

We're staying at the Hotel del Coronado, a mere twenty minutes from downtown. The rehearsal dinner is scheduled for tomorrow night, with the wedding taking place the following day, on Saturday. The bridal party will be here the whole weekend, along with Jackson and Cici's parents and Mia's mom. I've met everyone except for this Poppy chick, and unfortunately, it'll have to wait until the rehearsal since I'm running into work tomorrow.

Since the hotel grounds are vast, we're escorted in golf carts to our rooms. As I zombie-walk from the cart to the building, something catches my eye for a blink before it's gone. I swear I just saw a beautiful redhead walking from the hot tub between the buildings. The weird part is that it looked a lot like the girl from the plane.

When I turn to investigate, she's gone as quickly as she appeared. I shake my head and scold myself, needing to purge this girl from my mind. Damn. It was more than likely Cici's friend Poppy, not my sexy librarian, especially since she's staying here as well.

Ready to put this day behind me, I continue to my room and fall straight into bed, releasing a massive sigh when my head hits the pillow. Pulling my phone from my pocket, I immediately think of her, wondering what she's up to or if she might be reading another romance.

Suddenly, it hits me—she put the name of the book in my phone and might have given me her number. I eagerly open my notes app to look, only to be quickly disappointed, but laugh out loud, nonetheless.

Book Title: Last King Standing

Sequel: Dropping soon — like your jaw as you realize I didn't leave my number.

Cliffhangers are rough. So is emotional depth — you should try it sometime.

P.S. No name, no number — some characters are better left to the imagination.

Well fuck. That's the end of that. It doesn't mean I can't have one last fantasy, though.

Plugging my phone in next to the bed, I lie back, unbuckle my pants, and slip them off. My hand reaches down, grabbing my swollen cock that seemed to be semi-hard throughout the day because of my mousy librarian.

Right now, it's rock-hard, full, and dying to feel those plump, luscious lips wrapped around it. The thought of unpinning her hair and grabbing it with my fist while I lead her to my cock is almost enough to make me blow, but it's too soon, and I want more time with my illusion since it's all I've got.

She sticks her tongue out and licks the bead of pre-cum from my tip. The moan she releases is pure heaven. "That's it, Mouse, let me hear you do that around my cock." Her mouth opens wide while I feed it to her, lips pressing down my length. "Fuck, so good." I hold her firm as I work her, relishing the feel of her tongue lapping me while I thrust. Three more pumps and I'm releasing down her throat, making her gag as she swallows. My mousy librarian takes it so well. "That's it, baby. Yes. UH, FUCK. YES."

When I open my eyes back to reality after that mind-blowing orgasm, my stomach is covered in cum. Too exhausted to do anything more, I remove my shirt and wipe it away before rolling over and passing the fuck out.

3

DIGGING DEEPER

Poppy

I'M GIDDY WHEN I WAKE UP THE NEXT MORNING. THE HOTEL THEY chose for the wedding is out of this world. The bed, oh my God… it's so luxurious. I stretch out in every direction with a big smile on my face. The added bonus of a hot tub right outside my room is heavenly. You can watch the ocean and hear the sounds as you relax. I went straight in after the bachelorette party.

Which, as I expected, wasn't much of a party, since Cici and her bestie, Lily, are both pregnant, while Mia and her best friend, Walker, are underage. At least Lucy, the other bridesmaid, drank with me, and we made sure to drink enough for everyone.

It was so fun to meet Cici's friends. I've heard a lot about them over the last couple of years but hadn't met any, other than her fiancé, Eli, when he came to propose and help her pack. Her soon to be sister-in-law Mia, who is also the other bride, is adorably sweet. And I can't wait to meet Cici's brother Jackson, who Mia's marrying.

Eli, Cici, Jackson, and Mia are having a double wedding because Eli wanted to be married before their baby was born. So he poached

Jackson's wedding that was already scheduled. Yes, the pregnancy was a surprise. Note to future self, antibiotics can mess with your birth control.

Seeing my bestie again, who looks like she could give birth any day, was the highlight of the night. Although it made me sad to miss the last part of her pregnancy after being by her side for most of it. I wasn't sad for long, though, because as the night went on, laughter took over.

Lily was as adorable in real life as she is over FaceTime. Mia is a bit on the shy side, but her gay best friend, Walker, made up for that tenfold as one of the funniest people I've met, followed closely by Lucy, another bridesmaid. Man, those two are dangerous together. I laughed more than I can remember.

Partly from the story of the flight over, which they insisted on hearing every detail of. But it was mostly their running commentary that had us in tears. My God, the things that came out of their mouths—I'm still giggling at the memory.

Since Lucy and I were the only two drinking, we didn't stay out late. Knowing the hot tub was right outside my room, they received no complaints from me when the yawns began. No one chose to join me, so I was able to soak it in, pun intended.

Today, however, I can't wait to hit the beach. It's all I plan to do until the rehearsal dinner. I'll have to get through breakfast first, though, and meet the rest of the wedding party.

There's Cici's brother, Jackson—the other groom; Eli's brother and best man, Sebastian; another groomsman, Justin, who's Lucy's boyfriend; and last but not least, Braden—Jackson's best friend, best man, and the guy I'll be walking down the aisle with, who I've already been warned to steer clear of. Apparently, he's hot but a total player, which doesn't concern me after my test run yesterday. I can hold my own just fine, thank you very much.

Sure, Suit's advances almost had me crumbling at times, but that was my body talking—my mind was in complete control and dodged him at all costs. To which I flawlessly succeeded. Okay, confession time. I did use some of those naughty things he said as fuel after the hot tub, because why waste that dirty talk? Having a sexy man to imagine as well? Bonus.

That doesn't mean that I would ever give in to someone like that, though. Not a chance. This girl's holding out for the one who earns this sacred body. The one who works for it and proves he's worthy. Not some jerk-off whose sole purpose in life is how many women he can sink his dick into. That is certainly not the man for me.

So, yeah, I'm not worried about this Braden guy. I just hope it's not another repeat of yesterday with the relentless effort to get in my pants. Any more of that and I'll lose it. A girl can only put up with so much crap in the span of a weekend. Fingers crossed he's not as bad as Suits.

Taking my time this morning while indulging in this luxurious room, I pamper myself in the bathtub. Not one bone in my body feels rushed—that is, until I look at the clock and realize breakfast ends in twenty minutes. Shit.

I quickly finish, throwing on a sundress, before grabbing my sunglasses and walking to the restaurant. It's beautiful—sun, the ocean air, palm trees… I could easily live here. I can't believe Cici chose Bozeman over San Diego. It's August, and the weather is fricking fantastic.

As I reach for the door handle, the slightest flutter of butterflies sets in, knowing I'm about to meet more people, including the only single guy in the group. Although I've been warned, it doesn't stop the anticipation at the slim possibility of a connection. Isn't that what everyone hopes for when meeting a sexy, available man? I can't be alone in that.

"Poppy, there you are! Come meet my brother and parents." Cici calls out and waves me over as soon as I enter the dining room.

Heading over, I scan the room, smiling at Eli, who's with Lily, and I'm assuming her husband, Sebastian, Eli's twin. The man next to Lucy is probably Justin, her boyfriend, and since Walker's the only other one here, the third groomsman must be missing. My shoulders instantly relax, making me realize how nervous I actually was to meet him.

Cici hugs me before making introductions. "Poppy, this is my mom, Hazel, my dad, Jack, and that's my brother, Jackson. Oh, and that's Mia's mom, Sofia. Everyone, this is Poppy, my best friend from Bozeman," she says with a big smile.

I greet each one with a hug, along with Mia and Walker. We chat for a while, and it's nice how they all thank me for taking care of Cici during her pregnancy. None of them knew she was pregnant until she was almost seven months along. Miss Independent couldn't be talked into spilling the news. And not from the lack of Lily and me constantly trying.

After a few minutes, Cici tugs my arm and pulls me toward the other group.

"Guys, this is Poppy. That's Sebastian and that's Justin," she says without explanation, having already given me the details on everyone.

Justin runs a security and PI company that they've all used for various reasons and has become good friends with the guys. His girlfriend, Lucy is Sebastian's assistant and has become good friends with Lily and Cici.

"Hey, Poppy, it's good to see you again," Eli says in greeting.

After shaking hands with the other two men and hugging Lucy and Lily, I turn to Cici. "Braden isn't here?"

Justin hears the question and provides an answer. "Braden had to work. He just landed a new client and had to start on the case before the weekend. He'll be here tonight, but he wanted me to tell you he's *really* looking forward to making your acquaintance and sorry it had to wait." Justin shakes his head, then directs his attention to the guys. "Since he can't do his job without me, I'm taking off for a quick meeting at his office, but I'll see you at the shooting range."

The message from Braden was loud and clear. He sounds as equally douchey as Suits. And judging from the chuckles all around, it's typical behavior.

It's nice getting to know everyone. I'm still stunned Cici chose to leave such a great group of friends, but I suppose since I've never fought with my parents, I wouldn't understand, since that's why she left. I'm glad they've reconciled because it's easy to see how much they love their daughter.

Not long after brunch, all of us ladies and Walker are happily in lounge chairs on the beach, while the guys went to do manly things. I think it had something to do with a shooting range. This right here is precisely where I wanted to be today.

"So, are either of you nervous about tomorrow?" I ask Cici and Mia.

They answer at the same time, making us all laugh, before Cici goes first.

"It was so hard to make it to this moment, and now that it's here, I'm a nervous wreck. My heart wants this, but my mind tries to play tricks on me sometimes. Y'all will have to keep me in check to make sure we don't have a runaway bride on our hands." Cici laughs nervously.

"I'll chain you to the altar if I have to," Lily says. "Just remind yourself that you're only marrying him so we can be sisters and you'll be fine."

Cici swats her on the arm. "You're terrible. But seriously, I can't believe our kids will be cousins. Who would have predicted that you and I would marry twin brothers?" They both squeal as my heart swells with happiness for them.

Lucy and I continue to enjoy our Peachy Bottom cocktails. We're off the hook as bridesmaids, since Lily and Walker share the important maid of honor duties. Fortunately, one's pregnant and the other isn't old enough to drink, so everything's responsibly covered. I can simply sit back, relax, and enjoy a mini vacation with my BFF and new friends.

"What about you, Mia? How are you holding up?" Lucy asks.

"I'm scared out of my mind. Now that Eli and Cici are part of the wedding, which I'm thrilled about by the way, but a lot more people are attending, and I don't want people judging me for getting married so young."

"Do you feel like you're too young?" Cici asks her.

Mia doesn't hesitate before answering. "Not at all. I had to grow up sooner than most people, so I feel twenty years older with the amount of crap I've dealt with. Plus, I have zero doubts about being with Jackson for the rest of my life. I can't imagine otherwise."

Walker speaks up. "That's the only thing that matters, Mia. First of all, it's none of their business, and second, anyone who knows you and Jackson has no doubt you belong together. Don't let single-minded people dampen your day. Take it from me, it's not worth it."

Not only is he hilarious, but he's also a sweetheart, and it's easy to tell what a great friend he is to Mia. I'm seriously loving this whole group of people. I feel blessed to have been brought in and am so glad things worked out for Cici the way they did. She belongs here, surrounded by friends and family, with the man of her dreams. I'm so happy for her I could cry.

Which means I should slow down on the drinks, or we'll end up with a super sappy Poppy in a bit.

"You okay over there?" Cici asks, jolting me from my thoughts.

I giggle, "Yeah. Just getting sentimental and decided I'd better switch to water before it's out of hand. I'm so excited for the wedding."

I'm also looking forward to Matt's arrival tomorrow afternoon. It'll be nice to have another familiar face. Hopefully, some single ladies will be at the wedding for him. Maybe we can help each other out and do some scoping. We singles have to stick together.

"Do you guys have any girlfriends you could introduce to Matt?" I ask.

They're discussing the guest list when Lily excitedly says, "Ooh, I do have someone to introduce *you* to. His name is Jordan, and he's super cute. He works in the marketing department with me."

"If I hear my wife mention the attractiveness of another man one more time, there will be consequences." A voice comes from behind us.

We all turn around to the guys approaching from the hotel. Sebastian is in the lead and close enough to have heard Lily tell me about Jordan. Seriously, how did these women land such drop-dead gorgeous men? I mean, wow. Lucky bitches, I tell ya.

"Is that supposed to scare me?" Lily quips back as Sebastian leans down to kiss her.

They're a cute couple, but I've heard a few stories from Cici, and I'm not sure I'd be okay with a man like that. He seems a little too intense for my liking. He's formidable in person, that's for sure, and I can't imagine he's much different at home.

His twin Eli, however, is a puppy dog, which proves that Cici's commitment disorder is real because if it weren't, no way would she have held out so long before scooping him up.

Justin seems to be a mix of the two, but he certainly resembles his career in security well since he never lets his guard down.

And lastly, Jackson reminds me of a bodybuilder, but the only thing I've determined about him so far is that he's the most smitten. The way he looks at Mia makes my heart pitter-patter.

By the time this weekend is over, I'll need to find a man, because holy cow, am I a jealous bitch at the moment as the rest of the guys kiss and greet their ladies. Walker and I make eye contact, and we both crack up laughing, knowing we're thinking the exact same thing.

Braden

What a day. Warren and I pored through the information from Jim, the client I landed in Montana, while nursing the hangover from hell. It was necessary to get a jump start, though, since it's a nightmare of a divorce with the amount of assets involved. Now Warren can start gathering the additional data we need. Between that and the constant jabs about not scoring the librarian, it was a long fucking day.

Justin popped in to review the case and make a game plan for what he'll be investigating for us. He's the man who finds hidden assets, money trails, and is my best-kept secret around the office. I'm indebted to Eli and Jackson for the referral, which means I'll handle their divorces for free when the time comes. Not that it's inevitable, but we're dealing with a 50/50 chance, since those are the current statistics.

I won't tell my friends that. I'm not a total douchebag, simply an educated one. I'm happy for them. So I'm constantly reminding myself that just because it didn't work for me doesn't mean it won't for others, and I try to keep my thoughts in check. Otherwise, the words out of my mouth would be less than encouraging. Who can blame me, given my personal experience and occupation?

I'll be the model of positivity this weekend, though. Besides, not only is it Friday, but I'll be celebrating with friends with a sexy chick on my arm in… crap, looking at my watch, I realize I'm late to the rehearsal. Having just entered the room, I quickly remove my tie and undo the top two buttons of my dress shirt for a more casual look. It was a long day, but a quick glance in the mirror shows I've made it through all right.

My phone buzzes in my pocket. Shit.

> Jackson: Where are you? We're starting.

> Me: The room. Sorry, work went late. Leaving in seconds.

> Jackson: Hurry up. Cici's losing her shit.

> Me: Tell her to chill, this was your wedding to begin with.

> Jackson: Don't be an ass.

> Me: On my way.

Finishing up, I rush out of the room and jump in the golf cart they provided to hightail it over. I'm eager to meet this girl I'll be walking down the aisle with, especially after hearing that she's a looker from Justin. Not that Eli would've warned me off if she wasn't—he wouldn't have had to.

As I'm parking, I see the group in the distance. It's an outdoor wedding, and the rehearsal is taking place where the wedding will be held tomorrow afternoon. My partner isn't hard to spot, being the only redhead in attendance, and there's something vaguely familiar about her. I recognize that ass. And those legs…

Oh fuck, you've got to be shitting me.

I don't need any more evidence to know it's her.

Jackson's the only one facing my direction and calls me out. "Dude, it's about time you show up. We almost got a stand-in for you," he yells, causing everyone to turn.

The minute she sees me, her eyes go wide, and her jaw drops.

"And let Mouse walk down the aisle with a stranger? Not a chance."

"Who? What are you…" He trails off when he notices the recognition on her face and the smirk on mine.

"Wait. Have you two met?" Jackson asks skeptically, drawing the other's attention.

"We sat next to each other on the flight from Bozeman yesterday," she answers.

Her name is Poppy if I remember correctly. *I know her name now.*

"Oh shiiit," Eli says, then laughs as he continues, "This is the girl you struck out with?"

"Oh my gosh, it makes total sense now. That's the douchebag. How did I not put two and two together?" comes from Cici, who's next to Eli, smirking.

I glare at them but quickly recover. Poppy's eyebrows raise in surprise at our friends having heard both sides of the story. *Yeah, sugar, I did tell them about you.*

"How am I a douchebag for hitting on a hot chick? That shit happens every day. You should be flattered, Mouse."

"Flattered? Really? How about disgusted? Your pickup lines were enough to make any girl run for the hills," Poppy says with a hand on her jutted hip. She's annoyingly cute when irritated.

"Au contraire, most women are running straight to my bed," I state matter-of-factly.

"Well, I'm not a bimbo like the girls you're probably used to."

"Nope, you're just a meek little mouse who only reads about the good stuff instead of doing it."

She glares but doesn't reply, and the hurt is evident. Now I feel like a jerk. Especially with the evil eyes I'm getting from Cici, Lily, and Lucy. And the looks from the guys say I've definitely fucked up. Well, shit.

We're interrupted by the officiant, gratefully directing our attention away from each other. "All right, everyone. If Jackson and Eli come with me, I'll have the rest of you take your places so we can get started. I know you have a dinner to attend."

Cici whispers into Poppy's ear, then Poppy shakes her head with the words, "It's fine."

Great. Judging by the look of warning they gave me before walking off, Jackson and Eli are going to read me the riot act for that little show. As they take their places at the front of the aisle, Sebastian and Justin pull me aside.

"Dude, watch yourself. Cici's pregnant, hormonal, and it's her wedding. The last thing you want to do is piss her off. She'll hand you your balls," Sebastian offers.

"Yeah, if I were you, I'd take my word on things and wait for the next redhead to come along. I think your chances of landing this one are over. And you might want to do some groveling," Justin adds.

"Screw that. She dishes as much shit as I do. She'll be fine. And don't count me out yet, there's still plenty of time."

Sebastian shakes his head. "It's your balls, just be careful."

Justin claps me on the shoulder. "Good luck with that. And with Cici, if you succeed."

I scoff. "Whatever, we're all adults."

Both Justin and Sebastian's eyes go behind me as Poppy asks, "Does that mean you'll start behaving like one?"

Breathing deeply, I paste on a smile and turn to face my mouse. Her hair is up in a sleek ponytail, and the sundress she's wearing hugs her slender figure, accentuating her hips. She has no bra on, and the mounds of her breasts are peeking out enough at the top of her dress to make me want to uncover the rest.

"Now what would be the fun in that? Come on, sugar, let's do this." I grab her hand and bring it to my arm, stepping away from the others and the daggers Cici is shooting at me.

Poppy seems so prim and proper and, honestly, probably way too innocent for the likes of me. Dammit, I really should let this go, but I'm unaccustomed to losing and not quite sure I'm willing.

Sebastian and Lily take their place in front of Poppy and me. Justin and Lucy are behind us, followed by Cici and her dad, and lastly, Walker and Mia, who have graciously remained silent during the confrontation.

"What are the chances, huh? You know, if you'd told me your name, we could've avoided that," I whisper to Poppy.

"If you were capable of actual conversation and not just cheesy pickup lines, it probably would've come up," she whispers angrily.

Moments after the music starts, Sebastian and Lily begin walking.

"Something came up, that's for sure. Guess what I went to bed thinking about last night?"

"Stop it."

My shoulders shake as I chuckle silently. Riling her up is so much fun.

"I bet you had plenty of naughty thoughts. Tell me, have I starred in any of your fantasies?"

"Actually, you have—one where you got hit by a bus."

This time, the laugh escapes, causing Poppy to aggressively "shh" me.

As we proceed down the aisle, I can feel her seething the entire way, which in turn glues a smile to my face. When we arrive at the front, she yanks her hand from my arm and stomps toward the bride's side as I take my place next to Sebastian.

Eli gives me a warning look as Sebastian leans in to whisper, "You're digging yourself deeper, man."

"Nah, I'm having fun is all."

"It's your grave."

That it is. Or it could be my bed. Either way, I won't go lying down.

4

TRUCE

Poppy

IS IT POSSIBLE I'M STILL ASLEEP AND THIS IS ALL A DREAM? IF only. The sad reality is that I have to deal with this guy for the entire weekend. Even worse is that if he had an ounce of class and acted like a decent human being, I'd probably have been into him. He's hot as hell, no doubt about that, but damn—when Suits opens his mouth, his words overshadow his looks.

I'll have to tell Lily to introduce me to that Jordan guy right away. In the meantime, it'll take all my willpower to stay calm and make it through the next day and a half. *Shoot,* I wonder if they did a seating chart for dinner. If so, I hope we're at opposite ends. I'll be finding out soon since we're almost finished here. Until then—*I've got this.*

Annoyingly, Suits *did* star in my fantasies last night. Damn him and his filthy mouth. And double damn him for how he makes me feel, because the biggest problem of all is that my body is a traitor and can't be trusted, given its reaction to that filthiness.

I've held my own so far, thank God. And who knows, he may

give up soon, though it's doubtful considering his profession. His persistence makes sense, that's for sure. And coincidentally, so does the nickname I gave him.

I can't believe none of this came up on the way here. I could have at least braced myself. Regrets won't do any good, though, so I'll grin and bear it for Cici's sake. Starting now.

With a smile in place, Braden and I meet in the middle when it's our turn to exit down the aisle. My hand finds the crook of his arm, and he covers it with his. The feel of his touch makes my heart flutter, annoyingly so.

"Listen, let's rewind. How about you pretend I didn't say any of those things that offended you so much, and I'll pretend I don't want in your pants." I growl low, but he ignores me and continues, "We might as well attempt to get along, or it's going to be a frustrating few days. What do you say, Poppy? Truce?"

He's smooth when he wants to be, and hearing my name on his lips for the first time is… something I want to hear again.

"I think that's the most mature thing I've heard from you yet. But are you capable of watching your tongue?"

He shakes his head and chuckles. "Oh, Mouse, I'm not responsible for what comes out of my mouth when you talk like that."

Groaning, I elbow him, prompting a chuckle.

"You're hopeless. This truce of yours is probably a lost cause, but I'll give it a try," I agree for Cici's sake.

"That's the spirit." He nudges me with his shoulder, making me smile. Maybe everything will work out after all.

I wasn't as upset as I would have been without our chat when I found out that there is, in fact, a seating chart. Fourteen of us are seated at one long table, seven on each side. The parents and Walker are at one end, the two sets of brides and grooms are in the middle, and the rest of us are at the other end. Luckily, Braden and I are seated across from each other rather than side by side.

Way to look at the positive, Poppy. Score one for me. And

while I'm at it, I might as well attempt to play nice. Multiple conversations are happening at once, so I seize the opportunity.

"So, Braden, what were you doing in Bozeman?" I ask. He may not know how to have a normal conversation with a woman, but I'll help him out.

His head swivels in surprise, as if he didn't expect me to engage, but he recovers quickly. "I was interviewing a potential client in Big Sky."

That seems odd. "Why would you go to him and not the other way around, since he's the one hiring you? And shouldn't he be doing the interviewing to see if you're the right fit?" I'm genuinely curious.

"I'm a hot commodity, and I don't accept everyone who requests my services. I don't represent addicts, the unfaithful, or abusive assholes. The divorce has to be amicable or a result of the other spouse's fuckups." He shrugs. "And he chose to fly me over on his dime, including travel time. My clients are wealthy and generally get what they want."

"So did you take him as a client?"

"I did. His wife was having an affair."

"Is that common?"

"More than you can imagine."

"Now what happens?" I'm fascinated by the side of him that can actually converse and appears to be an upstanding guy.

"What do you mean? We sign a contract, and I handle the case."

"I mean, what do you do next—draw up papers to split everything?"

He chuckles. "If it were that easy, people wouldn't need lawyers. First, we review their assets and ensure everything's accounted for—on both sides. Just because my client isn't at fault doesn't guarantee he's not hiding things. We also have to make sure we have enough proof of the infidelity to hold up in court. Those two things alone take the most time. Then we begin negotiations, which may result in a court battle, typical of high-asset divorces."

Okaaay, so there *is* more to the guy than meets the eye. I should stop engaging in case I end up liking him. It might be best to stay in the dark. But before I redirect my attention elsewhere, he turns the tables.

"What about you? What do you do other than read romance?"

I can't tell if that was a dig or not, but at least it wasn't another sleazy pickup line, so I'll let it slide. "I'm a real estate agent like Cici. We were at the same office in Bozeman."

"Damn, you ruined my fantasy. I was hoping for the teacher."

He winks, and I shake my head.

"You just couldn't resist, could you?" I ask, making him laugh.

"No, I really couldn't. You're too easy," he says, smiling.

"You wish."

The rest of the evening goes better than expected. We all laugh, tell stories, learn more about each other, and by the end of the night, I forget all about being irritated with a certain someone.

Dinner is over, and we're wrapping up, ready to head to our rooms. Since tomorrow's the big day, we're calling it an early night. That's when I find out Suits is staying next to me.

"I saw you walking to your room last night, and you're right next door. Why don't I give you a ride?" Braden asks as we all make our way to the parking area.

"Uh… sure." Except I'm not sure—at all.

The girls all hug each other goodnight, and Lily whispers in my ear before she lets me go, "Hey, are you okay going with Braden?"

"It's fine. He's been better tonight," I respond.

"Well, let me know if he gives you any trouble."

"Don't worry. I can handle him." I assure her.

We all pile into our carts, and once we're alone, neither one of us speaks, creating an uncomfortable silence. But since I began the last conversation, I'm leaving it up to him this time. Seconds later, my patience is rewarded.

"Are you ready to call it a night, or do you want to go for a soak in the hot tub?" Braden asks as he parks the cart in front of his building.

"With you?" The shock in my voice is evident.

"Yeah, with me."

"Can you behave?" I ask teasingly.

"That depends on whether you want me to." He side-eyes me from the driver's seat.

"I think I've been crystal clear on that," I say, stepping out of the cart and facing him.

"I don't know… there's always room for interpretation."

My hand goes to my jutted hip. "I beg to differ. What part of *stop hitting on me* did you not understand?"

The infuriating man chuckles. "The part where your body reacts every time I do."

"It does not, and if it looks that way, it's because I'm repulsed."

We walk around the cart and meet on the sidewalk.

"I'll let you pretend for now. So are you joining me or what?" He holds his hand up, halting my reply. "And before you answer— yes, I'll behave… until you're ready for otherwise."

I roll my eyes. "Fine. Against my better judgment, I'll meet you out there." I give in, walking away before he utters more nonsense.

The question on repeat as I change into my swimsuit is: *Why did I agree to this?* I continue second-guessing myself while putting my hair up and checking my makeup because whether I'm interested in the guy or not doesn't change the fact that I'm still female and want to look my best.

I'm a nervous wreck on the way out, and I shouldn't be. It's not like this is a date or anything. We're simply two guests at a wedding who aren't ready to call it a night. No big deal. It means absolutely nothing. It definitely doesn't mean I'm into him.

I'll need to keep repeating this because when I make it to the hot tub, I'm instantly regretting my decision. This was a bad idea.

His chest is above the waterline, and holy hell, is he ripped. Not only is he an Adonis from the neck up, but he has a body to match.

Shit. I'm in trouble.

Braden

I'm making progress. That she even considered joining me in the hot tub was a surprise, and when she finally said yes, I about fell over. Now it's just a matter of playing my cards right. Regardless of what she says, I think she enjoys my dirty suggestions. Her body gives away what her words don't.

However, it'll still take some finesse to win her over. The right amount of naughty and nice should do the trick. I'll start with nice tonight and move on to the naughty tomorrow.

Thankfully, I'm already in the water by the time she makes her way out because when she steps shyly around the corner, appearing as if she's wearing nothing but the towel, my swim trunks immediately tent. And then when she drops it, holy shit, I could've busted a nut.

The strapless bikini leaves little to the imagination. A thin scrap of material barely covers her perky little tits, her nipples pebbling from the cool night air. Too bad she's facing me and not giving me a view of that ass.

"Hi," she says timidly, slinking into the water as far from me as possible.

"I was starting to think you ditched me."

"Nope. I just wasn't in a hurry. And don't forget, no funny business, I'm only here because I love hot tubs and the sound of the ocean."

Is she trying to convince herself or me? Rather than egg her on, I decide to keep the conversation casual and give her a reprieve.

"I'm sure it's nice, since you're not around it every day. But you're lucky to have mountains in your backyard. That drive to Big Sky is amazing."

"Yeah, but it's easy to take the beauty for granted when you've lived around them your whole life. Honestly, I'm drawn to the ocean more at this point."

"Makes sense. I don't know that I'd want to be landlocked. But I'm too busy with work at this stage in my life to be attracted to either." I shrug.

"The only thing you're attracted to is women, right?"

I chuckle. "If that was supposed to be a dig, you have major room for improvement."

She shakes her head. "Nope. Just a statement of fact."

"True, but you can't tell me you're not interested in men." I mock with a raise of my brow.

"I am, but it's different. I'm not into one-night stands or becoming a notch on some guy's bedpost. I want something meaningful like my parents have."

"How do you plan on finding that if you're unwilling to put yourself out there and date?"

"I didn't say anything about not dating. Obviously, it's part of the process, but it doesn't require sleeping with everyone. And if that's what a guy expects, they're not the one for me," she says haughtily.

"Well, I'm here to tell you you're missing out. Besides, you're too young to be settling down."

Her mouth drops open in disbelief. "I am not. If anything, I'm way behind. My parents were just out of high school when they got married and had kids."

I grunt at her statement. That's the most ridiculous notion I've heard. "You know, statistically speaking, 50% of marriages end in divorce, the leading cause being infidelity. Wouldn't you rather reduce the temptation later by sowing your oats before you limit yourself to one man?"

"Is that what you're doing, or will you be in such a habit of sleeping around that you won't ever be able to stay faithful?"

My blood boils immediately. "I would never cheat, and I think anyone who does is scum," I spit out.

She feigns shock. "We finally agree on something. Should we document it?"

Her sarcasm and adorable smile instantly cooled my anger. "We could seal it with a kiss." I wink.

She puffs out a breath. "I have seriously never met a more tenacious person."

"I didn't make partner at my firm by being a pushover."

"I suppose not. So why did you decide to become a divorce attorney anyway?"

"You heard a lot about my job earlier, so it's your turn. How is real estate working out?" I ask, redirecting the conversation. I'm not about to fill her in on the shit that went into my career choice. My childhood was less than ideal, and no one wants to hear the sad story of growing up penniless, without a father. Not many people know about my shitty upbringing, because it's best left in the past.

"It's good. I'm helping Cici finish up a few of her deals, so I'm a little busier than usual, but that's okay. With Cici gone, I've had more time on my hands anyway."

"How long have you been doing it?" I fire off the next question.

"I started as a receptionist at a real estate firm right after high school and was hired as an assistant by an agent in the office about a year later. I got my license three years ago."

"And it pays the bills?"

She smiles cutely. "That's a bit personal. Is that your way of asking if I'm successful?"

"Guilty as charged."

"It's lucrative. I've partnered with a few builders who work with me exclusively to list their properties, so I'm not a struggling agent who's barely making it. I've also built up a referral business, plus it helps to be in my hometown with old friends from high school who are starting to buy houses."

"Are you in love with being a realtor?"

She considers it before answering. "I wouldn't say that since I'm not sure I want to do it forever."

"What else are you interested in?"

"Getting married and having a family."

"Ahhh," I draw out slowly. Here's the crux of our differences.

"What? You sound like that's a bad thing."

"I don't know that that's the right word for it, but it's definitely not something *I'm* anxious to do anytime soon."

"Right. Because you're too egotistical to be responsible for anyone else, not to mention you'd have to limit yourself to one woman. Oh, the horror," she teases.

"I actually prefer my focus to be on one woman... *at a time.*" I smirk and wag my brows, then lower my voice to ask, "Would you like to be on the receiving end of that focus?"

In the blink of an eye, water is flying at me. "Does that answer your question?" she asks with a giggle.

"You won't be laughing in a minute," I say, wiping the water from my face.

She continues to laugh until I lunge, causing her to squeal, "I take it back. I'm sorry." She tries to get away in vain.

"Oh, you'll be sorry, all right." I wrap my arm around her middle and bring her onto my lap. Probably not the brightest idea I've had, but too late, because there's no way I'm letting go now that I have her. So much for sticking to nice.

The minute she realizes her precarious position, she stills. I'm sure she can feel my raging hard-on right under her ass. Only one thing comes to mind when that mouth is inches from mine. With no hesitation, I pounce, reaching my hand around the back of her neck, and pulling her toward me to seize the moment.

Oh fuck. She's as luscious as I imagined. Soft, pliable, plump, and the most kissable fucking lips I've ever felt. She's stiff at first, caught off guard, but returns the kiss within seconds. I squeeze her neck and angle my head, putting enough pressure into my lips to spread hers open for a taste.

The groan that escapes my mouth is feral, and I'm a goner for lifting the lid on Pandora's box. If I don't have this girl coming on my lap within minutes, then I'm losing my touch. My tongue begins a cautious dance as a rhythm is established.

I grab her hips and pull her tighter into me, her ass rubbing against my dick. Fuck, I need to feel her pussy and make her fall apart.

Trailing my mouth along her jaw while maintaining a firm grip on her neck, I whisper sensually into her ear. "Damn, baby, you're so fucking sexy." I lick and suck, and am rewarded with whimpers of desire.

"You feel so damn good. But I'm about to make you feel even better." I knead her ass and devour her neck as she pants in desperation and mewls with need.

My hand comes around to her stomach, quickly dipping into her swimsuit without resistance from the firecracker on my lap. The fuse has been lit and is about to be detonated. Before I know it, my fingers are grazing the tuft of hair above her mound.

I return to her lips, swallowing her gasp when my fingers find her clit and begin to circle it.

She moans deliciously into my mouth.

"That's right, baby. Let me take care of you," I breathe into the kiss, reaching farther south and pressing my fingers against her opening.

Her hips buck into my hand. "Fuck yeah. Spread your legs for me." I nudge her thigh with my wrist, and she complies, splaying her legs to give me access.

"That's it, such a good girl."

Her answering whimper tells me she enjoys the commentary.

My mouth travels back to her neck as she stretches for more, and her hips start rocking, seeking friction. I won't make her beg… this time. Beginning with one finger, I slowly penetrate the tightest fucking hole on the planet.

"Come on, Mouse, relax and let me in." I work it in and out with small movements until I'm as far as I can go and push a little harder.

"Oh my God," she moans.

"You like that, baby?" I ask as I move in and out a few more times. "Think you can take another?"

Her plea in response is all the answer I need to add a finger. Fuck, she's tight as hell. With my middle two fingers stretching her out, I rub her clit with my thumb as her hips go wild.

"Damn baby, your pussy feels so good."

The last thing I want to do is silence her, but it's probably necessary, since she'd be mortified if anyone heard us, so I claim her mouth again. Her walls begin to pulse, leaving no doubt she's close. To finish her off, I press in deep and curl my fingers to flick her G-spot, which sends her into orgasm bliss. She squeezes my arm hard enough to draw blood as she rides it out.

"That's it, baby. You're so sexy, fucking my hand, coming on my lap. I bet you taste like heaven."

Her entire body melts in my arms, and her muscles relax moments later.

I slowly withdraw from between her legs while wishing to God we weren't in the hot tub so I could lick my fingers clean and find out if she's as sweet as I imagine. Shit, that was hot. My little mouse has a bit of a minx in her. Taking her by surprise may be the key to unlocking that side.

"Did you enjoy having my focus, Mouse?"

The minute the words come out, she flinches. Miss Uptight just reentered the building.

"Oh my God." She practically leaps from my lap and scrambles to the other side. "I… that… we shouldn't have done that."

"*We* didn't do anything, but as for what *I* did? You seemed to enjoy it. I sure fucking did, and that orgasm says you did too, so cut the innocent act. You wanted it, babe. Hell, you came in less than three minutes flat."

"I'm going to bed. Don't mention this to anyone or get any ideas about it happening again."

"Come on, Mouse, don't be that way. We're both adults here."

She's out and wrapping the towel around her, already heading toward her room.

Damn this girl. How can she be so sensual one second, only to shut down in the next? I'm not sure what her problem is, but someone needs to loosen her up. Sounds like the perfect goal for the weekend.

"Good night," she calls over her shoulder before rounding the corner.

And that's the end of that. For now, anyway.

Currently, my only concern is handling the predicament I've been left in. I'm lucky no one else is around to witness the raging fucking boner I'm walking back with. Remembering the feel of her ass grinding on top of my cock a minute ago is enough to break me.

Luckily, it takes no time at all to make it inside the room and hang my wet shorts in the shower. I'm lying face up on the bed, hand working my cock while I envision that sexy-as-fuck climax play out. The way her body bowed and convulsed on my lap. Her moans of pleasure as her pussy squeezed the hell out of my finger, pulsing through her orgasm.

What tips me over the edge, though, is imagining my cock deep inside as she shatters around it, calling my name. Feeling her tight walls milk me dry. *Fuuuuck.* Cum shoots out as I squeeze tighter and pull, prolonging the pleasure.

Holy. Fucking. Shit. That's two fucking times in two fucking days over the same fucking girl. What the hell is happening to me?

5

NOT HAPPENING

Poppy

THAT DIDN'T HAPPEN LAST NIGHT. IT HAD TO HAVE BEEN A dream. Right? I huff as I roll over in bed. Oh my God, it did, though. It was a moment of weakness. That's all. I'm going to pretend we did not kiss—that I did not let him give me the best orgasm of my life. Nope. Did. Not. Happen.

The groan that escapes is one of frustration. Sexual? Possibly. Disappointment in myself? Most definitely. He came out of nowhere. One minute we were talking, and the next, well, that damn kiss. Who knew lips could be so fricking persuasive? And the hand on my neck was like a live wire straight to my nether region. His firm grip directed me where he wanted, making me hungry for more than ever before.

I may not be very experienced, but I've messed around. I've made it to third base but held back from bringing it home. Which, in all honesty, hasn't been much of a hardship considering the few encounters I've had were unimpressive to say the least. The only orgasms I've had have been self-administered.

Until last night, anyway. That was… otherworldly—unholy in

the best of ways. It's fair to assume Suits knows his way around a woman's body and should be avoided at all costs for that reason alone, which is precisely what I intend to do. Steer clear of the manwhore… magic fingers and all.

Besides, today's the big day. All focus needs to be on the happy couples. It's not about me. It's not about Braden and his relentless flirting. And it's certainly not about what occurred in the hot tub only hours ago. In fact, no one will find out. Because… It. Never. Happened.

My phone buzzes next to the bed, jolting me from my thoughts. It's Cici, along with a text from Matt that must have come through right before I woke up.

> Cici: Hey, did Braden give you any shit last night, or was everything okay?
>
> Me: It was fine.

Understatement of the year. It was incredible.

> Cici: Good. I was worried.
>
> Me: You shouldn't be worrying about anything. Today's your big day. Are you excited?
>
> Cici: So excited! You're coming to brunch, right?
>
> Me: Yep, somebody needs to drink the mimosas…

Going to Matt's text, I answer him next.

> Matt: I'm heading to the airport. Are you having fun so far?
>
> Me: So much. We were at the beach all day yesterday. It was awesome. Then we had the rehearsal and an amazing dinner afterward. Her friends and family are great.

No need to mention the end of the evening.

> Matt: Wish I was there. What's on the agenda today?
>
> Me: Mimosa brunch, then all afternoon at the spa.

Matt: Sucks to be you. I'm boarding in a bit.

Me: Yay. I'll leave a key under your name at the front desk.

Matt: Sounds good. Can't wait.

Me: Me too. See you at the wedding!

Since Matt will only be here for one night, I offered to share my room. I'm excited for him to be here, not only because he'll be a buffer in dealing with the Braden situation but also because he's a good friend. I've missed hanging out with Cici and him together.

Rousing myself from bed, I dress in the pajamas they provided for the ladies' brunch. At least getting through today will be relatively easy, considering the men and women are spending it apart. Apparently, Eli and Jackson are too possessive for a night without their women, but they did go their separate ways this morning and won't catch sight of their brides-to-be until they walk down the aisle.

Which is when I'll have to face Braden for the first time after the hot tub incident. Thank God I won't have to see him all day. That doesn't mean I won't be obsessing over that orgasm while attempting to conceal the tidbit of information from the girls. Ugh. The last thing I needed today was that hanging over my head.

Putting my hair in a messy bun and applying a layer of lip gloss, I exit my room to wait for the golf cart to arrive that will take me to brunch. I'd usually walk, but it felt weird to be wandering the posh resort in pajamas, so I called the front desk for a ride.

"Nice PJs. You need a lift?" comes from behind me.

Oh shit. My belly drops.

With a deep, calming breath, I turn around to Mr. Talented Fingers in the flesh, looking sexy in slacks and a short-sleeved button-down. He's smiling as if he's happy to see me—the complete opposite of my utter mortification. My body doesn't feel the same, however, as my core clenches in tribute to his pleasurable orgasm-inducing skills, and I can't help but examine the hand that administered that pleasure.

Shaking myself out of it, I respond, "Uh… no. Concierge is already on the way. Thanks, though."

"You sure? I'm heading to the main building anyway. We could flag them down as they pass."

"I'm good." This is *so* awkward. See? Bad idea. Bad, bad idea to give in to him.

He shrugs. "All right. Suit yourself. So I take it you're pretending nothing happened last night?"

Yep.

"I'm not sure what you're talking about," I answer instead.

"Hmph." His head bobs as he rocks back on his heels. "Well, enjoy the day with the ladies, then. And just so you know, I won't be joining you in the land of make-believe. I'm not through with you yet." He has the audacity to wink before getting in the cart and driving off.

By the third mimosa, I've mellowed out and managed not to blow my cover. It's been easier than I thought it would be with all the excitement from the pending nuptials. After brunch, we're scheduled at the spa for the full treatment… massage, facials, nails, makeup, and hair—the benefits of marrying a billionaire.

It's when our nails are being painted that Cici finally brings up the topic I've done so well to avoid. "I still can't believe Braden was the guy from the plane. It makes total sense, looking back on your story. So, how did the ride to your room go last night? Did he hit on you again?"

Shit. I was so close to making it through the day. I'm glad we're not sitting face-to-face, so she won't notice the inner turmoil from spouting a bald-faced lie. No way can I fess up to the truth when she specifically warned me about him. Not to mention, Cici was into him right before meeting Eli. Sure, that might have been years ago, but doesn't that break some sisterhood rule?

"It was fine. Just the usual Braden."

"Then he did. Did you set him straight?"

Oh boy.

"I think so, but I guess time will tell." That was pretty convincing if I do say so myself.

"Well, he'd better back off," Cici says angrily, and now I feel like shit for throwing him under the bus. It may have been his fault, but I *was* a willing participant… all too willing.

"Especially since I'm hooking you up with Jordan at the reception," Lily chimes in. "You're going to love him."

"I'll meet him, but don't get your hopes up. I'm only here for one more night."

"Girl, one night is all you need," Walker says, making everyone giggle while Mia smacks his shoulder.

"Not everyone gives it up as easily as you," she tells her best friend.

"Speaking of giving it up, tell me about this Matt guy. I've always wanted to ride a cowboy." Walker looks at me and Cici.

"I'm not sure he bats for the same team," I say while giggling at the thought.

"Firm or up for negotiation?" he asks.

Cici takes over. "Matt's definitely into women, but if anyone can turn someone, it would be you."

"Oh, I second that," Lucy interjects right before Matt responds, "Damn straight, as in he won't be for long."

We all burst into fits of giggles, even the moms joining in. Much to the makeup artist's dismay, the rest of the afternoon goes the same. Trying to get us to stay still becomes a job of its own, but by the time we're primped, plucked, and primed, we all look like we're ready for the runway. The photographer has certainly been busy capturing the day.

After finishing touches have been made, we head up to the bridal suite to get dressed. I feel like an absolute princess. I've never been so pampered or had that many things done in one sitting. The dresses Mia and Cici picked out are gorgeous, and thankfully, the colors for their wedding, sapphire blue and amethyst, couldn't have been better if I'd chosen myself. Sometimes it's hard to pair anything with fiery red hair.

When we're all dressed and minutes away from the ceremony, the nerves are starting to set in for everyone. Cici looks amazing in a fitted gown over the cutest pregnant belly a girl could ask for. You can't even tell she's pregnant when she's turned away from you. The V neckline accentuates her huge boobs in a classy way that doesn't dip too low, and the train that flares out under her fitted backside is beautiful.

Mia chose a strapless dress that perfectly flatters her tiny frame. Unlike Cici's more form-fitting gown, Mia's flares at the waist like a princess dress. They're both unique on their shared special day, and it's easy to see the love they have for each other and how excited they are to become family.

The wedding planner comes in to get our attention. "All right, ladies and gentle*man*, it's time to take your places. Cici, Mia, and Walker, you guys hang back a minute. Cici, your dad will meet you just outside."

We all squeal in unison before Lucy, Lily, and I grab our bouquets and head out. My nerves are more about the man I'll be walking with rather than the ceremony itself. The minute I round the corner, we make eye contact—his widening in surprise. I may do a better job at concealing my assessment, but holy shit does the man wear a tux well. This takes Suits to a whole new level—a sinfully sexy one.

"Wow. You're… stunning," he says, making me blush.

"You clean up pretty nicely yourself." I wouldn't want to inflate his ego more than it already is.

"That dress doesn't strike me as a bridesmaid dress. Not enough ruffles. It seems more fit for a gala."

"Brides are starting to pick dresses that can be used again these days."

"Well, that's… a great idea." He's staring at my cleavage, and I can't help but giggle at the absolute typicalness.

"Pervy much?" I ask.

"Sorry, it's just," he says quickly, then leans down and whispers in my ear. "I feel bad about not giving those any attention last night. I think they deserve a turn."

My breathing picked up the second he leaned in and only got worse with each word spoken. Speaking proves to be difficult as utter ridiculousness pours from my mouth. "Um… they're fine. I mean, no, they don't need any attention."

He chuckles in response before grabbing my hand, placing it in the crook of his arm, and leading me down the aisle.

My eyes roam the crowd and find Matt right away, who waves. I beam in his direction while noticing the scrutinizing side-eye from Braden. What's that about? He better not go all territorial on me after one brief interaction… no—after one brief *mistake* in the hot tub. He's got another thing coming if that's the case.

We make it to the end without incident and split off to take our places, allowing me to enjoy the moment. It's a beautiful wedding. Eli and Jackson look adorably nervous but stunning in their tuxes, as do all the men. The minute the wedding march begins, the guests stand, and Cici and Mia make their appearance. It's a sight to behold. The love between these two couples is palpable to every single person here.

The moisture in my eyes is unavoidable as I absorb the feelings pouring from all four. It becomes harder to control the tears as promises are made and the most beautiful vows I've heard are spoken. The moment each couple is pronounced as husband and wife, there's not a dry eye in the house. Thank God for the tissues tucked into the bouquet.

Cheers erupt as the happy couples are presented, and it's once again time to join my partner, who I couldn't help sneaking peaks at during the ceremony. The wink he shot me at one point caused my belly to dip, and I tried to refrain from making eye contact after that.

With the audience standing and talking, it's unnecessary to remain quiet as we return down the aisle, giving Braden the opportunity for the question I'm sure has been eating at him throughout.

"Is that your boyfriend?" he asks in the iciest whisper you could imagine. And I don't like his tone or the implication that he has a right to care.

"Wouldn't you like to know," I respond nonchalantly.

"Damn straight I would, since my fingers were in your pussy last night. Is it okay if I tell him that?" Even with the hushed voice, his underlying fury is evident.

"Are you serious right now? It shouldn't even matter to you. My personal life is not your concern, so mind your own business."

Thinking the conversation is over since we're around the corner and heading toward the rest of the wedding party, I yank my hand back, intending to stomp off. But before I do, he grabs my wrist and drags me through a door.

Braden

I'm furious. I won't rest if even a chance exists that *I* was the other man. No fucking way. When I saw the guy by himself in the back row wave to Poppy, and the smile she gave in return, my insides coiled. I noticed him earlier when returning to my room to grab something before the ceremony. Even though it was odd he was coming from Poppy's room, I didn't overthink it, assuming he was staff.

But my blood has been boiling ever since they made eye contact. I'd have never touched her if I thought for a second she had a boyfriend. It hit me then that she'd never answered the fucking question from the day we met.

"If you think I'm going to sit back and let you fuck someone over, you don't know me very well."

"Funny you say that. We don't know each other at all. And I'd like it to stay that way."

I lean down until I'm in front of her face. "Either you tell me right now if he's your boyfriend, or I'll find out myself. And I won't care who else is around to hear me explain why I'm asking," he snarls.

"You're an ass."

"At least I'm not a liar. And if you keep pushing me, you'll learn I don't make empty threats."

I'm about to march out when she gives me the answer I want. "No. He's not my boyfriend. He's mine and Cici's friend from Bozeman."

"Good enough friend to stay in the same room as you?" I'm still unconvinced, but her declaration took the edge off.

"Seriously? How do you even know that? And I already told you he's not my boyfriend, so whether we're in the same room or not is none of your business."

"It is when I want you in mine." With her mouth open in shock, I dive in, crashing my lips to hers. My hands automatically go to her neck, gripping her passionately and holding her steady while I take what I want. Her eager response tells me I'm not out of line and that she needs this as much as I do.

She whines into the kiss, meeting my tongue thrust for thrust. Reaching down to grip her ass, I pull her into me, seeking friction for my cock. Craving more, I shove her against the door, grinding into her. Christ, those sexy moans, along with her hips moving in tune to mine, could cause me to blow if I continue dry humping this woman.

Knowing we've been away too long and that if we keep this up, I'll have her bent over taking my cock, I decide we'd better stop before the search party arrives and catches us in the act. We have plenty of time for fucking later. And honestly, I'd rather savor this one.

Reluctantly, I pull away to a thoroughly ravished woman breathless with desire. I'm two seconds from making a bad decision and saying fuck it when she reaches up to slap me. I'm too shocked to avoid the blow, immediately stepping back while shaking my head.

"What the fuck was that for?" I ask.

"Why do you think? You can't just… do that."

"Do what? Kiss you? You didn't seem to mind, considering you were reciprocating."

"I—"

"Poppy? Braden? Where did you guys go? Everyone's waiting to do pictures." Lucy can be heard from outside.

"Shoot. What do we do? We can't be caught together," Poppy whispers, freaking out.

"Why the fuck not? We're adults. We can do whatever the hell we want."

"Because this is Cici's special day. She doesn't need to deal with drama."

"What drama?" *What the fuck is this girl's problem?*

"This." She motions back and forth between us. "You. Me. This can't happen. We… are *not* happening."

"It's happened twice now, baby. You can deny it all you want, but I bet if I feel your pussy it won't lie."

"You're disgusting. You don't have to be so vulgar."

"Ah, my poor little mouse. So skittish of a few dirty words." Closing the distance, I lean down to whisper. "You know what I think? I think you like my filthy mouth. But I promise you'd like it even better between your legs while I lap up all the evidence of your *non*arousal."

Her shiver tells me I'm right. Without another word, I straighten my bow tie and walk out the door, leaving her in a puddle of need that I'm positive has her panties soaking.

It didn't take long to find Lucy and tell her Poppy had to use the restroom and was delayed by a wardrobe malfunction. Women are constantly fixing something or another with their clothes, so I figured it was the most plausible excuse.

I couldn't give a shit if anyone knows we're messing around, but I'll indulge Mouse for now and go with a cover story. She'll eventually discover that it's futile. I'll have her sooner or later. Hopefully, it's before she leaves. Otherwise, the chase is on.

The photographer snaps pictures of the newlyweds while we wait for Poppy. When she rejoins the group, anxiety oozes from every cell in her body. When Cici sees her, she's immediately concerned.

"Is your dress okay?" Cici asks in concern.

Confusion flits across Poppy's face for the briefest moment before clarity sets in, and she glances my way in surprise.

Yeah, Mouse, I can be nice when I want to.

"Oh, it wasn't the dress, actually." She makes a face like it's obvious what the problem is, but doesn't want to say it out loud. I'm guessing she's indicating feminine issues, which is a useful cover as well. "But I'm fine. Sorry it took so long."

"No worries, we did some solo shots. You ready?" Cici asks.

"Yep," Poppy answers way too cheerfully.

After what feels like forever, we finish pictures and finally move on to the best part—the reception. Many of the guests are the Dubree brothers' business associates. A few are from Jackson and Cici's family business, and then a small number are Cici and Mia's school acquaintances. Those would typically be where my interest is, but my focus hasn't strayed from a mousy little redhead who lights up from my touch.

She immediately goes to the guy staying in her room, and from what it appears, she's telling the truth about him not being a boyfriend. She also doesn't seem to be the type to play around like that. I've done well not to be seen watching her, or so I thought.

Jackson leans on the bar next to me. "Dude, what's with you and Poppy? You've been stalking her like someone stole your favorite toy."

"That about sums it up. She could be my toy if she weren't so damn stubborn. She's skittish as hell, but she sure does respond nicely when caught off guard."

"You've sampled the goods then?" he asks.

Jackson and I have been best friends since college, and I'm not worried about hiding things with Poppy. He may be Cici's brother, but bros before hoes, sisters included. He won't stir the pot.

"Barely. We made out, and I gave her a hand job last night that was fucking out of this world. The problem is, we move one step forward, and she takes two back, and now that douchebag showed up, she's never alone. You know the guy?" I nudge my head in their direction. Cici and Eli are with them, and they all seem chummy.

"Yeah, that's Matt. It sounds like he helped her through some shit with the pregnancy. He seems okay."

"I don't like him. He hasn't left Poppy's side and is practically drooling over her."

Jackson snorts. "Man, you're pathetic. Go check out some of the other chicks here. Why work harder than you have to?"

"Because, like you said, I've sampled the goods, and now that I have, I want more." As in, I want it all.

Jackson smirks. "Well, looks like your competition is growing. Lily just brought another guy over to introduce her to. Good luck, buddy." He pats me on the back and walks off.

Fuck. Maybe he's right, and I should set my sights on another woman for the night. Though the problem as I study the room, is that I've already found what I'm looking for. Decision made—I'm not giving up until I have her.

Shit keeps interfering though. As I'm about to force myself into her orbit, the classic clinking of the wine glass signals it's time for toasts. With two nuptials, four of the wedding party, and the parents are making speeches. We agreed to keep them to a minimum with the number of people, but this is unfortunately prolonging my objective.

Parents go first, followed by Sebastian, Eli's best man, then Lily, Cici's maid of honor. Lily includes some humor, while Sebastian is completely serious. Walker is next as Mia's… best man, which leaves me, Jackson's best man. With Walker's ability to bring everyone to tears with laughter, he's a hard act to follow. Luckily, I'm used to speaking in front of people in the courtroom, so my confidence is natural as I take the microphone.

"This is a bit out of my wheelhouse, since typically I'm talking about why two people should be divorcing, not tying the knot, but I'm gonna give it my best shot. I'm here as Jackson's best man, but as I'm familiar with both couples, let me tell you, they had a heck of a time getting here. The fact that they've made it is a testament to how much they belong together."

"I first met Mia at a poker game. She was actually the shark who took me out. Jackson and Mia weren't together yet… okay, they basically couldn't stand each other. But even then, I saw something in Jackson's eyes that was inevitable—the game wasn't the only thing I lost that night—I lost my wingman. I'm still crying over both losses, but Mia, the joy you bring to Jackson far outweighs either one."

I turn my attention to the other couple. "And to Eli and Cici, I just want to remind you that Cici was into me first, so you're welcome for getting blackout drunk the night you met. Otherwise, you wouldn't have stood a chance." I wink in their direction. "Here's to the happy couples and to me, for being the last bachelor standing. Cheers." I raise my glass as everyone follows.

When the MC immediately announces it's time for the first dance, I groan at having to wait even longer to snag my sexy librarian away. Unless…

6

ONE TIME

Having Matt here has been a relief. It's not only saved me from any more encounters with Suits, but it's been nice having another familiar face around. Also, he was the perfect distraction after Braden's final words before walking away. Fricking A, how am I supposed to stop thinking about that kiss?

The subtle extra touches he snuck in throughout pictures didn't help. Whenever we were near enough, he would take the liberty of placing his hand on my back to guide me. And when we were next to each other for a photo, he wouldn't only have his arm around me but gently caress my skin with his thumb, causing flutters of desire.

Talk about sexual tension. Ugh. I'm not even interested in the guy. Okay, that *could* be a lie. But sometimes a lie is the truth you want to believe. And I'm trying desperately to believe it. The truth? I'm so insanely turned on by his advances and dirty words that I'm fairly certain I've been damp since walking down the aisle.

Lily brought Jordan over and introduced us, but we only had a moment to chat before the toasts began. He was sweet, offering to refill my champagne while I listened to everyone, and he's definitely easy on the eyes. It would be a great match if some other guy wasn't taking up all the space in my head. Consequently, I ended up comparing their features, musing over who had more appeal.

To make matters worse, Braden kept staring at me during the other speeches. I tried not to make eye contact, but it was too tempting to keep peeking, wondering if he was still looking at me. He was… every single time. He winked at one point, and heat rose to my cheeks.

Then he made his speech, and I was mesmerized. Not just the speech itself, but his voice, the confidence, and most of all, his charisma. I'm sure all the women in attendance were smitten by the time he was finished.

Now the four newlyweds are taking their first dance. After watching for a few minutes, Jordan resumes our conversation.

"You said you're leaving tomorrow and coming back after the baby's born?" he asks to kick us off.

"Yeah, I can't wait. I was there every step of the way until she moved."

"Nice. And are you staying here tonight?" Jordan asks, sounding hopeful.

"I am. I'm sharing a room with a friend who flew in today. That's Matt over there." I point in his direction.

He's been flirting with one of Cici's college girlfriends since Jordan was brought over and he took the opportunity to leave me. I'd been insisting he stay by my side all evening, fearing what would happen if he left me alone. The alcohol is weakening my resolve, and that damn kiss has me wanting things I shouldn't.

"Are you two together, together?" he asks, raising his brows.

"No. Just friends." I can tell Jordan's relieved at the answer.

"Well, in that case, may I have this dance?" He bows slightly, making me giggle—the champagne effect.

"Sure." Setting my glass down, I place my hand in his, and he leads me to the floor.

I catch sight of Cici and Lily beaming conspiratorially. Little do they know, I may be with Jordan, but my mind is elsewhere. Seconds later, however, the dance takes over any thoughts as Jordan leads me into a full-blown formal number.

"Uhm, wow. You really know what you're doing."

"I do. My mom's a traditional Southern belle and had me dancing from when I could walk. Made me take lessons and all," he says with a chuckle.

"How often do you use your skills?"

"Often enough. Weddings. Fundraisers. Parties my parents host."

"What kind of parties?"

"Wouldn't you like to know?" he asks, wiggling his brows.

My eyes go wide, wondering if he's implying what it sounds like.

He laughs. "I'm kidding. They're high society and enjoy hosting various social events: political fundraisers, holiday parties—pretty much any reason for a gathering. I go for the free booze and food, dancing with my mom as payment. She enjoys it, and I'll do anything to make her happy."

"That's sweet." And so perfect it hurts not to be as attracted to him as Braden. What is wrong with me?

"I'm lucky to have such amazing parents. How about you? Are you close to yours?"

See? Here's a guy who can carry on a conversation and isn't solely focused on sex. So why am I not responding to him like I do with Suits? It's like the man can hear my thoughts, because at that exact moment, Suits makes eye contact, conveying everything without words. My heart skips a beat before I give myself a mental shake, returning my attention to Jordan.

"I am. We live close by and have dinner together every Sunday."

He nods in acknowledgement and finishes the dance with vigor, gracefully leading us while twirling me around. When the song ends, my winded smile matches Jordan's.

"That was fun. Thank you," I say genuinely.

"My pleasure. Drink?"

"Absolutely," I reply, ready for a break.

"Come on, let's get a fresh one."

He takes my hand, pulling me through the crowd toward the bar. A minute later, we make our way to a table.

"When Lily told me she planned to introduce us, she never mentioned how gorgeous you are."

I smile and dip my head, embarrassed by the compliment. I take a sip of champagne for something to do other than reply.

He continues, "I wish she'd found me sooner so we could have had more time."

I'm not sure what to say. He's handsome, sweet, can dance like a pro, is obviously into me, and seems interested in messing around. Yet here I am still thinking about that kiss from Braden earlier. But I haven't really given this guy a chance. Who knows? Maybe kissing Jordan would be just as good. Should I make the first move to find out?

Deciding that's exactly what I should do, I take a deep breath. Here goes nothing. "Do you want to take a walk?"

"I'd love to. Lead the way." We stand, and his arm goes to my back as we weave through the tables.

OMG. What am I doing? I've never been so forward in my life. It's all Braden's fault. He's putting ideas in my head. Things I can't seem to shake off.

We're nearing the edge of the party area when I hear my name being called. I turn around to see Braden coming in hot, a man on a mission.

"Poppy. Hey, it's almost time for dessert, and Cici needs you to grab something from the bridal suite."

"Oh. Okay. What is it?"

"I'll explain on the way." He moves toward me and takes my hand, practically yanking me from Jordan's arm.

I look over apologetically. "I'm sorry. Can you give me a few minutes before we take a walk?"

"Definitely. Do what you need and come find me."

"Thank you. I won't be long."

As Braden pulls me along, I swear he mutters something that sounds a lot like '*Don't hold your breath.*'

"Excuse me?" I ask, snatching my hand back.

When we round the corner, he stops dead in his tracks and turns around, causing me to crash into him.

He grips my arms to steady me. "Were you seriously on your way to make out with someone who won't even come close to satisfying the need *I* filled you with?"

I cross my arms defiantly, but he doesn't release me. "You have no idea what you're talking about."

"Oh sugar, I've been watching you all fucking night. I know exactly what I'm talking about. I know you're not attracted to him, the same way I can tell you want me like I'm your favorite dessert. I know every time you think about that kiss because your face says so, and your body tells me the rest. Like how your legs squeeze together to ease the ache…" One hand slides down to slip under the high slit of my dress and is suddenly at my core. "Right here."

My mouth opens in a gasp when his other hand draws my head forward as our lips crash. I'm instantly craving more and ready to let him do anything he wants. I clutch his jacket to pull him closer. I've never responded this way to anyone. How is that possible?

"Are you done denying this?" he asks, breaking the kiss. "Admit you want me as much as I want you. Come on, Mouse. I'll satisfy that ache so good." He presses harder against my clit, and I melt, dropping my head to his chest and whimpering.

Leaning into my ear, he whispers, "Surrender yourself. Give me permission to fuck you and I promise you won't regret it. Say the word and we'll go to my room right now." His finger continues the assault on my clit.

"Come on, baby. I'll fuck you so hard and have you back before anyone notices we're gone."

I want it so badly. And while I have no idea what I'm doing, that's what's so appealing. I don't have to think about anything because he's controlling enough to take care of it all for me. He's perfect for my first time, and I bet he'll make it good.

Decision firmly made, the answer comes out in a whisper. "Okay."

His sigh of relief matches mine. "Thank fuck." He kisses the top of my head. "I'm not sure I could've survived if you said no. Goddamn, do I need to be inside you." He extracts himself, pulling me toward the parking lot. "Follow me."

"Wait. What about what Cici needed?" I remind him, tugging his hand to stop.

He turns and smirks. "I just made that up to get you alone. I was waiting for an opportunity all night, but your friend and that other guy didn't give me a chance. I wasn't about to stand by and let you sneak off with another man."

My jaw drops.

He continues on, talking over his shoulder as he drags me along. "Poppy, one thing you should know about me is that I'm used to getting what I want, and I've wanted you since I spotted you at the gate."

We make it to the cart, and I'm not sure why, probably nerves, but I decide to call him on his shit.

"Is this how you always treat women? Picking one out at random and chasing them until they give in?"

He answers as he backs out of the space, then onward to our building. "Sugar, I don't have to chase women. They come willingly. You, on the other hand, have been a challenge. It's refreshing."

"I'm honored," I say sarcastically, then add, "So now that you've won the battle, you'll be done with me?"

"You're leaving tomorrow, so yeah. That's generally how I work anyway." He's honest, I'll give him that.

For some reason, my chest tightens at his declaration rather than relief at being left alone. I'm sure it's because he'll be my first, not because I *like* him. Because I don't. He's crass. He's vulgar. He's the player of all players.

No. It's just sentiment, and I'll get over that. He's simply a means to an end—a way for me to experience my first time with someone who knows what they're doing. The last thing I need is him reading too much into this, which is why he can't find out I've never done it before. Plus, I don't think it would be as good if he knew I was a virgin. Hell, he'd probably run the other way, afraid that I'd cramp his style.

Thank goodness I grew up riding horses. They say you lose your hymen from it. I'm hoping it's not an old wives' tale, or he's in for quite the surprise. Fingers crossed the sheets remain clean, or rather, blood-less, because they better be dirty by the time we're finished.

"Having second thoughts? It's not like you didn't know this was a one-time thing. Although if you had given in sooner, we might've had time to play out all our fantasies. Listen, I live here, you live there. I'd say it's a perfect scenario for you."

"How so?" I ask as we exit the cart and walk toward his room, since I'm sharing mine.

"Bozeman's a small town, right? You've probably run through most of your options. I'm fresh meat. Someone to screw without over-thinking whether I'm husband material or not." He shrugs while open-ing the door. "Who knows, maybe this will be so much better than your supposed *meaningful sex* that you'll go home and start living like the rest of the single population."

"You're delusional." I shake my head at the ridiculous notion as we enter. Ridiculous because I have nothing to compare it to. I'm sure it won't change anything, but I hope he's right and it's at least pleasurable.

Grinning, he shuts the door, walks to the table to place his wallet down, and looks back at me, still standing in the doorway.

"I am delusional. You know what I've been doing these past cou-ple of nights?"

I shake my head.

"I've been jacking off to visions of your pussy wrapped around my cock instead of my hand. Ever heard the saying 'you bring about what you think about'?" He wiggles his brows. "I'm good at it."

He stalks closer and grabs my hand to remove my wristlet as he leads me into the room. Setting it on the table alongside his wallet, he continues, "I'm ready to make those visions a reality… right after I feast on your pussy until you're begging me for it. How does that sound?"

I gulp. I breathe. I open my mouth and close it—unsure what to say. The conversation on the way here gave me no chance to be nervous, but the minute the door clicked shut and the reality of what we're here to do kicked in, the nerves hit full force.

But uttering those words in that seductive tone, putting the images in my head—I'm once again putty in his hands and nodding in acceptance.

Braden

She froze the second we entered the room. My little mouse will be fun to coax out of her shell. Not that it's difficult with how she responds. Fuck, my words alone make her weak in the knees. Their effect on her is obvious in the flashes of desire that play out on her features.

She's stunning in the floor-length fitted gown. Her hair is up, showcasing her slender neck that I want to devour. I'm looking forward to dirtying up my wholesome little librarian, that's for sure. But first things first.

"I'm gonna need more than a nod of your head. Are you ready for me to have my way with you?"

"Yes," she says softly.

"Are you on birth control and been tested recently?"

She hesitates, her brows shifting in confusion as if the question is odd. "Uh…. Yes?"

"You don't sound very sure. I have, and I'd like to forgo condoms if you're okay with that, but I need you to elaborate."

It's strange, I usually wrap up automatically, but this one's fucking with me, and all I can think about is feeling her without a barrier between us. But only if I'm confident there won't be repercussions.

She jerks her head once up and down. "I get the shot, and I'm 100% STD free."

"Does that mean you're good with no protection?"

"Yes?" Her answer comes out as another question, and that's not good enough.

"Poppy," I say sternly.

"Yes. No protection. That's fine."

"You act like you've never had this conversation. Does no one ask you first?"

"Not… usually."

"Have you always used condoms then?"

She takes a second before answering, making me wonder why this is so hard for her. "This will be the first time without a condom." She smiles like she's proud.

Fuck. If that isn't the icing on the motherfucking cake.

"In that case, I'm ready to see if you're as sweet as I've imagined." I lead her further into the room and spin her around to face the bed. I bend down to place a kiss on her bare shoulder, trailing every inch of skin on the way to her ear, feeling her break out in goose bumps.

I whisper, "And I'll finally find out if our first toast was accurate."

"I did *not* toast to that," she protests adorably.

I chuckle behind her.

To think we've made it this far since our initial encounter. In my wildest dreams, I couldn't have pictured us here after she walked away that day. I recall how upset I was, but this more than makes up for it.

Reaching for her zipper, I slowly slide it down as my lips follow its descent, savoring the feel of her skin. As it reaches her panty line, I catch my first glimpse at the lace thong she's wearing, and my dick hardens a little more. I kiss each swell of her ass before rising.

The curve of her back is exquisite. I haven't been this focused on a woman's body in a very long time, besides getting my cock into them anyway. I had a feeling she would be different, and with the work I've put into this one, I'm going to savor the occasion, prolonging it for as long as possible, which unfortunately isn't long enough with the reception taking place.

I turn her around to face me, leaving the dress in place.

"In case I forgot to say, you look beautiful in this dress. But I'm more than ready for you to be out of it."

She swallows in response, and her cheeks go red.

"To put us on even ground, I'll meet you halfway." Taking a step back, I undo the bow tie and then quickly remove my shirt. Kicking off my shoes and unbuckling my belt simultaneously, I remove my pants, leaving the boxers on. If they come off now, there's no guarantee I won't fuck her first and play later. And I'd rather follow through on making her beg.

She's already panting in lust as it is, so it won't take much, but it won't be enough until she's screaming for it—only then will I fuck her like she's never been fucked before. Her hands are fidgeting, so I walk toward her and grab one, placing it over my throbbing cock.

She gasps.

"You feel that, baby? I want to fuck you so bad it hurts. The only problem is that I want to taste you even more, so let's get you naked and lying on that bed."

She nods. She won't be silent for long.

I reach for the tiny straps holding the dress up and begin to lower them. Inch by delicious inch, I slowly reveal my prize, exposing her strapless bra, her creamy alabaster skin to her belly button, and finally over her hips, where I release the straps, letting it pool to the ground.

With a full view of the white lace bra and panties, I'm reminded of innocence. With her pale, seemingly untouched skin, the white lingerie, and her shyness, that's precisely the vibe she puts off. She's basically every man's vision of a virgin sacrifice.

"Damn, baby, you're so fucking sexy it's taking every ounce of restraint not to throw you on the bed and fuck you right now. Why don't you distract me by removing your bra?"

She reaches back, doing as I ask, still not speaking.

"Good girl." Her pussy clenches, and damn if I'm not dying for a better look.

But all is forgotten except the sight before me the minute her bra falls. She's a goddess, exquisitely perfect in every way.

"Take your hair down," I demand.

She reaches up, working the pins out one by one, while I'm salivating in anticipation. She finishes and holds them out as her flaming red hair cascades down her back in waves.

"Drop them," I tell her, and as soon as she obeys, I lunge for her mouth while lowering her to the bed, leaving her panties in place. Maneuvering higher toward the pillows, I continue kissing as I palm her breasts.

"Has anyone told you how fucking perfect these are? I need my mouth on them."

Her moans are music to my ears as I give her neck attention on my way down. Once I reach her pert little nipple, I secure my lips around it and suck like I'm dying of thirst, her body bucking from my attack.

She whimpers as I explore, moving back and forth, my tongue flicking the tight nub, while I knead and pinch the other. They're not large but so fucking soft and just the right amount to play with. She's panting and distracted as I lower one hand to her mound and feel the heat emanating between her legs.

Unable to wait a second longer, I trail my mouth over her torso, licking along the way. Pausing at her belly button, I dip my tongue in and make eye contact as I gently slide her panties off, her hips rising to assist.

I sit up for a full view and revel in what a glorious pussy she has. "Damn, sugar. That's a sight to behold."

She looks away shyly.

"Don't be embarrassed. I'm serious, you're fucking sexy as hell." I reach forward and spread her open, exploring her folds.

"What are you doing?" she squeals.

"Taking my time. You're not in a hurry, are you?" My fingers run down her seam until finding the opening that's already slick and ready. Rimming the hole, I tease her. "Hm? Is this where you want me?"

Her hips move, begging for more as she bites her lip.

I slowly slide a finger into her snug channel as I watch her mouth part in a breath. I love that she takes everything I give her and doesn't rush for the main course like most women.

"You feel incredible. I can't wait to sink my cock inside this tight pussy. You're gonna squeeze the life out of me, aren't you?" My finger slides in and out as I speak, gently adding another.

She flinches at the addition. "Shh. You're okay. It's only two. It'll take more than that to get you ready for me. Let me help you relax." As my head lowers, her smell causes my cock to harden with each inhale.

The first swipe of my tongue and I'm a goner, throwing all restraint out the window as I dive in and devour. Holy fucking shit, she's sweeter than I ever imagined. Her pussy's fucking delicious, and I'm lost in the moment, my hand moving on its own, speeding up and finger-fucking her cunt with no pretenses.

I'm like a starving man who hasn't eaten in weeks, and when she starts undulating her hips, interfering with my feast, I press down on her abdomen to keep her still. Her voice cuts through my trance with cries of pleasure.

To stretch her further, I add a third finger. She's so gone, she doesn't notice as I pump my hand with short thrusts to work it in. Her pussy's so slick it hardly resists. I'm dying to feel this damn tightness around my cock.

But first, I need to bring her home. Sucking her clit into my mouth, I plunge into her farther than before and twist my hand for another angle.

"Oh my God. Oh God. I… Braden!" She detonates under me, pussy pulsing around my hand. Her screams pervade the room, and I'm filled with instant gratification.

I'm also sitting with a case of blue balls that need release.

Extracting my fingers before she comes completely down from her orgasm, I lift to slide my boxers off, finally releasing my dick that's about to explode.

Climbing up while she's still panting in ecstasy, I swipe my cock along her core to coat myself before plunging into the most resistant fucking hole I've ever felt. Goddamn. She's tight as hell, and fuck if it's not the best pussy I've experienced.

Poppy's eyes go wide as she raises her head in panic. Not gonna lie. It makes me a bit proud to have garnered that reaction from the size of my dick.

"This is a bad idea." She tries to clamor away, but can't with my arms blocking her in.

"It's a little late for that, Mouse. Just relax." She doesn't relax in the slightest.

"I take it you've been with pencil dicks up until now, but I promise you're meant for all sizes."

Remaining still, I bring my mouth down in a kiss to coax her out of her head. It's not long before she's kissing me back vigorously, moaning into my mouth. I move to her neck, making her crazy, hips rising in response. Exactly what I was going for.

I retract slightly, and she immediately tenses up.

"Shhh. Just breathe, Little Mouse. You can take it." I whisper into her ear, "You will take it because I'm not stopping until you're so full of my cock you'll be feeling it all night."

She whimpers in response. Fuck. All she needs is a little dirty talk and she's putty in my hands.

"You like the sound of that? You want me to fill you up and leave you dripping with cum?"

I barely retract only to push back in, hardly gaining any ground. Fucking hell, I've literally never had a tighter pussy. She really has been with pencil dicks, or it's been forever since she's had sex.

"That's it, baby. Let me in, just like that. You're doing so good." I continue making slight headway until I can't resist a moment longer.

"I can't wait any longer. I need to fuck you now, Poppy. Can you take it?"

Her needy moans are all the answer I need. I withdraw almost completely before slamming back to the hilt.

Her gasp of surprise, along with an enthusiastic "yes," dissolves any restraint I had.

"Oh fuck yeah. Thatta girl," I groan before repeating the motion.

"Braden!"

Picking up speed, I keep going. "That's right, baby, take it. Need this—can't hold back anymore."

I drive into her relentlessly, unleashing myself, her tight cunt squeezing the life out of me. She's so fucking slick it makes it easy, so I go for it, slamming into her repeatedly.

"Good girl taking it rough. Letting me fuck your tight pussy. You like that, baby? You like being fucked with a big cock?"

"Oh God. Yes. Oh God."

"That's right, let me hear how much you like it." I don't ease up, rutting so hard, she's almost to the headboard.

"Braden. Please…"

"Please what, baby? You need more? Is my dick not enough? Do you want another one in your ass? Two cocks fucking you?" Holy shit, the vision alone has me coming before I can stop myself, grunting and fucking her as I shoot my load.

She comes unglued with me, and the room fills with curses and moans as we lose ourselves to the moment. Her pussy coaxes every last drop as she pulses around me.

We're still panting, trying to catch our breath as my head hangs over her chest, and I can't help but take her nipple into my mouth. This is the first time in years that one time doesn't come close to being enough.

I'm already addicted, which means it's a damn good thing she leaves tomorrow.

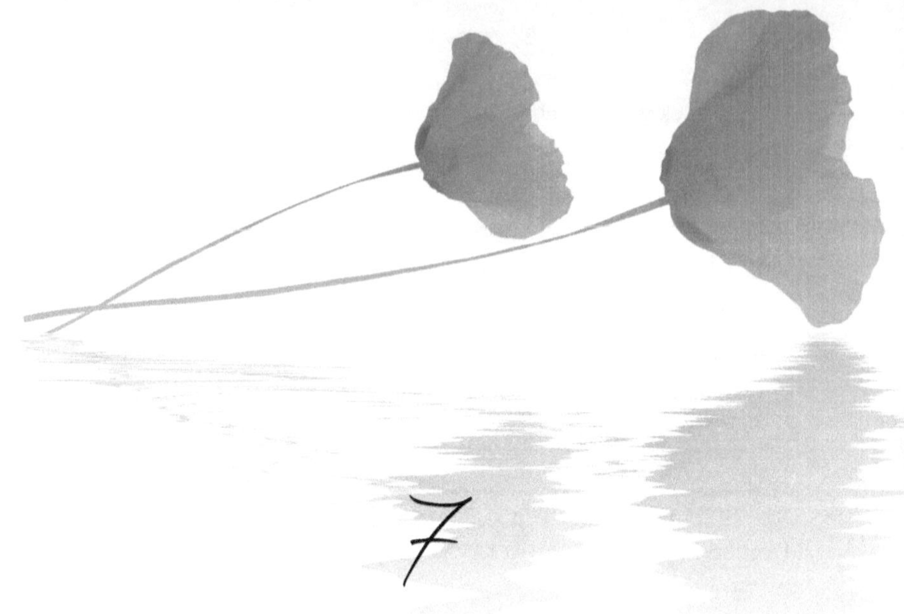

7

TERRIBLE IDEA

Poppy

"WHAT ARE YOU DOING?" I ASK IN SHOCK AS HE SUCKS MY breast.

He's finished. Shouldn't he be done with me? I was prepared for a quick exit, not for him to take his time afterward.

"Enjoying this buffet in front of me," he mumbles around my nipple.

"We have to go. Everyone's probably noticed we're gone. We'll have to come up with a story."

His head pops up. "Damn. That's what we should have done—role-played one of our stories. You could have been a teacher, and I could have bent you over that desk."

"Oh my God, seriously, move." I shove his chest with both hands.

He chuckles and rolls to his back, pulling out of me as he does. It's a weird sensation, especially when I feel his cum dripping between my legs.

"I need to clean up." I awkwardly rise, squeezing my core like I have to pee so no more leaks out. "Hurry and get dressed. We're leaving as soon as I'm ready," I say while gathering my clothes on the way to the bathroom.

Slamming the door in haste and twisting the lock, I set my things on the counter, run to the toilet, and drop my head into my hands with a smile. Oh my God, that was amazing. I did it. And now that I know what I've been missing, I can't believe I waited so long. I'm mind blown. Or is it cum drunk? I'm not sure, but holy shit… I'm something.

And did I hear him correctly before we finished? He mentioned having another guy at the same time. That's… weird. Why would he say that? More importantly, why did I orgasm while picturing it? I'll have to unpack that one later, because right now, we need to go.

Rushing to put myself together, I finally look in the mirror. Shit. My hair. I wouldn't say it's terrible, but the intricate updo I had is toast. I'll have to tell them the pins were giving me a headache. Running my hands through it will have to be enough. There's no time to go to my room for a more thorough job, so it'll have to do.

Taking a deep breath, I swing open the bathroom door to find Braden slipping his shoes on. He's wearing his pants and dress shirt, but no vest, jacket, or bow tie.

"Why isn't the rest of your stuff on? We need to leave—right now."

"This is fine. It's the reception—time to loosen up."

"They'll wonder why you're coming back half-dressed. Put it on," I insist.

"No. If anyone asks, we'll use female issues to explain why you needed a ride back to the room, and I'll say I stopped by mine to lose the suit. It's not a big deal." He shrugs.

It is plausible, considering I used the same excuse earlier. Okay, this could work. I'm impressed and instantly relieved we have something to go with. The last thing I want is gossip about Cici's friend being a hussy who shagged the first guy she came across. Not that I could've done better, since Braden happens to be the hottest one here.

"Fine. Let's go." I hastily put my shoes on before we file out the door.

"You won't go brag and tell your friends you scored, will you?" I glare as menacingly as possible and decide to add on a threat for good measure. "If you do, I'll tell everyone how awful it was."

"That's funny. Which part? The first orgasm on my tongue or the second with my cock?"

I huff in frustration for calling my bluff. "Just don't say anything. Got it?"

He shakes his head, chuckling. "You're the one who should be bragging about it. Finally experiencing a first-class fuck. I'm guessing you've been deeply deprived based on your…" He motions with his hand in my direction. "Lack of interest. I did you a favor. You might as well thank me for showing you what a real man can do and why you should be fucking on the regular instead of just reading about it. You're welcome."

The nerve of this jerk. "The only thing to thank you for is show-ing me what it's like to sleep with a certifiable asshole and why it was a terrible idea."

I'm relieved when he parks so I can be on my merry way and forget this ever happened.

"Oh, Little Mouse, sleeping is *not* what we did. And if I thought you actually believed it wasn't the best cock you've had, I'd take you right back to my room and prove otherwise."

"As if I'd let you."

"You really have no clue who you're up against, do you?"

Instead of answering, I exit the cart in a huff and walk back into the reception without uttering another word. He's impossible—cocky, rude, and so full of himself I'm shocked he has any friends at all.

"Where have you been, and why does it look like you and Braden were together?" Cici's voice is laced with suspicion as she catches me on the way in, noticing Braden behind me. We walk and talks toward the bar, since that's where I'm headed.

I'm sure it's easy for Braden to lie through his teeth, given his profession. Me? Not so much. But since the last thing Cici needs on her wedding night is to worry about me, I'll give it my best effort.

"Feminine emergency, and Braden was the closest one I could find to drive me to my room."

It seems like she bought it, but then she goes from skepticism to concern. "Is he harassing you again?"

"When is he not?" I laugh.

"True. Just let me know if you need me to step in."

"Don't worry about it. Did I miss anything while I was gone?" I ask as we make it to the bar, quickly changing the subject so as not to push my luck. The faster we talk about something else, the better.

The bartender comes over, and I quickly order my very much needed drink before she answers.

"Well, I'm not sure when you left, but Walker hit on Matt, and it was the funniest thing I've ever seen. Matt didn't take it very well and almost punched him in the face until Mia stepped in to smooth it over. They're getting along great now."

"Oh wow. Darn it that I missed it, but I bet I'll hear about it on the way home tomorrow."

Since Matt and I are on the same flight, I'll let him fill me in on the story then. It sounds like it'll be a good one.

"I'm sad you're already leaving. I've missed you," Cici pouts.

"Me too, but I'll be back before you know it… to meet this little one." I smile and rub her belly. "I can't wait."

"You and me both." She looks to the heavens.

"I'm so happy for you, Cici. Really. Congratulations. I'm so glad everything worked out with you and Eli. You guys are adorable together," I say genuinely.

"I heard my name. Are you talking shit about me already?" Eli asks sarcastically as he joins us, draping his arm around Cici and pulling her to his side.

"Of course we are. You better take care of my girl for me," I say sternly to Eli.

"She's my number one priority, which is why I'm bringing her to bed. You've been on your feet all day and need to rest." He leans in to kiss her temple. "Sebastian and Lily already called it. They said to tell you both good night and that they'd say goodbye in the morning." The last part is addressed to me.

"Wait! I have to throw my bouquet first," Cici exclaims.

"All right, cutie. I'll go have the MC announce it. But then we're going straight to the room." Eli kisses her forehead.

"You sure it's to rest?" Cici asks coyly.

"For you, yes." He kisses her cheek. "But I didn't say anything about me." He wags his brows and walks off toward the DJ booth.

"You're so lucky." I reach out to hug her.

"I really am." She beams. "You'll find your man soon. I can feel it. But you need to go on more than three dates a year. Make a goal of at least one per week maybe."

"How about you go throw your bouquet and I'll talk to you in the morning, Mom."

She leaves laughing, and with a fresh drink, I join the crowd around the dance floor when a hand lands on my back. Jerking away, thinking it's Braden, I'm surprised to find Jordan instead. That's when I remembered I'd left him waiting.

"Oh, sorry, I didn't realize it was you. And I'm *so* sorry I took so long. I ended up going back to my room for something." Using female issues as an excuse doesn't seem very smooth, so I leave that part off.

Oh, God. To think I could've been making out with this guy and missed out on having sex with the other. And who am I even having that thought pop into my brain? Braden truly has made a monster out of me.

He reaches up and touches a strand of hair. "Your hair's down. I like it."

"Thank you. The pins were bothering me."

"Would you be interested in that walk now?"

"I'd—"

"I don't think we've met. I'm Braden." Suddenly, he's between us, offering his hand to shake.

"Jordan." He reaches out, and it's obvious how hard Braden squeezes at the visible wince Jordan gives.

"So which bride and groom are you here for?" Braden asks casually.

"Eli and Cici. I work with Lily in the marketing department at Dubree Enterprises. How about you?" Jordan responds, completely oblivious to the testosterone rolling off of Braden.

"Both. Jackson and I go way back, and Eli and I have been friends for a couple of years now, and Poppy here," he turns to me, "was on the flight from Bozeman with me. We've been getting to know each other quite well over the weekend. Haven't we, Mouse?"

He has the audacity to wink at me—the absolute nerve of this man. Right after I told him I didn't want anyone finding out about us.

I fake a smile and force an answer while my blood boils. "We have been. Enough to know that I don't like you. If you'll excuse me, I'm going to catch the bouquet now."

To which—I did not.

Braden

I couldn't help it. The absolute nerve of this woman talking it up with another man minutes after I came in her. What the actual fuck?

"Hey man, we were just introduced tonight, but I'll back off if you two are…" Jordan trails off, unsure of what word to use.

Unlike me. "Fucking. Probably best not to double-dip. I'd offer to tag you in, but I'm not done with her yet." I wink and walk away. Hell, it's doubtful I'll see the guy again, so I don't give a fuck what he thinks of me. Mission accomplished.

After grabbing a drink and finding a seat to chill out, I can't help but follow the movements of one person in particular.

Jackson sits beside me. "Fuck man, you've got it bad. You do know you haven't taken your eyes off Poppy once tonight. What's the deal?"

"Fresh meat, that's all." He's my best friend, but he's still Cici's brother, so he might not be excited to hear I succeeded in banging her bridesmaid during the reception.

"You sure about that? I've never seen you so… attentive."

"Speaking of, shouldn't you be *attending* to your wife?"

"Fuck, I love hearing that."

"Which part? *Wife* or *attending* to her?"

"Both, but the fact that she's officially mine… damn. Nothing compares." He's staring at Mia with stars in his eyes while she shakes it on the dance floor with Walker.

"I'm happy for you. Cheers to making a man out of yourself." I hold my drink up.

He meets it. "Thanks. When will you do the same? You seem pretty interested in that Poppy chick."

"In one thing and one thing only. The word relationship isn't in my vocabulary. You know that."

"You need to let the past go. It's been years, and not all women are cheaters."

"Try telling that to my new client. They are if given the opportunity." I realized what I said a second too late. "Shit, I'm sorry. That's not true. You're right, not all women are. It's just hard to believe when not only did it happen to me, but it's the main reason I'm employed."

"Fair, but don't you want a family at some point?"

"Fuck no. I have no desire to screw up any more children—I wasn't meant to be a father." It's the most accurate statement I've made the whole conversation.

"Dude. Your upbringing has no bearing on your future children. If anything, it'll make you a better parent. Stop holding back just because you're afraid."

"What are you—my fucking therapist?"

He chuckles. "No, but maybe you need one. There's more to life than one-night stands."

"Says the guy who's been married for a few hours to the girl who broke him of the habit. Don't preach to the choir unless you have something worthwhile. And if it'll put your mind at ease, I'm happy with one-night stands. They leave time for my career, which is more important than any woman."

"You've already made partner, so that's a piss-poor excuse. And if work's your only focus, doesn't it look better to some of these clients to be in a solid relationship?"

I shake my head, exasperated and ready to be done with the conversation. "Man, you're relentless. Go take your wife to bed and consummate your marriage. I'll see you tomorrow."

Jackson gets to his feet and grips my shoulder. "Fine, I'll leave you alone. But at least be open to the possibility."

"Doubtful—unless you come to me in the morning and tell me that married sex is like nothing you've had before... then I'll consider it."

"I'm about to find out," he says, eyeing his woman with longing. "Night, man."

"Enjoy."

Damn. Your friends start settling down, and suddenly, they think everyone needs to. Fuck that shit. And on that note, rather than torture myself anymore by watching Poppy slip through my fingers, I decide it's time to leave, resigned to spend the night alone. The last thing I want is to witness her and her *friend* Matt go inside the room together. Motherfucker. I shouldn't give a shit, so why do I?

The following morning, I'm anxious to join the wedding party for breakfast after tossing and turning all night while my imagination ran wild about what could be happening next door. To my dismay, I miss saying goodbye to Poppy, along with the chance to rile her up some more, since she's already gone by the time I arrive. This is discovered by inquiring where she is, only to hear about their early flight back. Mistake number one: asking about her.

"Why? Did you do something? I swear I'll hurt you if you fucked with her." Cici scowls at me without waiting for an answer. At the same time, Jackson's subtle glance and muffled chuckle add to my pissy mood.

"I didn't do shit. She's in the room next to me, so I just wondered why she wasn't here. I figured her and that guy were still getting it on." I shrug as if it doesn't matter, when the thought alone has me seeing red.

"Matt? Seriously? Did you hear them doing it?" She seems genuinely shocked, and my blood boils that she even thinks it's possible.

"No. But two single people sharing a room and not fucking? Highly unlikely." I'm losing my mind, and it's my own damn fault. Why am I having this conversation again? Oh right, because I asked where Poppy was.

She rolls her eyes. "Says the manwhore of the century. Contrary to your beliefs, not every man has a one-track mind. Matt and Poppy are just friends. Besides, she was all about Jordan last night. That was more likely."

"So she did get with someone?" I can't help but ask the question—mistake number two.

Cici eyes me suspiciously. "Why do you care?"

Jackson isn't hiding the humor rolling off him at this point, and Eli is beside Cici, shaking his head, waiting for the bomb to drop, I'm sure. Oh, for fuck's sake.

"I don't. I'm only interested in finding out who got laid by whom. You're familiar with the term gossip. Isn't that what people do the day after a wedding?" I completely sold that.

"Well, I'm not gossiping about one of my best friends. And if any of you do, you're in trouble." She addresses the others around the table, then smirks at me. "So good luck with your *gossip sesh.*"

"Testy, testy. What does it matter? She doesn't even live here, she won't see us again."

"She's one of my best friends, dumbass. She's coming to visit after the baby's born."

Well, well, well.

That pleasant surprise keeps my mind occupied the rest of the day—all the way into Monday, when work takes over, giving me a reprieve from thoughts of Poppy until Warren wakes the sleeping giant.

"So did you bang any hot chicks at the reception this weekend?"

he asks while we're taking a short break to eat. It's not uncommon for working lunches more days than not.

Warren and I have a candid approach about our sexual conquests and aren't shy about bragging who and when we fuck. This time, however, I'm reluctant. Which is fucking weird. It was nothing special—at least that's what I've been trying to convince myself.

"Most of the women came with a date. It was slim pickings." Hopefully, he'll drop it.

"There had to be a few to choose from. How can you go to a wedding and not get your dick wet? Please tell me you didn't end up jerking yourself off?"

Can't do that, since that's precisely what I did after ending the night solo. So rather than spouting bullshit, I finally give in and go with the truth, starting with the plane, to fucking her during the reception, to wishing for round two.

"Dude. That doesn't sound like you. Why didn't you bang some other chick instead of calling it a night? Sounds like she might've done the same."

"She didn't," I state more forcefully than I should, willing myself to believe it.

"Oh fuck, does that piss you off? You catch feelings or some shit?" He laughs.

"Fuck no. I'd just like to assume I rocked her world enough that she didn't need to fuck anyone after." It's a half-truth. "And yeah, it was *that* good that I wasn't in the mood for sloppy seconds after I'd already had dessert."

"Hmmm. So you'd be into banging her again? That's rare for you."

"*She* was rare. It's not every day a mousy redhead turns into a siren in the sack."

"Well, too bad you didn't take advantage of round two before she left. But now that I know you have a thing for redheads, I'll be sure to tag you in next time I find one."

Do I have *a thing* for redheads, or is it one in particular?

"She's coming back in a few weeks to visit her friend." Something I'm once again thinking about.

"Perfect. You can tag *me* in, then."

Fuck. I should've anticipated this, considering that's our typical strategy. While the suggestion right before we climaxed turned me the fuck on, the reality of it doesn't excite me as much.

"Not sure this one fits the mold. I call her Mouse for a reason. She's skittish in the bedroom. Responsive as hell but doesn't have a forward bone in her body when it comes down to it."

"She just doesn't know what she's missing. That's the fun part—educating her. Come on, man. You'd be doing her a favor."

I laugh at the irony of his comment. "Funny. I already told her I did her a favor by fucking her, and it didn't go over well. I don't think that approach will work."

"Dude, you're killing me here. You at least have to give it a try. Take her out, and I'll magically show up. Once she has a taste, I guaran-fuckin'-tee she'll be in. What woman can resist two sets of mouths and hands making her feel good? Not a single one so far, and you know it." He points his finger at me.

Fuck. He's right, but that's not the problem—it's whether I'm willing to share.

Luckily, I'm forced to forget about the matter as the next few weeks fly by with work keeping me too busy to ruminate over my sudden greediness. The girl who rocked my world is on the back burner for now.

8

NEVER SAY NEVER

Poppy

"CONGRATULATIONS, CICI. I'M SO GLAD YOU ANSWERED, BUT I bet you're exhausted," I tell Cici over the phone. I'm in my office with the door shut. She gave birth the night before, and I didn't want to call too early, knowing she'd need her rest. Lily texted me updates all night, until Abigail Lily Dubree finally made her debut a week after she was supposed to arrive.

"No. I'm actually doing okay, and I'm so relieved it's over. Plus, there's no time to be tired since we have a room full of visitors. My parents, Braden, Jackson, and Mia are all here. And of course, Lily hasn't left since they let her in." She laughs on the other end. It's nice to hear.

What's not good to hear is that Braden is in the background. His name is all it takes for the guilt to set in about not telling Cici what happened. I always figured she'd be the first one I'd spill to about losing my virginity, but I can't bring myself to do it. It was during her reception, no less. I feel like a terrible friend.

"So everything went well?"

"It did. Epidurals are magic. I didn't feel any pain," Cici says excitedly.

"That's amazing. Ah, I can't wait to see her."

"Me too. I wish you were here. When are you coming? Have you booked your ticket yet?"

We'd already discussed waiting until a couple of weeks had passed. I didn't want to intrude right away, so they could adapt to being parents without a houseguest. I'm sure they'll be busy enough with all the family and friends around. But at least they don't share space with them, unlike when I visit.

"I'll come in two weeks. That'll give you some time to have Abby to yourselves first."

"Fine, but no later than that."

I laugh. "Depends on when the best price is, but I'll text you the details as soon as it's booked."

"Eli already said he's paying for your ticket. He said it's the least he can do since you took care of me during most of the pregnancy."

"Tell him he doesn't need to. I can afford a plane ticket."

"That's not the point."

"I know, but I've got it."

"Well, you two can argue about it later. Now take my video call so you can see Abby."

I pull the phone away from my ear to the request coming through and hit accept. The first thing that greets me is Cici's smiling face, which is as beautiful as ever. Only Cici could look like a million bucks after giving birth.

"How do you look that good after nine hours of labor?"

"Yeah right, I look like I ran a marathon yesterday, which I sort of feel like, actually. But it was worth it. Are you ready?" Cici asks while beaming.

The camera turns to reveal Abby, who Lily is holding. "Oh, Cici, she's adorable. You guys made the perfect angel. Hello, little Abby. You're such a pretty girl, aren't you?" I ask in baby talk.

"She is, isn't she?" Cici asks, turning the camera around to face her again.

It was only half a second, but the sight of Braden in the background makes my heart flutter.

"Can you believe it?" she continues, "All those months, and she's finally here. Thank you for helping me through everything. I couldn't have done it without you." Tears cloud her eyes as she declares her heartfelt appreciation, causing my own tears to gather.

"No thanks needed. I loved it and I can't wait to be there. I'll let you go since you have visitors and send a text when I'm booked. Love you, Cici. Congratulations to you and Eli."

"Thanks, Poppy," Eli shouts from the background.

"Let's talk soon, and if I don't have your flight details by the end of the day, I'll make Eli book a ticket for you," she threatens.

I smile at her persistence. "I'll do it right now. I promise. Bye." I wave and hang up, slumping in my chair as I sigh.

My mind is stuck on Braden and the fact that he was in the room. It only took one glimpse to realize I'm just as attracted to him as before. The sad truth is, I haven't been able to stop thinking about what we did, and if given the chance for a repeat, I'm scared I'll shamefully accept.

Seconds later, my phone buzzes with a text. I click on the notification to a picture from Cici. It's Abby… cradled in Braden's arms for the photo. No doubt he did it intentionally. His favorite thing to do is get under my skin, and I'm sure he knew that would do the trick.

Only this time, it's not because I can't stand the sight of him, but because the sight of him makes me yearn for something I shouldn't.

After a quick knock on the door, Matt peeks his head in, stopping me from delving deeper into that thought.

"Hey, it was quiet, so I figured you were off the phone. How's Cici doing?" he asks, walking in and taking a seat.

"She's so happy. Here, want to see baby Abby?" I show him the only picture I have so far.

"Wow, she's cute, but why is Braden holding her?" he asks, annoyance lacing his voice.

"He's visiting with Jackson and Mia. I'm positive he suggested it on purpose to annoy me."

"Or he did it because he's hoping for a repeat when you visit."

Matt called me out about disappearing with Braden during the reception when we were on the flight home. I figured since I couldn't talk to Cici about my indiscretion, Matt was the next best thing. It was a relief to have it off my chest, but it didn't do much to sort my feelings on the matter—not that I had any, other than wondering what the hell I was thinking.

Braden didn't make a great impression on Matt due to scowling at him most of the night, so Matt wasn't excited to hear that I'd given in to him. He wasn't rude about it, but he didn't high-five me, that's for sure. Thank God he didn't know it was my first time, or his reaction would have been much worse.

"He does have a one-track mind," I concede.

"I'd say it's working since he lured you in with it. And I bet you won't be able to withstand his charm any better next time."

"You don't know that. I've already decided I'm not giving in again."

"So you'd turn him down if he showed up tomorrow?" Matt asks knowingly, with raised brows.

I drop my head in my hands and groan.

"Just be careful. There's nothing wrong with having fun, but he doesn't seem like a relationship guy."

"I'm aware, trust me. But something about him drives me crazy—in a good and bad way."

"Yeah, it's called a dick. He has one, and he is one. It's guys like that you should be cautious with. I just don't want you to get hurt."

"I won't. I'm not stupid. I know exactly what type he is. My older brother has schooled me on dirtbags, and Braden undoubtedly falls into that category." I might be trying to convince myself simultaneously.

"Don't forget that when he says all the right things next time," Matt scolds.

"Okay, Dad." I give him the stink eye.

He laughs. "You're such a brat. When are you leaving? Did you get your ticket yet?"

"Shoot. No, I'm doing it now. It won't be for a couple of weeks, but I'll let you know the exact dates and leave plenty of notes for any files I need help with."

"Perfect. I'll give Cici's guests a little more time before I call to congratulate her."

"Good idea, and thanks for the lecture."

"Anytime. Not that it'll change anything." Matt shakes his head, smiling as he heads out the door.

Braden

I've decided to bite the bullet and make the call. What's the worst that can happen? If he realizes my obsession and shuts me down, so be it. It'll be the sign I need to let this go.

Eli picks up after the second ring. "Hey, Braden. How's it going?"

"Good. Really good. How about you? How's parenthood?"

"Crazy. I couldn't imagine life without Abby now that she's here, but man am I exhausted."

I laugh in response. That's exactly what I was hoping to hear to make my offer seem more plausible.

"I bet. Anything I can do to help?"

"Not unless you want to take night shifts."

"Dude, you're a billionaire. Hire a nanny."

He laughs. "Try talking Cici into that and tell me how it goes."

"Ahhh. Maybe she'll change her mind after a few more sleepless nights. Other than that, how's life? Are you guys finally slowing down on visitors?"

"Yeah. Lily's here every day, which I expect will be the norm, but Cici's parents have slowed down. Poppy's coming for a week starting tomorrow, so I'll work a bit more while she's here. It'll give me time to catch up on some things."

"Damn. It's crazy you're a dad now."

"No kidding. I literally couldn't imagine life without her, but a word from the wise, bag it up or you'll be in for a surprise."

A chuckle precedes the wistful memory of the last time I didn't. "No worries in that department, but thanks. Hey, would it help if I picked up Poppy tomorrow? I could pick her up from the airport and have an excuse to stop by and visit. I'm sure she'd rather be greeted by a familiar face over your driver." Fuck. That was smooth, if I do say so myself.

"That would be great, if you have time."

"Yeah, just text me her flight info."

"Thanks, man, I appreciate it," Eli says genuinely, prompting the slightest guilty conscience from ulterior motives.

"You bet. I was thinking I could also take her off your hands and show her a bit of San Diego if you want. We could go to the club since Cici's probably not up for that kind of entertaining yet."

"That's not a bad idea. I'll talk to Cici about it. I bet Justin and Lucy would go since she and Poppy hit it off."

"Perfect. I'll ask him. All right, send over the info, and I'll see you tomorrow."

I hang up with a satisfied smile. Mission accomplished. Minutes later, a text containing Poppy's flight appears with a message saying Cici wasn't happy to hear the plan and to behave. Now where's the fun in that?

After tossing and turning all night, playing out various scenarios about how her visit will go, I've come to the conclusion that I need to fuck her out of my system. I won't be free of her until I do. One time wasn't nearly enough to satisfy me and fulfill all the wicked fantasies she stars in. The anticipation is killing me.

I'm counting down the hours, and my concentration is total shit, which doesn't escape Warren.

"Does the blackout on your calendar starting at two today have anything to do with why you're distracted as hell?"

"It could be."

"And?"

I run my hand through my hair and sigh. I figured I'd have to fess up to Warren eventually. He practically runs my schedule, and there's no way he won't put it together, since he knows Poppy is coming back to visit.

"I'm picking up Poppy at the airport this afternoon."

"And you were going to tell me this when?"

"I'm telling you now."

"Fucker. Is this why you've been dodging drinks after work? Have you been saving your stamina?"

"Screw off. We've been slammed. I'm tired by the end of the day."

He coughs *bullshit*. "You're more hung up on this chick than you'll admit. She must have a magic pussy."

Hearing him talk about her like that makes me wince, although I've not been much better, but it's different coming from him and I don't like it. I shrug nonchalantly. "It's probably the chase. It's refreshing to work for it. She's not easy like the women we usually fuck. I think I just need to get her out of my system. Once she stops resisting, I'll be done with her."

"Riiight. Keep me posted on that. You gonna hit her up on letting me tag in?"

"I'm not sure. I'm taking her to the club this week, so maybe you can show up and we'll play it by ear."

"I'm pretty convincing. I'll have her eating out of my hand."

That's what I'm afraid of.

The following two hours pass in a blur, and before I know it, I'm outside of arrivals waiting to catch a glimpse of my redhead.

The minute she appears, it becomes clear that I'm not imagining this attraction or blowing it out of proportion; I'm unequivocally infatuated. Her hair is partially up but still full and wavy. She's in tight black leggings and a sweatshirt, which makes her look young and innocent—only I know she's not.

I'm surprised she's shocked to see me since I figured they would have told her I was picking her up, but the scowl on her face makes it obvious she had no idea.

"Why are you here?" she asks immediately, confirming my analysis.

I feign hurt with my hand over my chest. "Is that any way to greet your lover?"

She coughs incredulously. "Lover? Try again. How about my mistake?"

"Oh, Little Mouse, the only mistake was not doing it again."

"Which will never happen."

I lean down to whisper in her ear. "Never say never. I've been rubbing off every night to visions of your sweet pussy wrapped around my cock. And he missed out on so much more. Your mouth, your ass—"

She jerks back quickly and shoves me, making me chuckle. I had her until the word ass.

"Why are you here again?" she asks petulantly.

"Didn't Cici tell you I was picking you up?"

"No," she growls. "She probably knew I'd insist on an Uber instead. Why didn't they just send their driver?"

I grind my jaw. Her obstinance is beginning to irritate me. "Because I offered. Now let's go."

She has no choice but to follow when I grab the suitcase handle out of her grasp and start walking.

We're silent as we head to the car. I've been semi-hard since she came through the doors, and having her next to me, within reaching distance, isn't going to make it any easier on the way to Eli's. I need to get her under me, so I can get over her—and move the hell on. Then maybe I can scrape together some semblance of the life I had before this meek little mouse invaded it.

After loading her bag into the trunk, I can't help but stare at her perky ass in those pants and how badly I want to squeeze the hell out of it as she walks to the passenger door.

"Did you miss me?" I ask cheekily as I back out of the spot.

"I haven't even thought about you."

"That hurts. At least it would if I believed you. Tell me, is it my tongue or dick that takes the stage most nights?"

She scoffs and rolls her eyes. "Neither."

"So it's my hand you like the best, huh? I can work with that." I reach across the console and grab her leg, sliding up, but she flings it away before I even make it an inch.

"Hands off. What happened was a one-time thing and doesn't give you the right to touch me."

I tsk. "Oh, Little Mouse, I'll leave you alone for now, but be prepared to beg when you're ready for seconds."

"In your dreams."

"Damn straight, it is. It's all I've been dreaming about, and if you were being honest, you'd admit you have too."

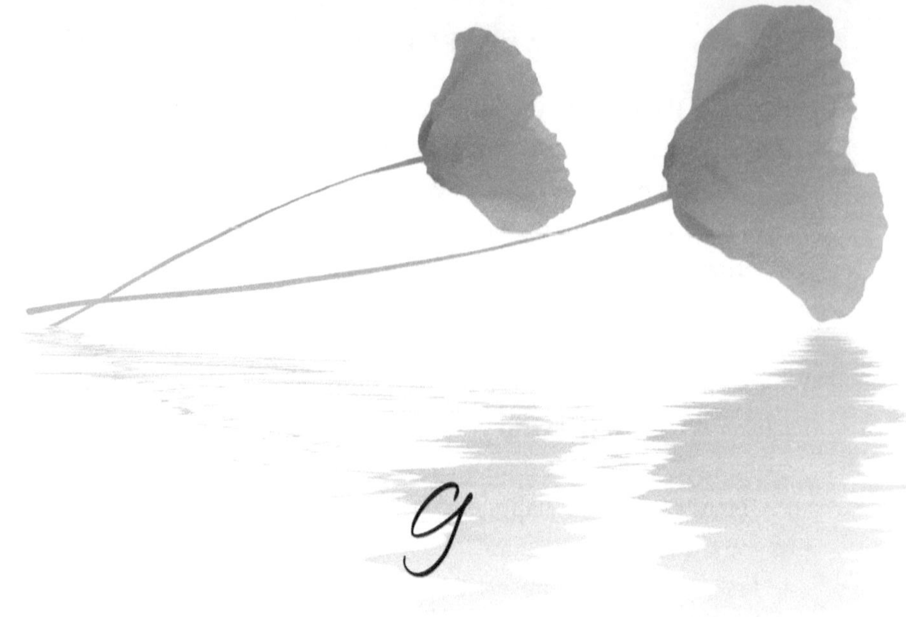

ROUND TWO

Poppy

"WHAT DO YOU MEAN I'M GOING OUT TONIGHT?" I ask Cici incredulously after the bomb she dropped in my lap. Evidently, Braden is picking me up at nine and taking me downtown to the nightclub that Eli and Sebastian own.

"You're here for a week, and last time, you didn't do anything but wedding stuff. I thought it would be fun for you to go out in the city."

"If you were going, it would be. I'm here to visit you and Abby."

"Abby and I will both be sleeping. Come on, you'll love it. And Lucy's going."

"I didn't bring anything to wear." Which is true, but I've also never been to a club. I mean, we have bars in Bozeman, but nothing remotely close to a dance club. Unless a barnwood floor and country music count. I suppose we have a couple of places with DJs on the weekends, but the barnwood floor doesn't magically disappear.

"Nice try, but I've got a closet full of clothes that have been gathering dust for months. I'm dressing you up, and you're going so I can hear all about it in the morning. I haven't gone dancing in ages," she says wistfully.

I groan my acceptance, "Fine. But I can just Uber. Braden doesn't need to pick me up. It's not a date."

"It was his idea to take you. He figured you'd want to do something other than hang out at our place every day. I thought you two were getting along," she says suspiciously.

"That's one way to put it," I mutter, realizing too late I said it out loud.

When he dropped me off two days ago, I was so consumed with Abby that I barely paid attention while he was there. Our interaction was minimal other than a quick thank you for the ride before he left. Not that I didn't notice him watching me the whole time.

"What do you mean? Is he still being rude and coming on to you? I thought he stopped."

Should I fess up to Cici about what happened? She is my best friend. And now that her life is in order, maybe it's okay to unload a little. It's now or never.

Taking a deep breath, I lead into it. "Please don't be mad for not telling you sooner, but I didn't want to say anything to distract you at your wedding."

"What? Just spit it out."

"Braden and I… we… went to his room during the reception and did it." I end up rushing the words out.

"Did it? As in, did it, did it? You lost your virginity? With Braden?" She's screeching at this point.

I nod as I cringe, knowing I should have told her right away, but also extremely relieved not to hide it anymore.

"Holy shit, Poppy! I can't believe you're just now telling me. What the hell. How? Oh my God, tell me everything. This is huge." She's smiling now, which is a positive sign she's not angry at me for keeping it from her.

"I don't know. I guess he just wore me down. We messed around a couple times and he—"

"Wait. What do you mean by *messed around*? When? Start at the beginning because I'm lost on how he went from a douchebag during the flight to the guy you had sex with *at my wedding*. You have a lot of explaining to do."

She listens over the next thirty minutes as I recount everything from the hot tub incident to stolen kisses to finally ending up in bed. Her interruptions are abundant, with embarrassing questions pulling more and more details from me. By the time we're finished, she knows every detail, including how incredible it was.

"Wow, so now what? Are you going to do it again?"

"Are you sure you're not mad at me? You specifically warned me away, not to mention you had a thing for him at one point."

"Oh my God, that was ages ago and so lame. I was a baby back then. And no, I'm not mad in the slightest. He's a charmer, all right, I'll give him that, and a very good-looking one. I just can't believe you went for it. I mean, I thought you had a five-date minimum? I hope you know he's not the relationship type."

"I do—100%. I think that's one of the reasons I did it, plus it was with someone I'd never have to see again. That was my thought process, anyway."

"Smart, except you are seeing him again. And it better not be the last time you visit." She scrunches her face.

I shake my head and groan. "I know. I wasn't thinking that far ahead at the moment. I was a little distracted."

Cici laughs. "Obviously. Well, you could always go for round two. This way, your body count will stay the same."

"Oh my God, you're terrible." Although the minute the words are spoken, my mind considers the possibility.

"Nope, just smart. I say go for it. If you end up at his place tonight, I won't hold it against you."

"Cici! Seriously, that's not happening. Besides, I don't want anyone else knowing, including Eli."

"He's friends with Braden. I wouldn't be surprised if Braden already told him." My eyes bug out of my head, but she waves me off and continues. "He won't care regardless. Eli and I had our fun back in the day. He'd never judge you."

"Still. It was a one-time thing. It won't happen again."

"Hm. If you say so, but I'll hold off the search party if you don't come home tonight."

I hit her with a pillow as she squeals, before we're laughing together. I feel lighter than I have in weeks, confirming my decision to tell her.

The rest of the afternoon is nice, spending time with Abby and taking a walk outside with her in the stroller. Lily joined us, so we didn't go very far since she's about to pop herself. It's so cool that they're having babies around the same time and that their kids will be cousins growing up next door to each other.

After dinner with Eli, who worked all day, Cici dragged me to her closet to pick out something to wear while Eli kept Abby. He's an adorable dad. I'm so glad everything worked out for them. Even though he missed most of the pregnancy, he's made up for it in spades.

The outfits she's pulling out are making me cringe. She has some seriously sexy clothes, most of which didn't make an appearance in Bozeman, but apparently, the dress code for this place is next level. I'm kind of excited to experience a real dance club with multiple floors and modern lighting.

Hanging out with Lucy will be fun too. What has me on edge is the sexual tension between Braden and me. Every innuendo he makes causes my insides to clench in desire, which is his intention, of course, and it's becoming more of a challenge to hold back. I'm afraid Cici's right and that it's only a matter of time before I give in.

"I don't think any of these will work. You seem to forget I'm not as endowed upstairs as you are. Plus, my ass is bigger." I whine to Cici as she piles more choices on the bed.

"We'll see. Strip, we have a lot to do, and your makeup will take a while."

Oh boy.

When she's finally through with me, I barely recognize myself as we stand in front of the full-length mirror in her bathroom. She didn't go over the top, but I look more… mature. And sexy as hell in this dress. If I went out at home like this, I might've already found someone. I seriously need to reevaluate my tactics.

"Braden's definitely putting the moves on you tonight. I wouldn't be surprised if you don't make it out of the club before you get down and dirty." She winks conspiratorially.

"I would never do anything in public."

"Who said in public? There are plenty of hidden alcoves, especially in the VIP section. I would know since that's where Eli and I became acquainted. Damn. Those were the days." She wistfully sighs.

"We'll be in VIP?" This is sounding cooler by the minute—a day in the life of Cici and her billionaire.

"Of course. All of Eli and Sebastian's close friends have a standing table anytime they want. Now that everyone's paired off and having babies, it's not used as much, but Braden still goes quite a bit."

"I'm sure he does." I cringe internally at my petulance.

"Hey, that just means he's better at pleasing a woman. Aren't you glad your first time was with someone who knew what he was doing and not fumbling around? You should take advantage of his skills while you can."

I shrug. "I guess you're right. It's just weird. I never saw myself being promiscuous."

She doubles over laughing. "Poppy, you are the furthest thing from promiscuous. One guy doesn't make you a slut. Hell, ten guys won't. It's your body, and you can do what you damn well please. When you settle down, it'll be that much more special that you've chosen one person to share the rest of your life with. And you'll bring experience to the table to boot. So don't slut shame yourself. You're young. Have some fun." She nudges me with her shoulder, smirking.

And that's why she's my best friend, because that's exactly what I needed to hear. A few more times and it might sink in, but it'll have to wait, because Eli knocks on the bedroom door.

He cracks it open enough to speak through. "Hey, ladies, are you almost done? Braden got here a while ago and is getting impatient."

"We're just finishing up. We'll be down in a sec. Tell him to hold his horses, beauty rushes for no one," Cici shouts.

"I'll pass on the message," Eli says before shutting the door.

"I'm ready, we can go down," I say.

"Nah, make him wait. It builds anticipation."

"I'm not sure that's wise. He's already a force to be reckoned with."

"Exactly, so this'll seal the deal."

"Cici, are you trying to get me laid or what?"

"Yes, duh. It's about time you had some fun. Okay. You need to make a grand entrance. Sashay into the room like this." She giggles as she walks, swaying her hips side to side exaggeratedly, causing me to join her in laughter.

"Yeah, right. Come on. Let's get this over with."

Braden

What the hell is taking so long? I've been waiting all day for this, and my patience is wearing thin. Hell, I've been waiting all damn week in anticipation of having her in my clutches again. And she will be by the end of the night, I have no doubt. Her body still betrays her denial.

"Cici said that beauty rushes for no one," Eli says as he returns to the kitchen, where we've been sipping the drinks he made us.

"Apparently. It's not like she didn't know what time I was coming. What's taking so long? She doesn't need to do anything to look better."

"Is that so?" Eli asks with a raised brow.

"Cici's probably done her up so much that she's not herself, which would be a shame, is all." I shake my head and take a sip.

"So what I hear you saying is that you're into her. Which means I'll be running interference between you and Cici if it blows up in your face."

"Don't worry, it's—" I pause mid-sentence when a bombshell in a tight red dress comes gliding into the room.

Holy fucking shit. My dick concurs with the sentiment as blood instantly rushes to it. Fuck. Reaching down to adjust myself, I stay behind the bar, staring at Poppy, eyes roaming from head to toe, while all the filthy things I want come to mind. It's not until Cici's smirk appears in the periphery that I snap out of it.

"Took you long enough. Ready to go?" I choose anger over lust to diffuse any suspicion.

Eli snickers beside me. "That's not what I would've started with."

I turn, glowering in his direction. His comment is aggravating. However, he made his point.

Turning back to Poppy, I try to save face. "You look great, by the way."

"Thank you." The reluctance in her voice is evident, making me feel like a jerk for not having said that to begin with, because she truly is a siren.

Her red hair is a blaze against the burgundy red dress that accentuates her figure. She may not have the largest tits in the world, but they're beautiful and damn—that ass. It's… fucking perfect, and I know exactly how it feels in the palm of my hand. Before my thoughts get too out of control, I move toward the door.

"Let's get going. Eli, thanks for the drink." I nod in his direction.

"Anytime. Don't be a stranger." Eli responds, winding his arm around Cici as they walk us out.

"Take care of Poppy tonight, will you?" Cici asks as I step outside, surprising me. That sounded like an innuendo, which tracks with the glare Poppy's giving her.

"I plan on it," I state bluntly as I place my hand on Poppy's back and lead her away.

"I can take care of myself," she says defensively.

"I'm sure you can, sugar, but not nearly as well as I can, and you know it."

Blake, the Dubree's full-time driver, stands at the back of their town car holding the door open.

"Thank you, Blake." I nod in greeting.

"My pleasure, Mr. Butcher, Miss Whitaker."

Poppy smiles as she ducks into the back seat.

"Would you mind raising the partition, Blake?" I ask quietly.

"Already done, sir." He winks knowingly.

"Thank you," I say, then join Poppy, sitting beside her. It won't be a long ride, but it's plenty of time to remind her how badly she wants me.

"You ready to have some fun tonight?" I ask to kick things off noncombatively. Because God knows it doesn't take much to provoke my little mouse.

"I'm excited to see the club. We don't have places like that back home."

"I'm glad I suggested it, then. You're in for a treat."

"I guess a thank you is in order. But I hope you're not expecting anything in return." She's stubborn, but her conviction is lacking.

"Enlighten me, what is it that I'd be expecting, Little Mouse?"

"Don't play dumb. You know what I mean. You have a one-track mind, and I'm sure you didn't offer to take me out on the town from the goodness of your heart."

"The club is full of ready and willing women to choose from. I certainly don't need to put all my eggs in one basket. Don't worry, Mouse. If you're determined to fight your attraction to me, I'll take my attention elsewhere."

"Good, you should do that." She sticks her nose in the air and turns her head to look out the window.

I stealthily move in close and grab her upper thigh, causing her to gasp. In a low voice, I growl into her ear. "I expect nothing from you other than honesty. And I highly doubt you can *honestly* tell me you haven't repeatedly thought of how good I make you feel." My hand begins to slide up, as her breath begins to quicken. "How hard I make you come."

She shoves me away and glares in my direction. "That might be all you think about, but I have better things to do with my time."

She says it with such conviction that she almost has me convinced. Almost.

Justin and Lucy are already upstairs when we arrive. It's fun to witness the awe written on Poppy's face from the moment we enter, all the way through the club, to the table we end up at.

I reach out to shake Justin's hand. "Hey, man, thanks for coming. Lucy, it's good to see you."

Justin returns the handshake. "Glad you asked. It's been a while."

"I'm so glad we're hanging out," Lucy says to Poppy, going in for a girl hug.

"Me too. I'm glad you're here. Hi, Justin," Poppy says, then takes a seat in an empty chair.

When we sit down, the waitress comes to take our drink orders. As one of the hottest clubs in the city, they don't have high turnover, which means Crystal and I are familiar and have used a few of the hidden alcoves.

She immediately steps around the table and embraces me in a hug. To avoid being a jerk, I return the gesture as casually as possible while Poppy watches the encounter with interest.

"Hey, Braden. It's been a while. Where've you been?"

"Work's been busy, so I'm not out as much."

"Well, I'm glad you're here. You want your regular?"

I cringe internally. That could mean a couple of different things if Poppy wasn't sitting next to me.

"Please. Poppy, what would you like to drink? It's on the house." I make a point of asking her, so Crystal takes the hint.

"I'll have a lemon drop."

That fits her perfectly.

"Are you guys still good?" Crystal asks Justin and Lucy.

"All good, thanks," Justin replies.

"Great. I'll have your drinks right up," Crystal says, tossing me a wink and walking away.

"Wow…" comes from Poppy when the coast is clear.

"Wow, what?" I ask her.

"Does every waitress here *know* you so well?"

"I'm here quite a bit, so if they work the VIP section, I'd say it's likely. Why? Are you jealous?" I jab, while Justin and Lucy sit back, amused.

"Uh, negative, just an observation."

I raise my eyebrows in her direction, calling bullshit, but don't have a chance to argue as Warren appears.

"Hey, buddy, glad you made it," I say in greeting, accompanied by a bro-shake.

"Yeah, me too." Warren goes to Justin next, a familiar face at the table. "Hey, Justin, good to see you out of the office for once."

Justin shakes his outstretched hand. "No shit. Lucy, this is Warren. He works with Braden. Warren, this is my girlfriend, Lucy."

When they're done exchanging pleasantries, I take the opportunity to introduce Poppy—the reason Warren showed up tonight.

"Warren, come meet Poppy." Then I tell Poppy, "Warren is my right-hand man in the office." Calling him my assistant never feels adequate to explain his position.

"Ah, so you're the guy who has to put up with Braden's crap every day. I'm sorry," Poppy says right out of the gate.

Warren laughs. "Well, aren't you a firecracker. I like you already. Braden's been feeding me lies about you."

"What did he say?" she asks accusingly.

"That you're on the shy side, but I think he's been holding out. I'm glad I came to see for myself. I figured you must be something special since he hasn't shut up about you." Warren, the smooth talker, needs to shut the fuck up.

"Hey, asshole. Go order your drink and give the girl a minute to breathe." I shove Warren's shoulder and note Poppy's blush. He's working his magic all right.

Warren goes to the bar to chat with the bartender when our drinks arrive, giving the girls time to talk while Justin and I discuss a few cases he's helping with. The second Lucy suggests they hit the dance floor, Justin's up and out of his seat in a heartbeat, and I'm following suit.

Poppy stops when I rise, turning to face me. "You don't have to come."

"Yes, I do."

"We'll meet you out there, Poppy," Lucy says before Justin leads her away.

"Okay, thanks," Poppy responds to Lucy, then turns back. "What about our drinks?"

"We'll order fresh ones. Come on." I place my arm over her shoulder and try walking us forward, but she digs her heels in and crawls out from under me.

She starts toward the dance floor, calling back, "I don't need you to watch over me. Especially since I want to dance with someone else."

Having had enough of that, I step alongside her, wrap an arm around her waist, then lean down and growl, "Listen, Little Mouse, only one person is putting their hands on you tonight, unless I decide to share, so you're sticking with me or sitting back down. Your choice."

She tries to break free, but I tighten my grip and propel us forward until we reach the dance floor. She's scowling as I turn her toward me and stiff as we start to move.

Then Lucy yells from the side of her. "Hey, you made it."

Poppy grins back at Lucy and relaxes a little. For the sake of Lucy or because she gives up, I'm not sure, but I'm glad she's done fighting me for the moment. While Lucy and Justin do their thing, Poppy and I begin to dance in sync.

I can't resist grabbing her hips and pulling her closer as we sway to the music. The feel of her body on mine causes my dick to respond, and it's not long before the bulge in my pants is unapologetically grinding against her stomach. It feels fucking fantastic, but it isn't near enough.

I snake a hand to her ass and squeeze, holding her tight when she raises her lustful gaze to mine, prompting me to grip her neck and lean in for a kiss. Damn. My memory is instantly validated the moment our lips meet.

Moments in, she jerks her head back as someone comes in from behind, sandwiching her between us, and I look over her shoulder at Warren. I tighten my grip, instinctively moving my hand up as he grabs her hips and matches our rhythm.

Her eyes go wide in shock, causing me to smile. "It's okay, Mouse, it's only Warren."

She's still unsure, so I distract her by picking up where we left off. It's not long before our kiss turns frantic, but when Warren starts working her neck, she stiffens. I double the assault on her lips, and within seconds, she melts once more, moaning in desire.

So far, so good, but it's time to take it up a notch.

10

FILTHY

Poppy

WHAT THE HELL IS HAPPENING RIGHT NOW? I'M sandwiched between two men on the dance floor, one grinding his package into my stomach and the other against my back. My body is on fricking fire. This is so not me. I'm in public for crying out loud.

"You're so fucking sexy," Warren rumbles into my ear while devouring my neck. His hot breath, his tongue, his lips—all feel amazing.

Braden's kiss puts me in sensory overload. I'm in a haze of lust and so wound up with this many sensations that I can't focus on anything. And that's when hands start wandering.

The one on my side comes around and palms my breast, massaging and grazing the nipple. My hips press forward, naturally searching for more, when the hand on my hip is suddenly lifting my skirt, dipping between my legs.

My core pulses in anticipation of what's coming, and as soon as I feel the first touch, I can't help the moan that escapes. Thank God it's too dark for anyone to notice anything other than the three of us dancing, because I don't have the strength to stop what's happening. Not when I've been craving it for weeks.

Fingers start circling my clit, driving me wild, and I pull back from Braden to breathe. He wastes no time moving to the opposite side of my neck as Warren. My head lifts toward the ceiling in ecstasy as we sway to the music, while I'm touched and kissed. The sensations are overwhelming, and I'm powerless to prevent the approaching orgasm.

My hips jerk forward when it hits, and my head drops to Braden's shoulder as I ride it out.

"Fuck that was hot," Braden says in my ear, while Warren asks if I'm ready for another drink.

All I can do is nod before they slowly lead me from the dance floor. My head hangs in shame at the sudden realization of what I just allowed them to do. I can only pray we weren't spotted by Justin and Lucy, which is highly probable. Though my hope lifts when they're already at the table with fresh drinks.

"Hey, I ordered you the same drink since we left them unattended. I hope that's okay," Lucy says as we take our seats.

"That's great, thank you," I reply a little too enthusiastically, because Lord knows, I could use it right now.

I can't even make eye contact with either man beside me. They must think I'm a total whore. I mean, who does that—lets two men grope and make out with her on the dance floor? Certainly not me… before tonight. Oh my God. Now what?

"Let's finish this one, and then it's *our* turn to dance. No boys allowed next time," Lucy says and holds her glass up to toast.

In full support, I eagerly meet hers with mine, then take down half the fresh lemon drop at once. While the rest of the table makes conversation, I'm stuck in my head panicking, sipping my cocktail like it's the cure. The next thing I know, my drink is gone and Lucy's grabbing my hand, yanking me out of the chair.

"Come on, Poppy. Let's leave them to their boring work and go dance." She drags me out of my seat. "Let's stop in the bathroom first," she says, pulling me in that direction.

The minute we're inside, she turns on me. "What's going on with you three? I thought there was something between you and Braden earlier, but then I saw you guys on the dance floor. Was that what I think it was?"

"What did you think it was?" I ask with a slight panic in my voice.

"A sexy man sandwich is what it looked like. I'm honestly a little jealous right now."

I laugh in relief, deciding to tell her the truth and get her advice. "Well, Braden and I had a fling at the wedding, and it was supposed to be a one-time thing, but he's been relentless. Then Warren showed up, and when he came up behind me, one thing led to another. Now I feel like a total slut." I drop my head into my hands and groan.

Lucy grabs my shoulders, and I look up to a stern face. "You are not a slut. You are one lucky bitch is what you are. That was fricking hot. So hot, I'm ready to go and have wild sex with Justin while imagining it. Damn girl. So what now? Are you going home with them?"

"As in plural? Uh, that would be a no."

"Why not?" she asks incredulously.

"Because that kind of thing doesn't happen."

"I'm pretty sure it does."

"Well, it's not supposed to."

"Says who?"

"Says everyone."

"Bullshit. You can do whatever you want with whoever you want. I wouldn't think twice if I were you. You might never have another chance."

"I didn't know I needed one. Normal people don't do that."

"Again, says who? Poppy, seriously, do you realize how hot that is?" She sees my hesitancy. "But, hey, don't let me pressure you. You shouldn't do it if you don't want to. You do you."

"Thanks. I guess it's not something I've thought about before."

"Then stop thinking and do what feels right. Or *good* rather." She winks, causing us to laugh.

"Now let's go dance our asses off and give them something to drool over."

After using the bathroom, we lose ourselves on the dance floor for who knows how long, until the guys run out of patience and join us. It doesn't slip into rated R this time, but they definitely don't keep their hands to themselves. I start to loosen up, enjoying them together instead of overthinking, and by the time we return to the table, I'm grinning from ear to ear.

Braden leans in. "That looks good on you."

"What does?"

He reaches up and brushes his thumb along my bottom lip. "This." Then he kisses me chastely before taking his seat.

"It's getting late. I think we're gonna head out after this drink," Justin says after another round is ordered.

I'm still in a daze from Braden's comment.

"Sounds like a great plan to me. Poppy?" Braden places his hand on my thigh, bringing me out of my stupor.

"Yeah. I'm ready. You guys wore me out."

Warren leans over and whispers in my ear. "Not yet, we haven't."

My cheeks heat as I catch Lucy watching. Her face tells me exactly what she's thinking, and I'm shocked to discover my mind moving in the same direction.

Once our drinks are finished, we all exit the club and say our goodbyes. Apparently, we're giving Warren a ride home, so the three of us pile into the back of the town car. Braden comes in last after telling Blake where to go, and when the door closes, the sexual tension is so thick you could cut it with a knife.

As we drive away, Warren wraps his hand around my neck and pulls me toward him. "I've been dying for a turn all night," he says before his mouth crashes into mine.

His kiss is more aggressive than Braden's, his lips slightly smaller but just as powerful, spreading me open for more. Not that he's forcing his way in by any means, since I'm eagerly matching his every move.

"So it's my turn back here then?" I hear Braden from behind as my hair is brushed to the side, and his lips graze my neck.

While Warren cups my breast, Braden's hand reaches between my legs and probes my aching core. "Ah fuck, sugar, you're soaking wet."

Warren breaks from the kiss. "I can't wait for a taste. See for myself how sweet you are."

"You want that, Mouse? Warren to lick your needy pussy… make you come on his tongue?" Braden asks seductively. It's not words that answer, it's the moan that leaks out along with the reaction my body makes of its own accord. My hips thrust into Braden's hand as he rubs my clit.

"Yeah, you do. Your pussy's begging for it. Turns out my little mouse is filthy," Braden says while pressing a finger inside, causing me to gasp at the intrusion.

"Damn right she is," Warren adds. "I'm ready to see how dirty we can get her. We headed to your place?"

I'm assuming he's talking to Braden, but I'm too distracted by their hands to pay attention as my head falls back in ecstasy.

"Give us another one, Mouse. We're not leaving the car until you come all over my hand." Braden licks my ear and nibbles the lobe.

"You better hurry, babe, we're getting close, and I need a sample." Warren's hand joins Braden's, and I feel another finger added.

Holy shit, they're both inside of me at once. My body detonates in no time, and I cry out as the most intense orgasm roars to life.

"Oh my God. Ahhh…"

"That's a good girl," Braden whispers into my ear as he caresses my forehead, causing my core to clench harder.

"We're lucky fuckers tonight," Warren says to Braden.

"You're damn lucky I'm sharing," Braden responds.

"True that." Warren removes his hand and licks his finger before sucking it clean. "Fuck, man, she's delicious. Damn lucky, is right."

Somehow, they help my lifeless body into Braden's place with not much assistance from me. I'm sitting on the couch watching them in the kitchen while they pour wine.

They've given no opportunity for doubt to creep in, and for some reason, it still doesn't come. They're seamless in their movements and technique, which suggests they've done this before. I should probably be worried about that… or jealous. But right now, I just want more, even if I don't quite understand what that means.

Although I'm pretty sure I don't need to worry about anything with these two. I'm sure they'll take the lead, and I'll eagerly follow, because, like Lucy said, do what feels good. And if what happened on the way here is any indication, they know how to deliver.

Braden

I was honestly surprised Poppy didn't hesitate when I suggested we go to my place. She's been quiet since we arrived and still hasn't said anything. Whether she's doubting her decision is yet to be seen, but we're about to find out.

Warren and I are in the kitchen, with a view of Poppy sitting on the couch through the archway. I'm stealthy as I pull him aside to clarify who's running the show tonight.

"If we're doing this, we're doing it my way."

"Since when? Normally, you like me taking charge."

"Not this time. I'm calling the shots," I say sternly.

He holds his hands up in defense. "Whatever you want, man. I'm at your command."

"Good. Let's not keep her waiting." Grabbing two filled glasses, I sit on the other side of the couch and pat the seat next to me. "Come here, Mouse."

Poppy scoots over, making room for Warren to plop down, enclosing her between us.

I hand her a glass and drape my arm around her waist. "How are you feeling?"

"Good. A little nervous," she answers, following with a timid sip of wine.

"I'd be worried you had Braden fooled if you weren't," Warren says.

"Fooled how?" she asks innocently.

Warren tucks a strand of hair behind her ear before answering. "Well, you've got him thinking you're a shy little thing, yet here you are trying something most people wouldn't even consider."

"What does that say about me then?" Her embarrassment is endearing, but it's the last thing I want her to feel.

"I think it shows that you're brave and more adventurous than I've given you credit for," I tell her sincerely.

"Or stupid for being promiscuous," she counters.

I chuckle. "You're far from. We're three single adults doing what we want. We won't do anything you're not okay with. All you have to do is say no, and we stop. If you follow my lead, I promise you'll walk away unscathed and more satisfied than you ever thought possible."

She takes a deep breath and nods once with a look of determination. "So where do we start?"

"Don't worry about that. Let's drink our wine, relax, and I'll take care of the rest. Deal?" I hold up my glass.

"Deal," Poppy agrees.

They both meet me in a toast to seal it.

After about twenty minutes of small talk, Poppy's shoulders have loosened, and she's calm, not worrying over what comes next, which is perfect timing to move forward.

Taking her glass, I set it on the side table, then turn to face her. "I think we've deprived Warren of dessert for long enough, wouldn't you agree?"

She doesn't answer but turns beet red as Warren says, "Fuck yeah, you have."

"What are you going to do about that, Mouse?" I ask.

"What should I do?" Her words are timid, nerves evident.

"Stand up and remove your dress," I instruct, trying to make it easier on her by taking the guesswork out of the equation.

It seems to do the trick. Without answering, she rises from the couch and shimmies it up from the bottom, revealing that luscious ass with full grabbable hips. The sexy black G-string panties don't leave much to the imagination, causing my dick to strain against my zipper, anxious to be released.

The dress continues to rise, unveiling the beautiful curve of her waist to her bare, braless back. When it's finally lifted over her head, she stands before us, her nearly naked body on display.

Warren whistles as she drops it to the floor. "Fuck me six ways to Sunday, that's the nicest ass I've seen. Fuck you for holding out on me, man."

"So you do this often, I take it." Poppy states, still facing away from us.

"Which means we know what we're doing. Turn around, Mouse, show us the rest," I demand.

She slowly rotates, her eyes widening at the large bulges we're both sporting.

"Yeah, sweetheart, you caused this." Warren grabs his cock and squeezes it through his pants. "Man… those tits are just as fine as that ass. I'd have considered keeping you to myself too. Now the real question is, what's underneath those panties?"

"You heard the man," I prompt, figuring she'll take the hint.

Which she does, lowering them to reveal the tiny patch of red hair atop the prettiest pussy I've laid eyes on.

Warren groans. "Fuuuck. You're killing me, man. If we don't get somewhere soon, I'm taking over."

"Come here, Mouse. Lay on the couch with your head in my lap and your feet on Warren."

She does as told, then looks up at me, waiting for the next instruction.

I brush her hair from her forehead. "Now bend your knees and open your legs, then reach down and spread your pussy lips. Let Warren take a good look at what he'll be feasting on."

Scarlet blooms in her cheeks while she timidly follows my instructions. "This is humiliating," she says, closing her eyes.

"Are you kidding me? This is hot as fuck." Warren tells her, giving her the encouragement she needs.

"Open your eyes, Mouse. See the lust in Warren's eyes. How you're teasing him, making him want you so badly."

She peels her lids up and looks straight at Warren, biting her bottom lip.

"Good girl," I say encouragingly, still caressing her hair.

"Fuck, man, don't make me wait any longer. I'm practically coming in my pants," Warren begs as he devours her with his eyes.

"Touch her. Tell me how wet she is."

Warren reaches forward and softly probes her entrance with a groan before slowly entering her. Poppy's eyes close, and her hips lift, already begging for more.

"Damn, baby, you need to be fucked." He looks up at me, pleading. "Why are we not?"

"Because you haven't eaten yet. Why don't you taste how sweet she is?" I give him the permission he's been waiting for.

"Goddamn, it's about time. You ready for me to rock your world?" he asks, receiving a nod in response.

He moves to his knees and lowers his head, not wasting any time as he licks her from bottom to top with one long swipe of his tongue.

"Oh, fuck, yeah. Even better than I expected. Hold on tight, sweetheart." Warren dives in after that and laps at her entrance, eating her out like a man starving. Her hands grip the cushions as she writhes from his attack.

Her eyes squeeze shut as she bites her lip. Fuck, I'm rock hard at seeing her reaction firsthand. It's just as enjoyable, if not more so, than being the one giving pleasure. I undo my pants and stroke my cock with one hand while the other plays with her breast. It's not long before I'm dripping with pre-cum. Wiping it with my thumb, I bring it to her mouth.

"Open." I push in past her lips. "Suck."

She does, and the moan she releases at the same time makes my dick twitch. Fuck. I could practically come from this alone. I swear every lap of her tongue goes straight to my cock, causing more pre-cum to leak out.

Removing the hand from her breast, I gather more and replace one thumb with the other. "Keep it up, baby, cause my cock is the next thing you'll be sucking."

With my free hand, I pump my shaft slowly, barely able to hold back from losing it. Warren's hands have joined the party with one working her clit while the other plunges into her cunt. Her cries of pleasure are intensifying, hips going crazy.

"Finish her off, Warren. I want to watch her fall apart."

He intensifies his thrusts, and seconds later, she comes with a cry, releasing my thumb, her hips jerking as she climaxes.

"Oh God. Yes. Oh my God." She moans the words between breaths as her face scrunches in ecstasy. Watching it play out first-hand is fucking phenomenal.

Warren works her through it and slowly retreats when she's fully spent. "That was the best dessert I've had in a long time. Your new nickname should be Sugar."

She giggles, probably too swept up from her orgasm to be shy.

"As sexy as that was, though, if my dick isn't milked in the next few minutes, I'll explode, so you better have a plan, dude," Warren says as he sits back.

"I do, and we're taking it to the bedroom." I grab under Poppy's arms and haul her off the couch over my shoulder.

"Braden, I can walk," she screeches in protest.

My hand delivers a slap to her ass. "Are you in charge, Mouse?"

She squeaks out a no in response.

"That's what I thought."

When we reach the bed, I climb on and scoot up to the headboard, setting Poppy on my lap.

"So here's what's gonna happen. While Warren undresses, you're going to assume the position on all fours and face me. Then, Warren's gonna fuck your sweet little pussy doggy style as you suck my cock. You're warmed up, so you should be nice and ready for him. We good?"

"Hell yeah. Is it my choice of holes?" Warren asks as he removes his clothes.

Poppy's eyes bug out of her head, confirming she's an anal virgin, which means double penetration is off the table. There's also no fucking way I'd allow him to have it before me. "No. Her ass is off-limits." I don't even want him *touching* it before I do. Nor am I letting him fuck her bare. I'm the only one to have that privilege.

"Grab a condom out of the drawer." I nod toward the nightstand.

"I'm sure her pussy will satisfy me just fine, considering *your* infatuation with it," he says, stroking himself as he reaches for protection while Poppy watches with interest, unmoving. "You ready for me to fill you, baby? I need your sexy body before I explode, since the only place I plan to come is inside that juicy cunt."

"Hop up, Mouse. Hands and knees, right here." I pat the bed, and as she gets into position, I quickly remove my shirt, followed by my pants.

Once she's settled, Warren climbs up behind her, rips the condom open, and sheathes himself. Poppy looks like a deer in headlights.

"Give her a lick, Warren, make sure she's drenched." I lean in and kiss her passionately to keep her mind distracted from overthinking.

Pulling back, I grab her chin. "Eyes on me while he feeds you his cock. Don't close them, I want to watch you take him in."

He lines up, waiting for my command.

"You know how fucking sexy you are, about to be filled with two cocks? Give her the first one, Warren."

"With pleasure." He slides in slowly, groaning along the way. "Holy fuck. This might be the tightest pussy I've ever had."

My cock twitches at the memory but more so from seeing her

reaction as he penetrates her—her eyes widening at the intrusion, mouth parting in surprise. It's so fucking hot. I don't think I've ever enjoyed watching this much.

"Dude, are you sure you fucked her? I swear this is a virgin pussy."

For some reason, she looks distressed by his comment.

"Oh, I'm sure. No way could I forget the best fuck I've had in ages."

"Damn. No kidding. I'm not gonna last long, you better get started."

"Let me worry about that. I'm enjoying this too much. Give it to her good so I can watch her take it."

She bites her lip as Warren grabs her hips tightly.

"Gladly." He unleashes in the next push, quickly withdrawing before relentlessly pounding her pussy as he grunts from the power of his thrusts.

Her eyes and mouth open wide, and she whimpers each time he bottoms out. I'm entranced as pre-cum leaks freely from my cock while I stroke it.

"Oh God," Poppy moans.

"You okay, Mouse?"

"Yes."

"You're so sexy. You like being fucked hard, don't you, Sugar?" Warren says as he pummels into her.

"Yes. It feels… so good," she answers, squeezing her eyes shut.

"Eyes on me, Poppy. Look at me while Warren fucks you."

She snaps them open.

"Good girl," I say and reach up to caress her hair.

Warren suddenly slows his pace. "Fuck man, stop with the dirty talk. She likes it too much. If her cunt squeezes me anymore, I'm gonna lose it."

I laugh. "Is that true? You like my filthy words?" I ask Poppy.

"Maybe," she answers shyly.

I can't help but lean forward and kiss her again.

Pulling away, I grab the steel rod between my legs. "All right, he's feeling left out." I squeeze her chin. "Time to put this mouth to good use. You okay if I'm in control?"

"What do you mean?" Poppy asks innocently, like she's never had her face fucked before.

"All you need to do is open wide and let me do the work. Can you do that?"

She nods.

My hand goes to the back of her head, pushing her to my cock as I guide it in. "Wider, Mouse. You're gonna take me all the way."

The minute I feel the soft heat of her mouth, I look up and groan in ecstasy. I've dreamed of her lips wrapped around my cock since the moment I caught sight of them. Holy shit. I won't last long.

"I don't have much left in me, dude. Hurry up." Warren says from behind while his eyes are focused on Poppy held over my dick. His movements are slow and controlled, like he's hanging on by a thread.

I'm so wound up, I don't need much time, but I'd rather prolong it. Unfortunately, I don't think that's possible.

"Don't worry. I'll be lucky to make it a whole minute. You ready, Poppy?"

She mumbles out an *ah-huh* as best she can with her mouth stuffed full.

"Just breathe through your nose, and I'll do the rest, baby." I start moving her head up and down, making her gag as I push her down farther and farther. "Oh fuck, that's it, Mouse. You've got this."

"Yeah, baby, suck that cock good while I wreck this pussy," Warren encourages, about causing me to blow.

"Look at you, taking both our cocks at once."

Watching Warren fuck her from behind while she sucks me off, I'm in absolute heaven. I still can't believe she's here—with both of us. She's spectacular and deserves to be rewarded.

"You're doing so good, baby. Warren, make her come. I'm almost there."

He reaches for her clit, and the minute he makes contact, she moans around my dick, bringing me even closer.

"So fucking sexy. Come for us, Mouse, so we can fill you up." My hips begin to thrust uncontrollably, the slurping sound, along with her whimpers, driving me wild.

"Fuck, man, she's squeezing me like a vise. I'm gonna blow. Oh fuck, oh fuck, I'm coming." Warren pumps his release into her as she screams out her climax around my cock, causing me to explode at the same time.

Cum floods her mouth as I hold her still, my cock pulsing inside her throat. "Oh fuck, yeah, swallow it, Poppy. That's it. Such a good girl. Fuck, fuck, fuck." I ride it out, chanting the whole way as she chokes down my release.

Warren hunches over her back as I lift her head to the sexiest cum-covered mouth I've ever seen. Her lips are swollen, tears streaking her cheeks.

"Fuck, baby. That was amazing," I tell her, wiping the tears away. I use my thumb to gather as much cum from her chin as possible and pop it in her mouth. She sucks it off without me telling her. That's how fucking perfect she is.

"My God," Warren breathes out as he drags himself to the bathroom, talking as he goes, "That was… epic. Damn, it's too bad you don't live here. We don't usually have repeat performances, but I'd be up for an encore."

Little does he know this would be a one-time thing even if she did live here. I'd covet the rest of her firsts, keeping them for myself. They'd all be mine. Unfortunately, that's not possible and probably for the best. Ultimately, she'd only end up hurt if I strung her along for more, so I'm glad it's not an option.

"Hey, grab a warm washcloth and bring it here," I yell to Warren.

Once Poppy is settled under the covers beside me, I brush the hair from her neck and check in. "Are you okay?"

"Yeah, I'm good. That was… fun." She smiles shyly.

"Fun? I'd say it was fucking fantastic. You were incredible."

Her cheeks flame, matching her hair.

Warren returns with a washcloth, handing it to Poppy.

"Thanks." She wipes her face, then passes it to me to clean the cum from my cock since it didn't all make it down her throat. Fuck, I'm hardening again at the thought.

Warren quickly dresses, then stands at the foot of the bed. "Well, I'd love to stay and sing Kumbaya, but I've got an early morning since I have a feeling this guy won't be in right away." He winks. "Okay, kids, don't have too much fun without me. Poppy, it was a pleasure. I'd be interested in round two if you're ever back in town."

I barely stop myself from declaring he's not invited, but refrain, knowing it doesn't matter since she won't be returning any time soon.

"Thanks, Warren. It was… nice to meet you?" She cringes and blushes again.

He laughs. "That's one way to put it." He walks out the door, saying goodbye and leaving us alone.

"So… I should probably find my clothes and—"

"You don't have to go." The words impulsively burst out without considering them.

Oh shit, did I just ask her to stay?

"Oh…" She looks at me in surprise, then adds, "I don't know…"

"You might as well stay. I can bring you back in the morning."

She contemplates for a moment. "I guess so, but only if you're sure."

The instant relief is all the assurance I need that it was the right choice, stirring feelings that have been dormant for years.

I cup her cheek and bring her lips toward mine. "I'd love nothing more," I say, then close the gap between us.

11

BLIND DATE

Poppy

"ALL RIGHT, TELL ME EVERYTHING, YOU LITTLE SLUT," CICI SAYS sarcastically while giggling.

"You might be saying that for real after you hear my story."

We're sitting on her couch after putting Abby down for a nap, since I said I couldn't hold her while talking about sex. Eli was at work already when Braden dropped me off, thank God. I think it would have been weird to be around him after screwing his friend, along with another guy. Way too awkward.

I had planned to call an Uber after Warren left, but was shocked when Braden asked me to stay. Instead of going right to sleep, we talked, made out like teenagers, then one thing led to another, and I ended up checking a new position off, as he spooned me from behind to my fifth orgasm of the night.

Something felt different about that last time. It was... intimate, almost as if feelings were involved, but I know better. I'm not that naïve. Even if my mind got confused or was playing tricks on me,

Braden for sure has no intentions other than sex when it comes to women.

"Since you'll probably hear about some of it from Lucy, I might as well tell you the rest."

So I recount everything in detail, starting with the incident on the dance floor until the end of the night, watching her eyes bug out during most of the one-sided conversation.

"Holy shit," she stammers once I finish the story.

"Yeah."

"I mean, holy shit. You are a fucking goddess. You went from losing your virginity one month to getting double-stuffed the next. Like, what the heck? Where were you when I was single and needed a partner in crime?"

"This doesn't change anything. I'm not gonna start sleeping around. In fact, I'm more determined than ever to find my person."

"I bet. So you can have sex all the time, huh?"

We both crack up laughing.

"Exactly," I say as soon as I catch my breath.

"Shoot. You'll need a guy who's capable of wild animal sex. So you'll have to test the waters before settling."

"True. But I won't do that unless someone is worthy of testing. And if he's perfect in every other way, can't they learn if they're not great at it?"

"Hm." Cici shrugs. "I'm not sure. But how will you find him in the first place?"

"Well, there's this new app I want to try."

Cici groans at my solution.

"It's not like I have friends setting me up all the time, and I don't go out very often, so my options are limited," I say defensively.

"Fine. Show me your profile."

I grab my phone and pull up the app. "I haven't done it yet, but it shouldn't be hard since it's without pictures."

"WHAT? You can't find someone without knowing what they look like. That's the most important part—you're crazy."

"It's perfect. They'll be searching for the same thing I am, and not just out for sex. Without pictures, it's about getting to know each other and connecting, rather than hooking up. Then, if you're still interested after the required number of conversations, you can exchange photos if you want. Or skip it altogether and just be surprised when you meet, sort of like a blind date."

To me, it sounds great, but leave it to Cici to point out the flaws.

"Yeah, but what if you totally hit it off with some guy and then he's hideous? What do you say? *Ohhh, sorry. You're great and all, but I'm looking for someone more attractive.*"

"Maybe it won't matter by then—I might like him so much that I'll think he's cute anyway."

"Then you need to enlist me to give you an unbiased opinion."

"Cici, it's not all about looks," I chide.

"Tell that to your future children," Cici deadpans.

I hit her with a pillow, and we fall into giggles again. "You're awful."

Abby's cry sounds from the baby monitor.

Cici rises from the couch. "I'm honest. Let me get Abby and then we'll do your profile. The sooner you find someone, the sooner I can say I told you so," she calls back before she rounds the corner.

"Bitch," I tease.

While she's gone, I look through the app again. When I first found it, I thought the same as Cici, but after reading the explanation along with the reviews, it made sense. My basic requirements are specified, so the profiles that appear on my feed will at least meet a certain criteria. If I put in that I want someone who's active, for example, they won't match me with a couch potato, and so on.

Now that Cici's filled my mind with doubts, though, I'm starting to have second thoughts. Still, it's not like I'm committing by signing up. Plus, do I really care if I tell them I'm not interested after seeing their picture if I've never met them in person anyway? I'd say it's worth a shot.

All I'm trying to do is prevent ending up with some manwhore like Braden, whose only interest is sex. Good sex. But still, that's not what I'm looking for. Well, I am, but to have that, I need to find someone special, and this is the first step to making that happen.

Cici comes back with a smiling Abby. I'm not sure if she's ever not smiling; she's such a happy baby. "All right, trade me. Take this little munchkin and hand me your phone. Let's do this."

I gladly hand it over and move to the floor with Abby to play with the little cutie. Rattling toys above her head and squeezing her little toes—I could stare at her forever. She's fricking adorable. I'm sad we live so far apart, and I won't be able to see her as often as I'd like. I'll miss a lot, so I'm soaking it all in before flying home tomorrow.

"Okay, I got the basics in. It's too bad you can't put a requirement for a stallion in the bedroom, but I guess that would defeat your purpose for choosing this app," Cici says as she continues with the phone.

"Plus, it would make me sound easy, and I'm not going for that."

"Yeah, yeah, I know. All right, so how can we make sure you don't get any losers?"

"Does it ask for income requirements or anything like that? Or profession preferences? What are all the options?"

"It looks like we can narrow it down for types of jobs, like professional versus just starting out, or student, which we'll ixnay, of course. They do have a box to check for self-employed, but you *could* end up with a guy who owns a pooper-scooper company."

"It doesn't have to be perfect. I'll still be able to choose the ones I want. We just need to specify the parameters for what appears on my feed. How about activity level, like whether they do sports or outdoorsy stuff?"

An hour later, I have a completed profile ready to submit. It takes twenty-four hours for them to approve it before it goes live. Then I'll be shown profiles that meet my requirements. When I like someone who likes me in return, a match is made, and we'll both be sent a notification.

After a certain number of messages back and forth, we're allowed to exchange pictures if we choose. I'm not sure why anyone wouldn't, unless they want to be surprised when they meet in person, but I think that would be worse—you'd have to suffer through the date at that point.

"All right, you ready?" Cici asks, holding my phone with her finger hovering over it, waiting for my approval to push the submit button.

Taking a deep breath, I nod, and she presses down. "Yay!" she exclaims. "You're one step closer to a lifetime of naughty, virtuous sex. You're welcome."

Braden

It's been two weeks, and I haven't stopped thinking about my little mouse. I've tried, God knows I have, but between work, extra gym time, and even a visit to the club for a hookup, I've had no reprieve. Not to mention, no hookup was had since the woman I wanted was a thousand miles away.

So I'm caving, arriving at Eli and Cici's under the pretense of visiting, so I can grill Cici about Poppy. I'm not sure what my goal is, but sitting around, obsessing over her isn't doing any good—maybe at least talking about her will help. Fuck. Who am I kidding? Nothing can pull me out of this except the woman herself.

"Good to see you," Eli says as we exchange a manly bro hug on my way in.

"You too. How's the little one?"

"She's great. Cici will bring Abby out in a minute. She's just feeding her. Let's grab a drink and sit on the patio." He opens the fridge and removes two beers, handing me one before we head outside.

"I didn't think you were a glutton for punishment, but here you are," Eli says cryptically once we're settled.

"What is that supposed to mean?" My brows rise in question.

"My wife and I tell each other everything. Cici and Poppy tell each other everything." He looks at me pointedly. "Which means I know what happened that night. You can imagine the shit she's gonna give you, right?"

"Fuck." It hadn't occurred to me she heard the details of our last night together, which makes this more awkward than I anticipated.

Quickly moving on to other topics, we catch up on life as we wait for Cici to join us.

It's not long until she opens the slider and steps out. "This is a surprise. Two visits in two weeks. You must love babies, huh?" She smirks mockingly as she holds Abby up.

"Well, she is why I have to visit you now, since you guys don't go out anymore."

"We'll start having Cici's parents watch her at some point," Eli says.

"But I'm not ready for that yet, am I?" Cici says in baby talk as she nuzzles her nose against Abby's face and kisses her. Then she settles her into the contraption next to her.

"Soon, everyone will have kids, and I'll be making the rounds to all of you. Mia and Jackson probably aren't too far behind after spending time with you guys and Lily."

"She's so young, but maybe." Cici shrugs. "I'm sure Jackson would be up for starting a family. What about you? Are you ever gonna date someone for longer than one night?" she asks before quickly adding, "Oh, wait, you spent two with Poppy. Is that a record?"

I knew this was coming, so I shouldn't be surprised. And honestly, it works to my advantage since I'm not the one who brought her up, so now I can roll with it.

"You're hilarious," I say sarcastically, when an idea suddenly hits me. "Speaking of Poppy, can I get her phone number? She left something at my place that I need to return."

"You can just give it to me, and I'll take care of it."

The problem is, she didn't leave anything. Damn, Cici, for making it complicated.

"I'll handle it, since it's my responsibility. Warren can mail it— that's what assistants are for."

"Among other things, I've heard," she says pointedly, causing Eli to snicker.

Yep, I walked into that one.

"Right. So what's her number so I can reach out?" I try again, pulling my phone out this time, hoping she'll spill it already.

She does, thank God, and I'm instantly anxious to wrap this up so I can go text her. *I'm so fucked.*

After Cici rattles it off, she catches me off guard. "By the way, you must have had quite the impact on her. She's suddenly pretty serious about *finding* someone serious. Listen to this. She signed up for this dating app without pictures. I still can't believe something like that even exists."

Eli disagrees. "I don't know. It made sense when she explained it to me. It's more about the relationship rather than a quick fuck." He shrugs.

"Screw that. I'm siding with Cici. No pictures? No, thank you. That's fricking insane. But enlighten me on what I had to do with it." I raise my brows at Cici.

I can't imagine our interaction inspiring a longing for commitment when that was the last thing I was offering.

"Sex. She wants to find a husband so she can do it all the time." She laughs as I internally cringe at the thought of Poppy with another man, shocked at the rage it fills me with.

"Nice, dude. You should start a service for women. Your ad can be: One night with me is all the inspiration it takes to walk down the aisle." Eli's busting up.

I need to get out of here. That new tidbit of information has me spiraling out of control. How the fuck can she already be dying to sleep with someone else so soon after we were together? It obviously meant nothing to her, since she's looking for another bed to jump into. Fuck, what is wrong with me? I'm acting like a pussy.

That last time, though, seemed different. Almost like it was more than just sex, which is insane considering we barely know each other.

I didn't know what to say or how to leave things, and figured it was best just to let it be, but now I wish I hadn't.

Steering the conversation to safer subjects and doing my best to remain calm, I stay long enough to finish my drink before making an excuse to head out.

I almost sent a text right when I reached the car, but decided to wait, obsessing about it the entire drive home. Thus, it's ready to send the minute my front door shuts behind me. Not that it's any better for having waited.

Braden: Hey, this is Braden. Cici gave me your number.

It doesn't take long for her response to come over.

Poppy: Hi?

Braden: I wanted to check in and make sure you're still feeling okay about that night.

Poppy: Yeah. Why wouldn't I be?

Braden: It seemed a bit out of your wheelhouse. Hoping you weren't regretting it or beating yourself up.

Poppy: Nothing you need to worry about.

Braden: I disagree, since I'm the cause.

Poppy: I'm an adult. I could've said no.

Braden: But you didn't.

Poppy: Nope, I didn't

Braden: I'm glad.

Poppy: Me too.

Relief floods my system. I didn't realize how worried I'd been, wondering if she regretted our last night together. But now that I have the answer, what do I do with it?

It's not like I can ask her why she's so eager to replace me. She'd know I was talking to Cici about her, and that would give too much away. I'm not sure what else to say—having no excuse to keep the conversation going. And when nothing comes to mind, I decide to let it die.

But as days pass and I'm still perseverating over what feels like unfinished business, I know I need to think of something. Inspiration finally hits, and although it seems drastic, I'm getting desperate at this point.

> Braden: Would you be open to some company next week?

> Poppy: Why?

> Braden: I'll be in Bozeman for a meeting and thought we could see each other.

I don't have any such plans yet. But it wouldn't take long to make a trip happen. She doesn't answer right away, and my palms sweat as I wait. Damn, this woman drives me crazy.

> Poppy: Probably not a good idea.

> Braden: Why?

> Poppy: Because we had our fun, and now we're done.

> Braden: We don't have to be.

> Poppy: Yes, we do. You don't do relationships, remember? Enjoy your time in Bozeman, but it won't be with me.

Fuck. So much for that. I certainly can't show up after she blatantly turned me down. It's not until I'm putting myself through another grueling workout at the gym that I'm struck by pure genius.

When I type the words *"dating app with no picture"* into Google, two different options appear on the screen. Not bad odds, but why make a profile on both when I can simply ask Eli which site she used? Time is money.

> Braden: What's the name of the dating app you guys were telling me about? The one Poppy's doing with no pictures? Warren is interested.

It's a great excuse if I do say so myself. It's not like I could tell him my plan. If anyone knew what I was about to do, they'd think I was certifiable. Hell, maybe I am.

> Eli: Warren, your assistant? Weird. I'm not sure, but it had the word blind in it.

> Braden: Thanks, that should be enough to go on.

> Eli: Good luck.

> Braden: I'll pass it on.

Perfect. That gives me exactly what I need. The next thing I know, I'm creating a dating profile, focusing on the details I think Poppy will be looking for while being careful not to use anything that could blow my cover. I decide to go with my middle name, Owen, and last initial to make myself feel better about not lying... per se.

The tricky part will be making sure we match, which means we'll have to choose each other's profiles. Poppy comes up quickly because my preferences all point to her. Now that I've selected hers, it'll be up to fate whether she chooses mine in return.

A week later, fate still hasn't stepped in, and I'm starting to get nervous. I'm headed to Jackson's for Thanksgiving as I do most years. My mom has her husband and his family to celebrate with. We talked this morning, of course, but stuffing myself with turkey isn't enough of a reason to fly to the other side of the country, so I'll visit at Christmas like I always do.

I'm looking forward to spending the day with friends. I've shared many holidays with the Solomans since Jackson and I met, and now that Lily *and* Cici married the Dubree brothers, they're all included. Lily's practically one of their own, having lived with them through-out high school, and Sebastian and Eli's parents are deceased. We're just one big collection of misfits that they've graciously embraced into their family.

I'm the last one to arrive, as usual, and let myself in, greeting Mr. and Mrs. Soloman, who are busy in the kitchen, before heading out back, where the three couples are. Man, does it hit home that I'm alone now that they're all married, two of them even starting a family. Holy shit.

"Braden, you made it. Glad you're here, buddy." Jackson's the first to welcome me with a hug. His wife, Mia, is next. I inspect her stomach for the telltale sign of pregnancy, but don't notice anything yet. I'm sure it won't be long with baby fever running rampant.

Eli and Cici are next, along with Abby, followed by Sebastian and Lily with their days-old baby, Samantha, nestled in the crook of Sebastian's arm. Man, is that a sight to see. He was probably voted the most likely to end up in the mafia in high school, and here he is, the doting dad.

"Congratulations, man. Fatherhood looks good on you," I tell him as we lock arms in a bro hug.

"Thanks. Feels good, too."

Then I turn to his wife, Lily, the last to greet. "Congrats, Lily. She's beautiful. And so are you, I might add."

"Careful," Sebastian says, giving me the stink eye as I shake my head.

She slaps his arm, the one not holding their daughter. "Stop it. He was just being sweet. I gave birth a few days ago, so I obviously look like crap and six months pregnant still."

"You're more beautiful than ever," Sebastian tells her with a kiss to the forehead.

"And that's why I love you." She looks at him adoringly enough to make me slightly envious.

"That and my baby-making skills." He smirks at her.

Lily rolls her eyes, causing Sebastian to narrow his in return. I don't even want to know what that's about. But Lily ignores him and scoops up her daughter. "Don't say those things around Samantha," she chastises before joining the other ladies.

"See what you have to look forward to? You can never win with them," Sebastian says, sipping his drink.

It's crazy that it's only been three years since we've been hanging out together. I feel like I've known these guys forever. Though Jackson and I go further back, and Mia joined us a year ago, they're like family, and I couldn't imagine a better group of friends.

"I'd say you're pretty lucky in my opinion. It's hard to find someone worthy enough to spend the rest of your life with, so you're all winning in my book." Shit, that's not like me. I'm usually the one telling everyone that marriage is crap, but seeing my friends this happy is making me rethink that notion.

Eli raises his glass. "Cheers to that. Where's your drink?"

"I came out to say hi first. I'll get it in a minute."

Sebastian jumps at the task. "Let me grab you one. I need a refill anyway."

"Thanks," I say as he walks off, leaving me, Jackson, and Eli.

"Speaking of finding someone worthy, did you find that dating app?" Eli asks.

"What the fuck, dude? You signed up on a dating site?" Jackson injects, laughing.

I shake my head. "No. It was for Warren. Eli and Cici told me about some pictureless dating app that Poppy went on. Warren wanted to know what it was, so I found it for him."

"No pictures? That's fucked up," Jackson says.

"No shit, but whatever." I shrug.

"So, did he sign up?" Eli stays on topic, and I don't miss the skepticism in his voice that implies he still thinks the information was for me.

I shrug again, feigning ignorance. "I passed on the info. I'm sure I'll hear about it if he does."

"Let me know how it goes," he says with a hint of something that indicates he knows I'm full of shit.

"What about Poppy? Did she find anyone yet?" I was nervous about being called out when he first brought it up, but this couldn't have worked out better if I'd planned it myself.

"Not sure," he says, then yells out to Cici. "Hey, babe, how's Poppy doing on that app she went on?"

Shit. Cici's already questioning my motives, and this won't help. I figured Cici would've kept Eli up to speed, but I guess they're too busy parenting these days to talk about trivial things.

"I haven't heard yet. Why?" she asks accusingly while giving me the stink eye.

"Warren was thinking about signing up, so I thought I'd check if it worked for Poppy or not."

Hopefully, he doesn't end up around any of these guys soon, since I'm throwing him under the bus.

My response must work as she shrugs it off before answering. "She's been busy, and we haven't talked much. I'll have to give her a call and see. I wish she lived here, so I could just set her up with someone."

"Jordan would have been perfect," Lily adds.

I'm standing right fucking here. Why not set her up with me? Whatever. That fucker wouldn't get within ten feet of her, anyway. She's already mine.

I don't know where this possessiveness is coming from, but I don't altogether hate it. What bothers me more is that they don't think of *me* as an option, which is the exact problem someone else seems to have.

"Well, too bad for Jordan she doesn't live here," I spit out a little more aggressively than necessary.

"Too bad for Poppy. He'd be a catch," Mia counters, to the raised brows of Jackson.

Fucking serious?

12

A PERFECT MATCH

Poppy

AFTER RETURNING FROM MY VISIT LAST MONTH WITH CICI, clients suddenly came out of the woodwork. Along with the catching up I had to do, it wasn't possible to focus on my new endeavor to find a man. But since it's Thanksgiving weekend, I have no showings or plans for the next couple of days.

It's nice having a moment to finally breathe, and after stuffing myself with turkey yesterday, I'll need the whole weekend to recover. With our offices closed and most people on vacation for the holiday, I might as well get started on my manhunt.

Getting comfy in an oversized T-shirt and grabbing a beer, I settle on the couch with a blanket, then open the app for the first time since being approved. I'm seriously nervous. What if Cici's right and I'm crazy to think this could work without knowing what the guy looks like?

Okay, pull it together, Poppy. You can do this.

At least their height, weight, hair, eye and skin color are listed, and luckily, it's required to submit a picture to the company for verification. Plus, even if I have a match, that doesn't mean I have to engage. Although that is the reason I'm doing this.

Chugging some of my beer, I steel my resolve and focus on the first profile. He seems normal with no red flags, but I won't make any choices until I've seen a few more.

I like that you don't have to choose immediately and can save profiles you want to go back to. That way, you can pick one or two at a time to talk to, while having the rest to refer to when ready for someone else.

So far, I've saved three out of ten when I come across a profile that makes my skin prickle. It's… perfect. Almost too perfect. It seems impossible for anyone to tick this many boxes and be real.

He's fit, according to his activity level, height, and size. They don't ask for weight but use words like curvy, medium build, or svelte. He's a regular at the gym and says he's of medium build. He drinks socially but no drugs or smoking. He's a career-minded professional and is ready for a relationship.

I'm squealing in delight as I read on.

His signature physical trait is sideburns, which I've recently become a fan of. On a side note, we put freckles on mine, but didn't indicate red hair. Less chance of creeps like Braden, who might only want the answer to the same question he had.

It's like this guy was made for me, and I'm filled with hope, wondering if I'm finally on the right track. With nervous excitement, I take a deep breath while hovering over the button to like the profile, willing myself to press it.

After I do, only a second passes before a message pops up on the screen saying we've matched. Oh my God. The first one, and it's *the* one. Mr. Perfect.

I'm not sure what happens next. Does he reach out, or should I? I don't want to be the one to make the first move. I guess I could start by clicking on the notification.

It opens a chat window that says, *"Congratulations! You've made a match. Take this opportunity to say hi."* While I stare at it, contemplating what to do, a message appears.

Owen: Hey, Poppy. It seems we've matched.

Oh my God. Oh my God. I'm hyperventilating, bouncing on the couch. Shit. I need another beer for this. Plus, I can't look too eager, so I set the phone down and go to the kitchen to grab one before replying.

Poppy: Hi, Owen. This is my first match so I'm not sure how it works.

Dots appear, showing he's typing.

Owen: I suppose we should get to know each other. How about we play one of my favorite games? Truth or dare?

I giggle. Oh, good lord, he's already got me laughing.

Poppy: We're not with each other, so how would we do the dare part?

Owen: It takes a certain level of trust.

Poppy: I don't know you enough to trust you.

Owen: Let's change that. You up for it?

Poppy: Who goes first?

Owen: You go ahead.

Poppy: All right, Truth or dare?

Owen: Oooh, tough choice. I don't know you well enough to decide.

Okay, I'm laughing again.

Owen: Let's start with a truth.

Poppy: Why did you sign up for a dating app?

Owen: Great question. To meet you, of course.

Oh God. I'm grinning from ear to ear.

Owen: Okay, my turn. Truth or dare?

Poppy: Dare

Owen: Risky. Text your last hookup that your feet smell, with no other explanation.

Poppy: No way. What if I don't do hookups?

Owen: Then the last person you slept with. Are you forfeiting out of the gate?

Poppy: Ugh. No, I'll do it.

I can't believe this. What if I just say I did it but don't? He'd never know. But then, if we end up together, I'd have lied, and what if he asks to see the text?

Owen: Are you chickening out?

Poppy: Just give me a minute. I'm doing it.

Here goes nothing. Taking a deep breath, I type out the message to Braden, wondering how this will go after I shut him down last week. The crazy thing is, a part of me wanted to meet up with him since I haven't stopped thinking about what we did. But I know it would bite me in the ass if I gave in. Booty calls may be the norm for him, but I couldn't keep my heart out of it if they became a habit.

Poppy to Braden: My feet smell.

Poppy: All right. I did it.

Owen: Good girl. Your turn.

Poppy: That's it? You're just going to trust me?

Owen: Isn't that what all solid relationships are based on?

Oh. My. God. A '*good girl*' and a meaningful statement back-to-back. I'm swooning over here.

Braden: I'm sorry to hear that, Mouse. Too bad I'm not with you.

Poppy: How would that help?

Braden: I'd wash your feet.

WTH? He can't be serious.

Owen: Are you there?

Oh shit, what have I gotten myself into? I'm talking to two men at once. This is wrong on so many levels. Not to mention, really difficult to keep track of.

Poppy: Sorry. Truth or dare? Though I think you owe me a dare after that.

Owen: LOL, I'll indulge you this time. Dare.

Ugh. I wasn't ready. I have no idea what to make him do, and I can't copy him. However, giving him a taste of his own medicine sounds good. Hmmm, it's too easy to pass up.

Poppy: Text your last hookup that you want to wash her feet.

Owen: Cute. And completely unoriginal.

Poppy: You started it.

Shoot. I left Braden hanging, but another text shows up anyway. I must've taken too long.

Braden: Is this a bad time to share my foot fetish? I'd love to wash your feet. I'm hard just thinking about it.

Wait. What the hell? I screwed up with that dare, since now it's even harder to keep each conversation straight. I'm so confused.

Owen: Done. Truth or dare?

Poppy: Truth

Owen: Best sexual experience.

Poppy: Uh...

Braden: Did the foot fetish scare you away?

Poppy: Shouldn't the threesome have done that already?

Braden: Did it?

Owen: Too soon? Rewind. What's your relationship dealbreaker?

Poppy: Liars. Your turn, truth or dare?

Owen: Don't I deserve a follow-up question to that?

Poppy: Rules are rules. One question per turn.

Owen: Ah... so you're a stickler for rules, I'll remember that. Fine, I'll go with a truth.

Poppy: Give me a minute. I need to think of something and grab another beer.

Owen: I'll grab one too. We can have a drink together.

Poppy: For some reason, no.

Braden: I'm glad. But regardless, I don't plan on sharing you again.

Poppy: I'm not yours to share.

Braden: Not yet.

Poppy: Not ever.

Baden: We'll see about that.

What the heck? I pad into the kitchen for my third beer, completely perplexed at the situation. Tossing my empty bottle into the trash, I open the fridge for another and return to the couch. If someone had told me I'd be sitting here talking with a potential date and a past hookup, I'd have called them insane. Even crazier is that *"past hookup"* is a phrase in my vocabulary.

At least this is fun. I like the option of chatting through text, rather than the stress of meeting in person and having to be *on*. It's easier to be myself and not panic over my appearance or how I sound.

But whatever this is with Braden is crazy. I figured I'd never talk to him again, let alone be bantering back and forth. I'm not sure what this means, or where to go from here, but I'm already in this mess, so I'll see it through. At least it's only over the phone.

Owen: Did I lose you?

Poppy: I'm here. Just had to get settled. What's the biggest misconception about you? Cheers, by the way.

Owen: Cheers to you. Let me think about it. Don't go anywhere.

Poppy: I'll be waiting.

I've got to be quicker at transitioning between conversations.

Braden: What are you doing tonight other than texting me about your stinky feet?

Visiting the Twilight Zone. Having a conversation with two men at once like some hussy. Wondering what the hell is happening right now.

Poppy: Relaxing. I've hardly been able to since I've been back.

Braden: I wish I could help you with that.

Poppy: I don't think you'd be much of a help.

Braden: You were pretty relaxed after I made you come.

I can't believe he said that. I'm fanning myself, suddenly too hot, and removing the blanket covering me. That he can provoke a reaction from a thousand miles away is insane.

Owen: That I have no heart. Truth or dare?

Wait… what? I scroll up to look at my question. Oh. That sounds bad. Why would people think he has no heart? Is it because he's mean? That was too ambiguous. I need to make a list of concerns for later.

Poppy: Truth. We should keep learning more about each other.

Owen: It's okay to admit you're scared of another dare.

Poppy: As if…

Shoot, I have to respond to Braden, but I can't let him think he got to me with that comment. Maybe I'll take a page from his book.

Poppy: Yeah, but I don't need you for that.

Braden

Damn. My dick goes rock-hard as I lie in bed at the vision conjured by her retort. I like the direction this is taking. I've been trying to keep things PG with *Owen,* but the conversation with Braden allows me to spice things up.

I was frustrated after she shut down a trip to Bozeman, so the notification of our match couldn't have been better timing. I'd begun to worry something was wrong—that she might not have liked my profile—so when my phone pinged, I responded immediately.

Texting her as Braden at the same time as Owen wasn't part of the plan, but when the idea came to me, I couldn't resist. However, keeping the two conversations straight is more difficult than I imagined. But I won't waste the opportunity for the perfect excuse to keep her talking to Braden. To what end, I'm unsure.

I'm still wondering what my goal is. We don't live near each other. She wants love. I've sworn it off. She doesn't do casual. I don't do relationships. So why am I pursuing her? I wish I knew. But after having my mind consumed by this woman for the last few weeks, possessing her by any means necessary became a need I couldn't ignore.

Until I figure out why that is, I'll enjoy the journey and worry about the destination later. For now, it's time to have some fun along the way.

Owen: What's your ideal date?

Poppy: With someone new or been dating a while?

Owen: Hit me with both.

Braden: I'm sure you don't. I'd bet money you've been using thoughts of me to take care of yourself for weeks.

Poppy: Wow. Love yourself much?

Poppy: A round-robin night out with someone new. So one place for drinks, another for an appetizer, and so on. With a person I trust, a home-cooked meal and board games.

Owen: Then I'm looking forward to gaining your trust for a home-cooked meal.

Poppy: Who said I'd be cooking?

Owen: Not me. A night in my kitchen and you won't ever want to leave.

Poppy: That's a bold statement.

Owen: That I can fully back up.

Poppy: All right, Mr. Confident, truth or dare?

Braden: What I love is watching you come for me. And since I can't do that, I might as well imagine it. Moment of truth...I've pictured you while "relaxing" more than I care to admit.

Owen: Truth, since you're trying to get to know me ;)

Poppy: Why did your last relationship end?

Owen: She cheated on me.

Poppy: I'm sorry. That sucks.

Owen: My turn.

Poppy: Truth.

Owen: What's something you can't live without?

Poppy: Let me think about that while I grab another beer.

Braden: But I'd like more than a picture. How do you feel about a video call?

Poppy: No way! You'd probably end up recording it somehow.

Braden: Only so I could watch it every night.

Poppy: You're terrible. I'd never do that anyway.

Braden: Funny, I seem to remember you doing something else you said you'd never do. I'd say that turned out well.

Poppy: Still, I am not having phone sex.

Braden: So you don't want to know where my hand is right now?

Poppy: Stop it. You're so full of crap.

I text her a picture.

Poppy: You did not just send me a dick pic!

Braden: It's blurred… you can hardly tell what it is.

Poppy: Still, you can't do that.

Braden: Don't doubt me next time. If I say something, it's true.

Poppy: Lesson learned. Thank God I have beer for this.

Braden: What are you wearing?

Poppy: I'm not doing this with you.

Braden: You started it the second you texted me about your feet.

Poppy: Well, now I'm finishing it.

Braden: I'd rather we reach the finish together. Why don't you start by telling me what you're wearing. I'll go first—sweatpants and a T-shirt.

Poppy: I'm back.

Owen: What did you come up with that you can't live without?

Poppy: Rules.

Owen: LOL… I should have figured that one.

Poppy: JK, well, it is true, but the answer is my Kindle. Do you read?

Owen: Is that your question?

Poppy: Sure.

Owen: As far as reading goes, I recently became a fan. But since my time is limited, I've realized I enjoy listening to audiobooks instead.

Poppy: What do you read?

Owen: Uh, uh. My turn. Who was the last person you kissed, and how was it?

Poppy: That's a double question.

Owen: Only one and in the sentence is okay. Two would be a violation.

Poppy: You're making that up.

Owen: Are you trying to avoid answering?

Poppy: I kissed a guy I met at a wedding, and it was fantastic. So, there. Now give me a minute to think of something.

Hm. I like that response.

Poppy's cute when she's tipsy—I could almost envision her sticking her tongue out at the same time. I'm having more fun than I've had with a woman in ages. In fact, I can't remember the last time I enjoyed one outside of fucking them. While I'd love to engage in some naughty phone sex, I can honestly say I'd be happy with simply talking all night.

Braden: How's that beer tasting?

Poppy: Good, but the bad news is I'm out.

Braden: Sorry to hear that. Have you made it to your bed yet?

Poppy: When did you have sex last, and how was it?

Owen: Copycat.

Poppy: You started it.

Owen: About a month ago, and it was quite possibly the best. My turn. How did you lose your virginity?

Braden: You're an expert at avoiding my questions, Mouse.

Poppy: Yes, I'm in bed.

Braden: Will you be reading yourself to sleep? Any sexy parts coming up?

Poppy: Bet you wish you could read over my shoulder again.

Braden: What book are you reading? I'll download it and follow along.

Poppy: You read faster than me. It wouldn't work.

Braden: I'll slow down and wait if I get too far ahead. Come on. It'll be a book club.

Poppy: A two-person book club?

Braden: You and me, Mouse. Think about it.

Poppy: Hmmm… okay. Answer's still no.

Owen: I hope you didn't fall asleep on me.

Poppy: Nope, it takes me a lot longer to do that.

Owen: We have that in common. I'm sure the beers make it easier, though. You ready to tell me about your first time?

Poppy: Not really, but I suppose I have to. Rules and all. It's kind of embarrassing.

Owen: Most are. If it makes you feel better, mine was awful.

Poppy: Luckily, that wasn't my issue. It's just that it was pretty recent. That's the embarrassing part. Remember the guy I kissed that I met at the wedding? My first time was during the reception.

Owen: You're joking, right?

Hell to the no. What the fuck? Is this the same Poppy? Shit, obviously it is. She texted *me* when I dared her to. But that means… *oh fuck.* My mind spins, going back to that night, running through scene by scene. *Oh fuck.* How is that possible? She didn't say anything. She didn't act like a virgin.

It can't be true. She's gotta be messing with me. That's it. She knows I'm Owen.

Poppy: Is that a problem?

Dammit. That probably wasn't the best response. I need to cover my tracks in case she's serious.

Owen: No. Sorry. Just surprised. Is your age correct on your profile, or did you embellish it? Not interested in dating a teenager.

Poppy: LOL. It's right.

Owen: What made you give it up to some random guy you met at a wedding and not someone you were dating? Did you feel forced?

Oh God. I'm not sure I can handle it if her answer is yes. I'm not that guy. Fuck. I'd never have tried so hard if I'd known.

> Poppy: Absolutely not. I just wanted to see what all the fuss was about and get it out of the way. And he knew what he was doing, so that was nice.
>
> Owen: Was it what you expected?
>
> Poppy: It was way better. I have no regrets, other than taking it too seriously before knowing what I was missing. I still won't be the girl who sleeps around. I'm not saying I won't have sex again until marriage, but it needs to be with someone I'm serious about.

I'm not sure how to respond… as Owen or Braden. I'm at a loss for words—shell-shocked from the truth. Why wouldn't she have told me? That's the number one question plaguing my mind. I could've done things so differently, been gentler, slower, more caring. Fuck. I'm an asshole. A total fucking prick.

Christ. Her second time, and I fucking tag-teamed her. Her *second time*. My hand is practically pulling my hair out from the turmoil.

> Poppy: Sorry, I know that's a lot to digest, and you probably want someone more experienced. Don't worry, you won't hurt my feelings if that's the case. We haven't even met yet. You're my first match, so really, it's okay. I didn't mean for that to come out right away. Or at all, actually. Lesson learned for the next one, huh? LOL Note to self: don't play Truth or Dare on a first date. Not that that's even what this is.

Fuck. She's spiraling. I'm spiraling. I need to respond.

> Owen: No, wait. I'm sorry. Just taking it all in, and putting myself in your shoes, trying to figure you out. I'm not on this app for a quick fuck. If I were, I'd be scrolling through pictures. It threw me for a loop, is all.
>
> Poppy: Thanks, but I promise it's fine if I'm not what you're looking for.

Owen: One thing to know about me, I don't lie. I'm very straightforward, so if something bothers me, you'll know. And you're exactly what I'm looking for.

After ending Owen's conversation with plans to pick it up the following night, I'm reeling from Poppy's revelation and can barely sleep. My mind won't stop replaying all our interactions, searching for signs, racking my brain as I try to remember if I coerced her somehow.

Throughout the next day, guilt completely takes over, along with an unexpected emotion—possessiveness—pure and utter possessiveness of my sexy little mouse and her body. The problem is, I'm not sure what to do with it.

When she texted Owen this afternoon that she'd be out tonight and might not be home to chat as planned, it gutted me. After refusing to go out with me, who the hell is she seeing? I need answers, which means it's time to pick up where we left off.

Braden: How about we start our book club tonight?

Poppy: You don't give up, do you?

Braden: I thought you knew that about me already.

Shit. Immediately, my mind goes to the fact that I was so persistent in luring her into bed.

Poppy: How would we make it work?

Braden: Book club, or you and me?

Poppy: Well, since only one of those is on the table...

Braden: Hmmm... I like the sound of that. You'd make a delicious meal.

Poppy: I'm blocking your number if you keep it up.

Braden: Alright, alright. You choose a book, and we'll only read it when we're reading together. We can start tonight.

Poppy: Can't. I'm headed to dinner with a friend.

Braden: Male or female?

Poppy: Why does that matter?

Braden: So it's a male. Oh well. A little competition isn't a bad thing.

Poppy: You're delusional. There's no competition.

Braden: I'm flattered.

Poppy: Meaning, you're not in the running. Five states away, remember? A player interested in notches on his bedpost versus one who's ready to settle down.

Braden: We could negotiate.

Poppy: Stop it. If you want to read, I'm open to the idea. Anything else and I'm serious about blocking you.

Braden: When can we start?

Poppy: We can talk about it tomorrow. I've got to finish getting ready.

Braden: Send me a picture of what you're wearing.

Dammit. She's going out. On a date. What if someone else touches what's mine? I shake my head in disbelief. *Mine?*

Fine, that may be a stretch, but I can't stand the thought of another man's hands on her. And now I'll be stuck thinking about it until I hear from her. It's insane that this is what I'm reduced to—on a Saturday night, no less.

Rather than sit here and stew for God knows how long, I decide a distraction is in order.

Braden: Anyone free tonight?

Jackson: Nope, headed to the parents. It's been a while, though. What about Tuesday?

Eli: Abby's been running a fever, but Tuesday works.

Sebastian: Keep me posted. I should be able to.

Braden: Tuesday it is. No pussying out.

Hopefully, Warren's available.

Braden: You up for drinks?

Warren: I thought you'd never ask.

Braden: The club in thirty?

Warren: You got it.

My phone pings again while walking into the bedroom to change. It's a text from Poppy—she actually sent me a picture. A smile instantly breaks out as I stare at her, standing in front of a full-length mirror wearing jeans, ankle boots, a modest sweater, and those glasses that make me want to bend her over a desk and fuck her.

No one would call her plain, but it's not your typical dress-to-impress attire. So maybe it's not a date. Or she isn't the type to flaunt herself, which is more likely. Other than when we went to the club. That was a smokin' hot Poppy, and I'm certainly glad it was me who benefited.

This Poppy is subtle, but if you take the time to look, you can't miss the shape of the long, slender legs leading up to her hips, which are the perfect size to grip. The modest neckline still shows enough of her alabaster neck that I'd give anything to taste right now.

But the real prize is higher. Those fucking full lips that happen to be smirking. Those would be the first things I would worship if she were here. That luscious mouth would be devoured within seconds.

I'm hard at the thought but need to get a move on, so I toss my phone on the bed and enter the closet. I'm a suit and tie guy—goes with the profession. The slacks seem to stick when I go out, and my shirt collection rivals a clothing store. Needless to say, I'm a snazzy dresser.

Next is the bathroom to style my hair. Since it's only fair to send a picture in return, I spend an extra minute making it perfect before grabbing my phone to snap one in front of the mirror with a smirk of my own. Might as well give her something to think about during her date.

13

RIGHT TRACK

Poppy

DAMN, THAT MAN IS SEXY. I WASN'T EXPECTING HIM TO SEND a picture in return. Heck, I can hardly believe I sent him one to begin with. It's so unlike me, but the one he sent back makes it very worth it. He's obviously going out tonight with how well he's dressed, and I'm surprised at the pangs of jealousy that creates. Which is crazy, mind you, since he's absolutely *not* who I'm looking for.

Although the more I think about it, the more I'm considering giving in to Braden's book club proposal. It might be fun to have a long-distance fling. Practice for the real thing, maybe?

Thank goodness I ran out of beer last night because my head could have been much worse today. As it was, the first thing I did when I got out of bed this morning was head for the medicine cabinet for ibuprofen so I could clean the house. Luckily, I muddled through. Now, I'll still have my whole Sunday tomorrow to relax.

Part of me is mortified at everything I told Owen, and part of me is relieved. Confessing to my inexperience early on is probably for the best, and the fact that he's still interested makes it even better. Owen was so sweet after my awkward *first-time* revelation.

Braden, on the other hand, was an unexpected spinoff. I'm not sure what to think about him. He oddly stopped texting after suggesting we start a book club together, so I figured he must've fallen asleep or given up on me knowing I wouldn't cave to phone sex. But then he surprised me with his text a bit ago, doubling his efforts about this club he's trying to convince me of.

When the ping sounded and I saw his name, I was shocked at how giddy it made me. Maybe I have Stockholm Syndrome. Yeah, yeah, I know… that's when someone kidnaps you. But he sort of did kidnap my body because it certainly hasn't felt the same since he had his way with it.

I'm not sure how to proceed with either of them from here. Owen asked for another chat date tonight, to which I agreed. Unfortunately, I had to postpone, since Matt and I made dinner plans, but I told him I'd text him afterward if it wasn't too late.

We decided not to do Truth or Dare again, which honestly makes me nervous. The game made it easier to break the ice, giving us a framework to follow. I'm a little worried if the conversation will flow as smoothly without it.

However, things with Braden were left unfinished. Surprisingly, I enjoyed the banter with Braden as much as Owen. The question is whether texting two guys at once is the same as dating two guys, and if so, is that wrong? Since I'm completely out of my element, I'm consulting an expert before dinner.

"Poppy! I was just telling my parents that I feel like we haven't talked in forever," Cici says, answering my call.

"That's because we haven't. How is Abby? You're not sending enough pictures."

"She's amazing, and I know. I'm sorry. My brain shut off the minute she was born, and I became a walking zombie. I'll send a few right now." She puts me on speaker to hunt for the perfect ones.

I laugh. "While you're doing that, tell me about Thanksgiving."

"It was great. Lily and Sebastian came, and oh my God, I forgot to tell you, Lily had her baby two weeks early. They named her Samantha, and she's fricking adorable."

"Oh, how sweet. I'll text her congratulations. How about Mia? Is she pregnant yet?" I figured she'd be right behind them. It's like a virus—once one gets pregnant, they all do. Maybe I should move to San Diego.

"No. I don't think they're trying yet. But who knows? They're in the longest honeymoon phase in the world and still spend most of their time at home." She giggles.

"Makes sense after the struggle they had to be together."

"No kidding. What about your Thanksgiving? How was it?"

"It was okay. I'm glad it's the last one without Grayson. And it was nice having Matt with us."

"Yeah, he never got into the whole thing with his parents, and why he doesn't go home anymore, did he? He's a mystery, I tell ya. Oh. Speaking of mysteries, have you met anyone on the pictureless app yet? Braden asked me yesterday if you did," she says nonchalantly, tossing that bomb out like it's no big deal.

"Wait, how does he even know about it, and why is he asking?"

"He said Warren was interested in trying it out and wanted to know if it was working for you."

I harrumph. "That's weird. Warren seems like the least likely person to sign up for a dating app."

Is that really why he asked, or does he want to know if I'm sleeping with anyone else? No, I'm sure he doesn't care. This is where women go wrong: thinking every man is obsessed with them and reading too much into things.

"I know, right? So, tell me how it's going."

"Well, I finally went on last night—"

"Wait, for the first time since you signed up?"

"Yes." I groan. "I've been too busy. Then I'm always tired after work and end up reading myself to sleep. So I—"

"Hang on. I just sent some pictures. Look."

This girl's killing me. Laughing, I pull the phone from my ear and put it on speaker. "Oh my God, she's adorable. She's so smiley. I wish I could visit more."

"Like my mom once said, you can do real estate anywhere."

"It's tempting, but Grayson will finally be home. That would be sad if he got here and I left."

"Or… it would be perfect. Your parents would have a replacement."

"Rude. But back to my story… I finally started scrolling through profiles last night, and after about ten, I came across one I swear was meant for me. He checked all my boxes, and something about him… just stuck out."

"Even without knowing if he has missing teeth or three eyeballs?" she jests.

"Shut up, that's not possible. Anyway… I liked his profile, and bam, we were an instant match. Within seconds, I shit you not, he messaged me, and we ended up talking the rest of the night."

"Oooh. This is so exciting." I can hear her clapping in the background while I picture her bouncing up and down. "What did you talk about?"

"We played Truth or Dare, which—"

She cuts me off. "Uh… how exactly did you do that through a chat window?"

I explain how well it worked and tell her some of the questions we asked. Then I drop the bombshell about bringing Braden into the mix.

"I can't believe you really did it. You could've said you texted him without actually doing it."

"Lying isn't the way to begin a relationship."

"Seriously? What relationship? It was the first five minutes of a non-date. Did you end up exchanging pictures?"

"No! That's not how it works. You need so many interactions before you're even allowed to send a photo. Anyway, I couldn't lie because what if he ends up being the one, and he found out? He'd lose any respect for me."

"Fine. You're right. So what did Braden say after you texted something so crazy?"

"Well…"

I recount the entire situation, then finally get to why I called in the first place.

"So now I'm talking to two guys at once, and I'm not sure if that's okay."

"That's what you're worried about?" She screeches through the phone. "Poppy, you could be sleeping with two different guys and still not be doing anything wrong. You can't put all your eggs in one basket."

Funny, that's exactly the term Braden used when we first met. So maybe this is okay. But…

"Am I leading them on if I'm not up-front about it?"

"Nobody expects you to be exclusive off the bat. But what's going on with Braden? I thought you couldn't stand him outside his *'find-a-husband-for-sex'* inspiring bedroom skills?"

"I can't most of the time. But I can't shake the guy, and honestly, I like his persistence. Something about it makes me feel, I don't know… wanted? Also, I can't put my finger on it, but he was different last night. I mean, don't get me wrong, he was still the same Braden, trying hard to have phone sex, but beyond that, he was… cute."

She laughs on the other end. "Cute? I never thought I'd hear that word to describe Braden. Hmmm. I wonder what he's playing at. It's not like you guys could be serious, though. He's five states away."

"I know, right? And now he's trying to start this book club thing where we read together. But it was weird how he stopped texting last night and then picked right back up today like he didn't ghost me the night before. You know what? I'm probably stressed for nothing, and he'll give up anyway."

"Well, even if he doesn't, you shouldn't worry about talking to both of them. You've got to play the field while looking for a man."

"I just wish I'd put myself out there sooner. I want a family, and now you guys are all having babies, and I feel like I'm even later to the game. My parents were already married with kids at my age, and here I am, unable to hold onto a guy past a few dates."

"That's because you always let them go. You need to find someone worth keeping, but until then, have fun and stop overthinking it."

I stifle a groan. "Easier said than done."

"You're right, which is why you should continue to practice," she says mischievously, causing my eyes to roll even though she can't see me.

We chat for a bit longer, talking about motherhood and married life, before saying goodbye and promising to call more often. I'm so happy for her and her new life, but boy, do I miss having her here.

I'm in good spirits when I hop into Matt's car and am glad we're doing this. I'm excited for another opinion on the whole two-men-at-once thing. Though it takes until we're sipping drinks, waiting for our meal, to finally work up the courage to bring up my so-called dating life.

"So, do you remember that app I signed up for? The one without the pictures?" I ask nonchalantly

"Oh yeah, how's it going?"

"Friday was the first time I went on since they approved my profile, and I matched with the first guy I chose."

He chuckles. "Of course you did."

"What does that mean?"

"That you're a catch. Who wouldn't pick you?"

"Well, I'm not sure about that, but anyway, he messaged me right away, and we ended up chatting the rest of the night. The weird thing is, I was texting Braden the whole time too," I say sheepishly.

Matt's brows drew together condemningly. "The guy from Cici's wedding? The one you had the fling with?"

"Yeah. We went out to a club when I was there last time, and he's been messaging me since." It comes out in a rush, omitting our extracurricular activities.

"I thought it was a one-time thing." His contempt is evident.

"It was."

"Then why have you been talking to him?"

I'm not sure how to answer. Why *am* I? I'm obviously sexually attracted to Braden, but am I willing to admit that I might like the guy?

I sigh loudly before answering. "Because I'm having fun, and there's more to him than first meets the eye." As soon as the words are out, I know they're true, and my whole body feels lighter—like I've passed some test I was agonizing over. I'm relieved to have put that out in the universe, and any hesitation I felt is suddenly gone with the simplicity of the truth.

"I wouldn't let your guard down around him, that's for sure. He seemed like the *use her and lose her* type."

Our meal is delivered, pausing the conversation, thank God. Is it weird to tell a guy friend about my sex life? Yeah. But if I want real advice, then I need to be up front about the situation, and give him the whole picture, or I'm wasting my time.

After focusing on the food for a bit and chugging the rest of my margarita, I take a deep breath and spill, fessing up about the repeat performance with Braden, leaving out the additional participant. I'm sure it's unnecessary to the story and definitely TMI. Matt's eyes convey enough surprise already.

"And I don't want to hear it if you think I'm crazy. If I were a guy and told you that, you'd be high-fiving me, so no lecture. I'm only telling you because I feel weird talking to Braden while I'm starting something with someone else. So, from a guy's perspective, what do you think?"

He takes in a deep breath, letting it out slowly. "Wow. Not what I was expecting. I just… shit, Poppy. I can't believe you gave into him again."

"Matt!" I sit back and cross my arms over my chest in defense.

His head drops. "I'm sorry, I'm not trying to be an ass. I'm just surprised. And you're right, it's a double standard. But if you're still talking to him, feelings might be involved, and if that's the case, you should be careful. You could get hurt, especially since he doesn't even live here. He could be keeping you on the line for a booty call whenever you visit Cici."

"Maybe I want *him* for a booty call. Huh? Then would it be okay?"

His hands go up in defense. "All right, point made. I'm sorry. So what is it you're worried about?"

"Well, I feel like I'm doing something wrong by talking to both of them, almost like I'm being deceptive or something."

The waitress comes to clear our plates, and we order more drinks since Matt says he needs another for this conversation.

"So, what do you think? Would it be bad if you were Braden or the guy from the dating app and found out about someone else?"

"I'm positive Braden isn't a one-woman sort of guy. And you just met this other dude, so I'd say it's too early to feel guilty about anything. And the app guy is probably already talking to other women. Most people don't limit themselves to one at a time if they're on an app, do they?"

I shrug. "I guess not."

"Then, for now, I'd say you're fine, but if it becomes serious, then you'll have to make a decision. Until you decide to be exclusive, you're not doing anything wrong. You should be cautious giving too much information about yourself online. He could end up being some psycho and start stalking you. Poppy isn't a common name. You'd be easy to find."

"True. I'll keep that in mind."

"And, you know, if you do become more involved, then be careful with—" Matt grimaces as his voice lowers. "—protection and shit."

I burst out laughing. "Oh my God. Okay. Thanks, Dad. Let's cheers to that," I say, still chuckling and raising my glass for a toast.

Braden

"Dude, what's up with you tonight?" Warren scrutinizes me while waiting for an answer.

Considering he's all too familiar with the woman I'm preoccupied with, I'm not inclined to unload on him. It's probably wise to let sleeping dogs lie where that's concerned. So I go with the next best thing, which is way more believable than being troubled by a woman.

"Just work shit. The Marlow case has been dragging. We're expecting the final documents this week, so I'm anxious to have the opposition filed. I think the wife's gonna try to pull some more crap, and I'd like to put this last motion behind us so we can move on."

"It's Saturday, Braden. Take it easy. You should be focused on pussy, not paperwork. Speaking of… two chicks have been eyeing our table since we walked in. You game for a foursome?" He cocks his head in their direction, leading my gaze to the women he's referring to, their eagerness evident with flirty looks.

I'd usually be all over that, but the only woman I'm eager for may currently be with another man. Sinking my dick into someone else might take her off my mind, but for the first time I can remember, it's not appealing.

I shake my head to decline. "Nah, I'll pass tonight."

"Seriously? Who are you, and what have you done with Braden? They're hotter than fuck. Plus, I owe you one for that last hottie we tag-teamed. She was a sweet piece of ass, man. I'd love to get my hands on her again."

Damn it. Hearing him talk about Poppy like that makes my blood boil, and before I can stop myself, I open a can of worms.

"You won't be, so forget it." I chug my drink in disgust for allowing it in the first place. Was it hot? Fuck yeah. But knowing what I do about her brings guilt instead of pleasure from the memory.

Warren's eyes go wide. "Dude. What crawled up your ass? Is something going on between you and that chick? Is that what you're brooding about?"

"Her name is Poppy, and I'm not brooding. I'm just not in the mood tonight."

He laughs loudly. "You're not in the mood? You're full of shit, is what you are. Oh, fuck, this is classic. Who's the pussy now, huh?" He's still laughing uncontrollably.

Although I'm irritated, I can't help but chuckle along. He's right. I'm acting like a fucking chick. This is pathetic.

"Enough already. She's obviously gotten under my skin. As of now, there's nothing between us, but…fuck." I shake my head, submitting to the truth. "I'd like there to be."

"I thought she lived in Bozeman. Didn't you meet her when you went to interview Marlow?"

Right when he says it, the light bulb goes on. I know exactly what my next move is. With a clear objective and renewed purpose, I'm ready to go. The second phase of my plan will have to wait until Monday to enact, but that doesn't mean I can't continue what I've started. It's Owen's turn to woo her tonight.

"Yeah. We've been talking through text, but it's complicated. Anyway, I'm gonna head out and leave those two for you. Thanks for joining me. Sorry I was such a buzzkill," I say before tipping my glass back and standing.

"Fuck. You're serious. Okay, well… good luck with the girl, I guess."

After saying a quick goodbye, I met my Uber out front while contemplating my initial message. She said she'd text me, well, Owen, after dinner, but I decided not to wait and caved on the way home.

Owen: Hey, beautiful, did you have fun at dinner tonight?

She doesn't respond, and I'm antsy as I hop into bed. My gut coils at the thought that she may have ended up at some guy's place. I'm spiraling, about to send another text, when the app finally pings with a message.

Poppy: How do you know I'm beautiful? I could be hideous.

Owen: It's a hunch to go along with your personality. Besides, you're beautiful to me, regardless. So how was dinner?

I'll lose it if she evades the question again.

Poppy: It was nice. I met with a friend of mine from work. It's been a while since we've been out.

My entire body sags in relief. But it doesn't escape me that the little brat completely led me on and made me think it was a date.

Owen: I'm glad. Are you up for chatting or ready to call it a night?

Poppy: I'm snuggled in bed, so I'm all yours until we tire out.

Owen: Do you know how many things that brings to mind?

Poppy: LOL. How about we start with some follow-up questions from last night?

Owen: Go for it.

Poppy: You said people think you don't have a heart. Why?

Owen: I'm ruthless in my line of work. I also haven't dated since I was cheated on. I'm not celibate, though, if you catch my drift.

Poppy: I do. What kind of job requires you to be ruthless?

This is where it becomes sticky. I'm not sure how to answer without giving myself away. I'd call this farce off now if I had a chance with her as Braden. The problem is, she's still under the impression that Braden's a womanizing manwhore. Until I prove otherwise, I'm stuck letting her learn about me through Owen and pray she understands when I tell her we're one and the same.

Or maybe she'll miraculously fall for the real Braden, and I'll never need to come clean. That split-second thought goes to ashes when I realize everything she's learning from Owen is true, so she'll eventually clue in. The only way out is the truth. I just hope she's so head over heels for me by then that the deception won't matter.

Owen: I'm in law. It's a shrewd business. What do you do for work?

Poppy: Professional sales. A friend just reminded me to be careful online, so we should go back to safer topics. When were you cheated on?

She may be talking to other people on the app, so I'm glad she's being smart. Not to mention, it saves my ass from hitting too close to home. But I do wonder what other advice this *friend* is giving her these days and whether any of it concerns Braden.

Owen: Probably a good idea.

Poppy: When did you stop dating?

Owen: Three years ago.

Poppy: Whoa, that's a long time. So what are your relationship goals then? Do you eventually want to get married or start a family?

Owen: Straight to the point, huh?

Poppy: Might as well.

Owen: I was about to propose to the girl who cheated on me, but after that, I swore off dating until recently. I'm not eager to walk down the aisle, but I'm not as opposed as I was before.

Poppy: Is that because you're getting older, or what?

Owen: Let's go with "or what". My turn now. I want to hear more about your first time and why you waited so long.

Poppy: I knew we'd end up on this topic again.

Owen: I'd say it's a pretty big deal.

Poppy: Deal-breaker?

Owen: I already told you it wasn't. I'm just trying to understand where you're coming from.

Poppy: That's fair. It's mainly because my brother scared me away from guys all through high school, while my parents inspired me to want someone special, and no one was ever special enough, or like I said, anyone who made me want to.

Owen: Then you've been dating the wrong men.

She doesn't argue.

We chat a bit longer about trivial things, favorite foods, thrills, hobbies, and the like until she's practically falling asleep. I told her I'd be with family tomorrow, and we could pick up again on Monday, since I want all her focus on Braden for the day. If I have my way, she'll forget Owen even exists by the time I'm through with her.

The next morning, it takes serious willpower not to text her the second my eyes open as I reach for the phone. If I do it as Owen, I'm only strengthening a false relationship, but I'm afraid to scare her away if I do it as Braden. This entire situation is fucked up. Which means I'm fucked.

The hole is getting deeper with each passing conversation, but I haven't found a way out yet, nor have I stopped digging. Talking to her as Owen gives me insight I wouldn't have, and Braden allows me to bring out the fun in her otherwise reserved self.

I manage to make it to the gym for a quick workout while my wheels spin about scheduling a meeting with my client *in Bozeman*. It's a dirty move, but I need to be with Poppy in person to prove I'm not the man she thinks I am. Plus, a do-over is in order… to show her what her first time *should* have been like.

14

BOOK CLUB

Poppy

I WOKE UP WITH A SMILE ON MY FACE THIS MORNING. TALKING to Owen last night wasn't as awkward as I thought it would be with no rules to follow. We learned a lot about each other and elaborated on things more than the night before, which was nice. My first impression is that he's a good guy, but we've only scratched the surface.

I'm feeling hopeful after two long chats, along with all the information in our profiles. That's two of the five conversations we need to exchange pictures. I'd be lying if I said I wasn't nervous about that part—and not just because of what he looks like but also because of what he'll think of me.

> Braden: Good morning, Mouse. Sleep well?
>
> Poppy: I did. Plus, I'm still in bed.
>
> Braden: That's a great place to be.

I don't know if I'm ready for Braden yet. He confuses me, and I'm not sure how to handle him. Should I go along with this crazy book club idea or let it go and stop talking to him? It wouldn't be smart to indulge him at this point, considering A, he doesn't live here, and B, he's not at the same stage as I am, as in wanting a relationship.

He's only after sex, and in hindsight, I probably messed up by making him think I was a no-strings-attached type of girl. I may have started with that, but it doesn't mean I'll continue down that path. It's simply not in my DNA. But then, like I said, it could be good practice for the real thing.

I'd be opening the door for heartbreak if I go down this road with him, though, and it's certainly not *his* heart that'll be on the line. I've no doubt this book club idea is only to get what he wants, even though we're miles apart. He already tried once for phone sex, and I'm sure he won't give up, especially during the spicy scenes.

> Braden: So tell me, sleepyhead, are you planning to stay in bed all day? We could read a book together.
>
> Poppy: Since I cleaned the house yesterday, that was the plan, but you weren't part of it.
>
> Braden: It's a perfect day to kick off our book club.
>
> Poppy: Did you miss the bit where I said you're not part of it? Besides, don't you have anything better to do?
>
> Braden: Not that I can think of. Well, there is, but it would require teleportation. Damn that it's not invented yet.

Okay, so he's fun… and somewhat growing on me. But I'm not equipped to handle a guy like him. I don't know how long I'll be able to ward off his advances until I crack. And then what? If I'm already feeling guilty for simply talking to two guys, how will I feel if something inappropriate happens?

> Poppy: I need caffeine to deal with you and your innuendos.
>
> Braden: Get some coffee and sustenance and come back to bed with a book picked out. No cheating. You can't start it until I'm ready.

Poppy: When did I agree to this?

Braden: Baby, you agreed the instant you responded to my text this morning. Don't deny it. Now go get your coffee. Eat. Send me the book title. And we'll talk in a bit.

He's so bossy. And infuriating. And deviant. And apparently, I'm drawn to those characteristics because I'm strangely giddy at the prospect of spending the day reading together. I'm in way over my head here.

I'm prolonging the inevitable by taking my time in the kitchen. I'm not a big breakfast eater, but I'll do anything in the name of stalling. While the bread is toasting, I grab my phone to peruse my endless Kindle library.

I'm not sure what he's expecting, but I want a book he'll enjoy for more than just sex. I'm giggling at the irony. He liked what I was reading on the plane, but he came in during a spicy scene, so that made it easy to hook him.

I wonder if he'd want a sports romance or if sticking to fantasy is the way to go. Better yet, I could find an office romance with lawyers. However, that could backfire if he starts thinking about someone from *his* office. Then again, that shouldn't bother me, right? Ugh, this man has me second-guessing myself at every turn.

Sitting at the table while eating my toast, I continue scrolling through options until finally settling on a mafia romance. Nothing too crazy, but something he won't know about, so he won't annoyingly comment on everything.

Texting him the book title, I leave my phone on the nightstand and go brush my teeth as slowly as possible. I could take a shower, but that might be overkill in the avoidance department since I don't need one to sit in bed all day.

After running out of things to do, I climb under the covers and grab my phone to a message from Braden waiting for me.

Braden: Ready when you are, Mouse.

Poppy: So, how are we doing this?

Braden: Let's just start at the same time and text each other if we need a break.

Poppy: What if you read a ton faster and are ten pages ahead when we stop? Would I have to stay after class to catch up?

Braden: Boy, do I like the sound of that. We'll play out that teacher fantasy one of these days.

Poppy: You're such a cad.

Braden: You know you like it.

Poppy: Moving on, what's your solution?

Braden: How about we get started and see how it goes. Ready? Set…

Poppy: Go.

I dive right in, considering this was what I'd be doing with or without Braden, and I'm immediately sucked into the story. It's about a girl who's been promised to a rival family's son as a peace offering. She's innocent and beautiful, and of course, he's attracted to her at first sight, but hates her father and thus hates her—typical enemies-to-lovers.

Twenty minutes later, I'm deep into their first encounter when my phone pings with a text.

Braden: When do we get to the good stuff?

Poppy: Seriously?

Braden: No. But I love riling you up. How far are you?

Poppy: Page 23. You?

Braden: I'm not telling.

Poppy: God, you're annoying.

Braden: LOL, you're just too easy. I'm on 25. Not too bad. What do you think of the book?

Poppy: So far, so good. You?

Braden: I'm digging it.

Poppy: Can we go back to reading now?

Braden: Already am. I'm multitasking.

Poppy: You drive me nuts.

Poppy: Pause, I need more coffee. I'm on page 29

Braden: Page 31, tell me when you catch up.

Poppy: Ready.

Braden: Let's go.

Braden: I'm hungry. Should we break for lunch?

Poppy: Sure.

Braden: What do you feel like? It's my treat.

Poppy: That's okay, I've got it.

I end up losing the battle, and Braden orders Uber Eats. He's sooo stubborn. He said it was the least he could do for commandeering my Sunday. We eat, chat, and then read some more until late in the afternoon, when we finally come to the first full-blown sex scene. There was plenty of sexual buildup before that, but this is intense.

Naturally, I'm aroused, but knowing Braden is reading the same thing has me more worked up than usual. Curiosity plagues my mind whether he's thinking about me. He hasn't chimed in during the previous parts leading up to this, but I wonder if he will now. I'm struggling to focus on the words as the anticipation builds.

My heart is hammering, and the familiar clench of my core increases as I picture the scene. I'm so tightly wound that I jump at the ping from my phone.

Braden: What page are you on?

Poppy: 143

Braden: How are you feeling, Mouse? Needy?

Poppy: I'm fine.

Braden: I'm not. I'm sitting here remembering how it felt to have your tight pussy wrapped around my cock.

Oh God. What do I say to that? I know where he's going with this, and I don't think I have the willpower to stop it. Mainly, because I'd really like it to happen.

Braden: What do you usually do during these scenes?

Poppy: Nothing.

Braden: Liar. Home alone, reading in bed, hot and horny, and you're telling me you wouldn't be sliding your hand inside your panties to relieve the ache between your legs?

Poppy: That's none of your business.

Braden: Read another page, and then I'm making it my business.

Poppy: You can't do that.

Braden: Read, Poppy.

So I do, and am even more turned on knowing what we're about to do. I'm so keyed up that I barely refrain from reaching my hand down. I'm just about to, when his next message halts me in my tracks.

Braden: My cock is so hard for you. Each stroke reminds me how good you feel. Can you picture my hand gliding over my shaft while I think of you and your tight pussy?

Braden: Are you aching for it? Do you need to touch yourself as you imagine my cock, dripping for you?

Braden: Take your panties off and spread your legs for me, Mouse.

Each text comes through with a few seconds in between. Like he's letting me soak in each one. I hesitate for the briefest moment before I follow his instructions, mainly because I want this just as badly as he does, if not more so.

Braden: Did you take them off?

Poppy: Yes.

Braden: Good girl. Now reach down and tell me if you're wet for me.

Braden: How wet are you, Mouse?

Poppy: Really wet.

Braden: I bet you're sopping, wishing my cock could fill you up.

Braden: Do you miss my cock, baby?

More than he could imagine.

Poppy: Yes.

Braden: Fuck, Poppy. Rub that cunt for me. Pretend it's my tongue. Picture my head between your legs, eating you out.

Braden: I'd be balls deep by now. I bet I'd slide right in, wouldn't I?

Poppy: Yes.

Braden: Are you taking care of that sweet pussy for me, since I can't be there to fuck you hard, the way you like it?

Poppy: Yes.

Braden: Tell me what you're thinking about.

Poppy: I'm pretending it's you, that you're the one touching me.

Braden: Good girl. I'm close, baby. I'm about to explode, all this cum could be yours if I were there. I'd fill you so full. Would you like that?

Poppy: Yes. I'm close.

Braden: Come with me, Poppy. Oh fuck, I'm coming.

Poppy: Me too.

Oh my God. That was so fricking good. So much better than on my own. Like wow…. How can I ever go back to doing it by myself? Great. Not only has he ruined me for other men, but now he's made it so *I* don't even stack up. Dammit. So, what happens next?

To my relief, since I wasn't sure where to go with the conversation, we called it a night after agreeing on how hot that was. And I must say, I slept well.

We can't do that every time, though, so when he suggests a repeat the following evening, I quickly shut him down. And after having last night on constant replay throughout the day at work, it was no easy feat.

Instead, we ended up chatting about random things for a while, taking the night off from book club, which worked out since Owen started messaging right after.

Owen: How did Monday treat you? And before I forget to say, I'm enjoying our conversations.

Poppy: Thanks. Me too. Today went well. I'm finally catching up at work. How about you?

Owen: Couldn't be better. So tell me more about your family. The parents who inspired your relationship goals and the brother who scared you away from boys. I take it you're close. Do you all live in the same city? What do they do?

Poppy: LOL. Well summarized. My parents are here. We have dinner every Sunday. They're both teachers. My brother, Grayson, has been in the military for twelve years but is finally moving home right before Christmas. I'm excited to have him back. What about yours?

Owen: Sounds like a solid family. Must be where your aspirations came from. I'm an only child. My dad is out of the picture, and my mom lives across the country with her husband. We talk on the phone once a week or so. What I lack in family, I make up for in friends. I'm fortunate in that regard.

Poppy: That's nice. I'm lacking in the friend department. My best friend moved away, and the guy I had dinner with this weekend is my only other close friend. I've lived here my whole life, so I obviously know people but they're more like acquaintances.

The night goes on, asking questions back and forth. Owen is easy to talk to. He's sweet, and he's constantly making me laugh. He's perfect, yet there's no way of knowing if we'll be attracted to each other.

I'll find out soon enough with only two more conversations before exchanging pictures. If anything, we could always end up as friends, but I'm hoping for more at this point and excited for our next chat on Wednesday.

Braden

I'm at dinner with the guys after work on Tuesday. It feels like it's been forever since we've gone out, but finding a time that works for everyone is difficult. Between work, Eli's and Sebastian's newborns, and Jackson's new marriage, we have a lot of obstacles.

When I made partner, I became busier and slowed down on going out. I didn't notice how much I'd neglected my friends until we weren't hanging out at all, and I miss it. However, I'm expecting a shit ton of crap when they hear about my trip this coming Thursday.

I called Jim Marlow first thing yesterday to schedule an in-person deposition. It could easily be done from here with the help of a local source, but hey, I'm a hands-on type of guy—or at least I'm hoping to be—with a certain redhead I'll be paying a visit to.

Poppy and I enjoyed our lazy Sunday in bed, where the texting was hotter than the book. The next day, when she shut me down for more sexy times, we briefly chatted about mundane things before she convinced me to take the night off from reading.

But I hadn't had my fill, so Owen got in touch shortly after. Neither of us will be talking to her tonight, since I'll be out with the guys. I'm still not sure how I'll dig myself out of this mess, but at this point, I'm enjoying it too much to quit. Conversation number five is when I'll have to worry. That's when exchanging photos won't work without revealing who I am.

What I like about having Owen is learning about each other on a deeper level. I've kept mental notes about what I've shared to avoid doubling up. The thing is, I've revealed more to Poppy than to any other woman since Layla. Except it's all been through Owen, and she has no idea he's really me.

Hanging with the guys tonight is the distraction I needed, and an hour into dinner, I'm relaxed for the first time in weeks. As our meals are cleared and we're three drinks in, distraction is thrown out the window when the shit-talking starts. As I'm the only single one left, they're enjoying it a bit too much.

"I never thought the day would come when Braden the Butcher was chasing a woman," Eli jests.

"Not just chasing. He's traveling thousands of miles for one. She must have a damn fine pussy." Sebastian never did lose his crassness even after settling down.

"Hey, I'm just glad you've finally realized not all women are bitches like Layla. Even if it doesn't work out, at least you're moving on." Jackson and I have the most history, and he saw firsthand the Layla shitstorm.

Eli points his beer in my direction. "Remember, you're walking the line. If you screw her over, you'll pay for it. Cici will have your balls. So basically, don't fuck it up."

I point mine right back at him. "I guess you'd better wish me luck then. She doesn't know I'm coming yet, so don't go home and blab to your wife. Let me have the element of surprise. It'll end well, I promise."

"Care to make a wager on that?" Eli raises his brows in question. "From what I've heard, she doesn't have the highest opinion of you."

"I'd love to. I'll hit record next time we're in bed together."

Their chuckles and whistles of approval accompany glasses being raised in cheers.

Eli, however, is shaking his head, smirking. "Dude. We all know the bedroom isn't the problem. It's everything else I'm worried about. Seriously, man, I'm not covering for you if this goes south."

Jackson intervenes. "Go get your woman. I'll handle my sister."

After that, the conversation fortunately moves to less stressful topics. No one knows I've been talking to Poppy through the dating app, although if Warren and Eli were to end up in the same room, I might be outed, which is why Warren wasn't invited tonight.

The last thing I want is a lecture—I'm aware how fucked up it is and don't need to feel worse than I already do. So why am I continuing the charade and not making Owen go away? Because I'm convinced she wouldn't be as forthcoming with me as with Owen, so he's still needed.

Maybe after a few days in Bozeman, I'll sweep Owen under the rug. If all goes well, she might even make the decision herself and decide I'm the one she wants. The distance may be an issue, but we'll address that later.

We call it a night after one more drink, and by the time I crawl into bed, I'm powerless from sending a message, even though she'll probably be asleep, since she's an hour ahead. Lucky for me, she's not.

Braden: It was unfortunate to miss book club tonight.

Poppy: For you maybe…

Braden: Is that so? Did you do something without me?

Poppy: Thankfully, I have more books, and I certainly don't need your assistance for other things.

Braden: That may be true, but is it as good?

Poppy: I plead the fifth.

Braden: Hey, that's my line.

Poppy: How was your night?

Braden: It was nice. I missed you, though…

Shit, I regret it the minute I hit send. What am I doing? It's too soon for that.

Poppy: Oh, I know what you missed, all right. On that note, good night.

Braden: Good night, Poppy.

The next day was hell after barely sleeping. That last text had me tossing and turning, regretting the admission, while at the same time wishing it were something she could actually believe. Her opinion of Braden is still complete shit.

But really, I haven't done much to correct it, which is my priority for tomorrow's visit: show her another side of me—a softer side.

In the meantime, it was Owen's turn tonight. We ended up talking about our choice of dating apps and agreed that it's been easier getting to know one another this way, without the typical awkwardness or distractions. We discussed hobbies, places we've traveled, and where we'd like to go. It was another perfect interaction between the two.

We've yet to disagree on anything, which is insane considering that she and I started out so terribly in real life. I royally fucked up from the beginning as Braden. In all fairness, I *was* only trying to fuck her. Now, I can't imagine that ever being enough.

I've got a lot of ground to cover to change her perception of me, and it will be much easier to do in person, but first, I need to put the wheels in motion for it to work.

After crawling into bed and setting my alarm for five in the morning, I pull her name up to send one last text before closing my eyes.

Braden: I have a surprise for you tomorrow.

Poppy: Oh yeah? What kind of surprise?

Braden: The surprise kind.

Poppy: How am I getting this surprise?

Braden: I'm glad you asked. I was hoping you were free for dinner tomorrow night.

Poppy: Why? Are we doing book club and ordering in at the same time again?

Braden: Something like that. Are you available at six-thirty?

Poppy: Sure.

Braden: Go to Plonk and give your name to the hostess. They'll direct you from there. Do you know the place?

Poppy: Of course I do, I live here. So you're buying me dinner. That's the surprise?

Braden: Do you need a vocabulary lesson?

Poppy: Fine, don't tell me. I'm going to sleep now, anyway. G'night.

Braden: Sweet dreams, Mouse. Text me when you're at the restaurant.

With the early morning flight, I arrive in time for the two o'clock meeting with Jim this afternoon. I wanted it out of the way before focusing on the main reason for my visit. His offer to meet here rather than me driving to Big Sky was helpful.

I'd called in a favor earlier this week to a local downtown law firm for the use of their conference room and arranged to have one of their clerks transcribe and act as a witness. They had the room prepared, and the clerk waiting when I walked in, just in time to greet my client.

"Good to see you again, Mr. Marlow. I appreciate you making the trek to Bozeman," I say as we shake hands.

"My pleasure, Braden. And please, call me Jim. Big Sky has too few restaurants to choose from, so it's nice to come down the mountain."

"I'm glad it worked out then. Should we get started?"

"Lead the way." He motions his arm to proceed.

The deposition took place over the next two hours and couldn't have gone better—not that I was worried about it. The only reason I came in person was to kill two birds with one stone and figure out what this is with Poppy, what our potential is, and why I can't stop chasing her.

I close the folio before me and nod to the clerk in dismissal, calling it a wrap.

"Well, Jim, that should do it. Thanks again for accommodating my schedule."

His smile is kind in return. "No worries at all. I'm happy you made it up here again. Why don't you join me for dinner while you're in town? No sense dining alone after coming so far."

"I appreciate the offer, but I've already got plans with a woman who lives here," I say with a devious grin.

"Well, I won't stand in the way of that." He winks. "How about a drink then? One of my favorite bars is one block away if you have time."

Glancing at my watch tells me it's still two hours before my date. "Let's do it. Give me a minute to wrap things up here, and I'll be ready. Feel free to wait in the lobby. I won't be long."

"I'm in no hurry."

A little while later, we're sitting with drinks at none other than Plonk on Main Street with a cheese tray on the way. I'm not worried Poppy will notice me since I discreetly chose a corner booth, and now I'll be able to watch her when she comes in.

"So how is it you know a woman from Bozeman? Friend from college?"

"We met on the flight back to San Diego after I came out for our initial meeting. We didn't hit it off at first, but then she happened to be the maid of honor at the same wedding I was in that weekend."

"Proves what a small world we live in. So why does it sound like there's more to the story?"

For some reason, I find myself opening up and describing the entire thing in detail, which is way too much information to share with a client, but something about Jim Marlow makes me want to spill my guts. Of course, I leave out the raunchier details and Owen's involvement.

"That's quite the tale. I take it you like this girl?"

"That's what I'm trying to figure out, sir. Truth be told, I'm not a big fan of relationships. Between being jilted by a woman, a dad who left my mom for an affair, and the line of work I'm in, I've steered clear of them."

"Would you be open to some wisdom from an old man who's been around the block?" he asks shrewdly.

I nod. "I'd love it. What do you got for me?" I ask, then sip my drink, wondering where he's going with this, considering his wife recently cheated on him.

He chuckles, then goes in the opposite direction than expected.

"Well, son, you know my current situation would suggest a different take on things, but I'll tell you something, living without love isn't a life worth living. To appreciate someone, to worship, to strive to be better for another person, fills you with purpose and inspires compassion. There's nothing like having a woman you're excited to come home to every day." He gazes into the room, lost in his own thoughts, before continuing.

"If you came back for her, which I'm assuming is what prompted this meeting, then it might be the start of something here." He points to his heart. "And if that's the case, it's worth pursuing."

"That wasn't what I expected, given your circumstances, but I appreciate the advice. Can't say it's up to me anyhow. She's not exactly a huge fan of mine. In fact, she doesn't even know I'm here yet."

He laughs. "That surprises me. You seem like you could charm the pants off anybody. Where did you go wrong with this one, and how in the world are you taking her to dinner if she doesn't know you're here?"

"I may have come on a little too strong initially and not in the best way." I chuckle and tell him my plans for the night and how I arranged our date without her knowing I'm here. After a hearty laugh, he leaves me to wait for my redheaded beauty, but not before wishing me luck.

And boy, will I need it.

15

SURPRISE

Poppy

'M FEELING ALL SORTS OF STUPID AS I WALK INTO THE restaurant. It's weird going out alone. The only thing I can come up with is that we'll FaceTime each other during dinner, which is equally strange, especially in a place like Plonk that has no privacy.

I guess it's one way to have a long-distance date, but then, is that what this is… a date? I have no idea, but I'm about to find out since I just texted Braden to let him know I'm here.

After giving my name to the hostess, I'm led to a low oblong table with a couch on one side and two plush chairs on the other. Strange to take up such a large space for one person, but at least I won't be right next to someone while I'm on the phone.

Moments after being seated, the waiter arrives, saying a bottle of champagne has been pre-ordered and asks if I'd like it now or to start with something else. Hm, the night might not be so bad after all. Though I'm still unsure what to make of it.

It's been a week since I've been talking with Braden, and it's strange how different we started out. Rather than date before doing the deed, we did the deed, and now we're dating. Although I'm not sure if reading together or phone sex is considered dating. We might need to backtrack a bit. But why bother when we live so far away?

And what about Owen? He's everything I would want, except I have no idea what he looks like. It's one thing to get to know somebody that you've seen pictures of and be nervous they may not live up to them, but another thing altogether not to have a clue what to expect.

I'm still feeling guilty for talking to two people at once, but Matt and Cici are right, this is just part of the process. It's not like we're serious. I haven't even gone on a date with either of them, so both situations have issues.

The waiter interrupts my thoughts, arriving with the champagne, a bucket, and two glasses.

"Oh, I'm here alone," I say, embarrassed as he sets it down.

He looks at me quizzically. "Hm. Somehow, I had this down as a table for two."

"Nope, just me," I restate, becoming more uncomfortable by the minute.

"I'm sorry, Miss. I apologize for the misunderstanding," he says as he pops the bottle and proceeds to fill one glass. "Enjoy that for now, and I'll be back with a cheese tray that's finishing up."

"Thank you," I say, instantly impressed that Braden had all this set up. He doesn't exactly strike me as the thoughtful type, which makes me wonder what he's up to.

I'm thankful for the champagne, but I'm beginning to feel even more awkward being alone. It shouldn't bother me so much since the restaurant side is nearly empty. But I've been here for ten minutes already with no response from Braden, and it's making me antsy. I've never been the one to reach out first to either him or Owen.

Maybe that's one of my problems. Should I be more forward? Not that I would ever need to be with Braden—he's forward enough for both of us. Plus, that's not what this is between us, so I shouldn't even be stressing about it.

I'm preoccupied as I stare at my phone, impatiently waiting, when someone approaches from the side. Turning my head, expecting the waiter, my jaw drops to see Braden in the flesh. The first thing to hit me is how unbelievably hot he is in a suit with his signature sexy smirk, and immediately following that thought is utter confusion.

"What are you doing here?" I stammer.

"I had a meeting in Bozeman and wanted to surprise you," he says with a devastating smile.

If the smirk was sexy, the smile is downright sinful.

"Wow. This is… crazy."

Some sense of manners returns, and I stand to hug him in greeting. This is so weird. The last time we were together was in bed, and we weren't alone for part of it. Just thinking about it makes me flush.

He whispers in my ear. "Hopefully, it's a good crazy."

I'm still too shocked to respond with anything clever so I stay silent. As soon as we pull apart, he sits on the couch next to me, and the waiter appears with the glass he removed moments ago.

"Ah, so there are two of you this evening," he says while filling it with champagne. "I'll check on that cheese tray and have it out shortly."

Braden thanks him before returning his attention to me and raising his flute in a toast. "To new beginnings."

I repeat his words, meeting him in the middle. Once we each take a sip, he simply says, "Hi," with that damn panty-melting smirk again.

"Hi," I respond shyly.

This is a different version of Braden, and I'm not sure what to make of it. He's not being… *Braden-like*. He's more subdued, prompting me to ask if something is wrong.

"No. I'm just out of practice. Sorry." He grins adorably, almost appearing shy.

"With what?"

"Dating?" He smiles nervously, and it's impossibly endearing. That, in addition to his answer, causes me to laugh.

"What?" he asks.

"Nothing." I shake my head. *I still can't believe he's here.* "So is that what this is? A date?" I can't help but ask.

"I'd like it to be. If that's okay with you?" He quirks an eyebrow.

"Um, I guess." I shrug, not having a reason otherwise and wondering if that small spark of hope is dangerous. I'm choosing to ignore it for now. "You said you had a meeting?"

"Yeah. The same client I came to interview when we first met. We did his deposition today."

"How did it go?" Not that I know what that is or anything, but I figure it's polite to ask.

"It went well, and then we came here for a drink afterwards. I like the guy."

"That probably makes it easier to work his case." Then what he says registers. "Wait. Have you been here watching me the entire time?" This is so strange, I'm not sure what to think.

"Yes. It was harder than hell to stay in my seat and not come over, but I wanted to give you a minute to get comfortable."

"How long are you in town for?"

"Until Sunday, if all goes as planned." He winks at me, and I can't help the butterflies that come to life.

"Did you decide all this yesterday?"

"I scheduled the deposition on Monday. These arrangements came next."

"What if I was already busy tonight?"

"That would have been a problem." He smirks. "Lucky for me, it worked out."

"But what if it hadn't? Would it have stopped you from

coming?" I ask, realizing my mistake in verbiage the second his expression changes, and roll my eyes.

"Oh, Mouse, you make it so difficult to behave. It's hard to resist goading you when you give me such perfect opportunities."

"Don't worry. I don't expect anything less from you."

"Yeah, but my goal is to have you expecting more."

"What does that mean?"

"It means I'd like you not to think of me as *only* a player."

"Why?"

Before he has a chance to answer, the waiter arrives. "Here you are. Would you like me to go over the selections for you?"

"Yes, please, that would be great," Braden answers.

While the waiter talks about the various cheeses and meats, my mind spins. With him showing up like this, I wonder more than ever what's happening. Is this a booty call or an actual date? I can't figure him out. He's always been easy to read, so to speak—out for one thing and one thing only. But we already did that. And he certainly doesn't need to travel a thousand miles for sex. Braden could have any woman he wanted.

Unless he's hoping to share me again, since I bet most women are averse to that. That's probably it. I'm so stupid for thinking anything else. I wonder if he brought Warren along and is buttering me up for later when we go to his room where Warren is waiting. Not that I'm even considering going to his room.

This is so fucked up. Why am I letting myself be played like this? I'm spiraling, so I reach for my glass, needing some liquid courage to give him a piece of my mind—or to stop from continuing down this rabbit hole.

When the waiter leaves, Braden immediately realizes my shift in attitude and calls me out.

"Hey, what happened? Are you upset I'm here?"

"No. I just can't figure out why you asked me to dinner. Is Warren with you? Were you hoping for round two?"

"Shit, that's what you think? God." He sits up straight and runs his hand through his hair with a loud sigh. "Fuck, no. That won't happen again. I mean, yeah, it was hot, but no—you're…" He shakes his head. "I won't be sharing you. I came to spend time together… get to know one another."

"But why?"

He looks straight at me in complete seriousness. "Because I like you."

My head jerks back in shock. "Seriously? But you're constantly telling me what a mouse I am. Obviously, you're way out of my league. Plus, we don't even live near each other. What's the point?" He's got to be playing me. He can't be interested in anything more than sex.

"Dammit, I have a lot to remedy." He drops his head before looking up with remorse. "You may have been mousy when we first met, but in all fairness, I came on pretty strong. The nickname stuck, but only as an endearment because you're cute. It's not meant to be derogatory. I'm sorry you've been taking it like that. I won't use it anymore if you want."

"No, it's fine now that you explained it." I don't have a chance to say anything else as he continues.

"And as for being out of your league—you're crazy. I'd say you're out of mine. And yeah, we don't live in the same city, but… I don't know… I can't stop thinking about you." He grabs the back of his neck and pulls. "I'm not sure what this is, but I'd like to explore what it could be if you're willing to give me a shot."

I don't know what to say. This is the most nonsexual conversation we've had, and it's taking me off guard. I've sort of grown fond of flirty Braden, and I certainly can't complain about the orgasms he delivers. But maybe he could be more. Do I want that?

I'm silent for too long.

"I've completely freaked you out, haven't I?" he asks.

"No. I'm just processing." I take a sip of my drink for something to do while I think. He silently watches, patiently waiting for an answer.

Finally, after a slow inhale, I take the plunge. "I'm open to that idea, but after this weekend, I'm not sure how it's even possible with the distance issue."

"How about we worry about that when we need to? For now, let's pretend we don't live miles away." He points to the dish in the middle of the table. "We should probably give this a try. But first, a new toast," he lifts his glass and holds it out. "Cheers to possibilities."

Clinking mine with his, I repeat the words, smiling shyly, before we each take a sip and then dig into the cheese tray.

This is so weird. I didn't think of Braden as more than a fleeting moment. I figured we'd have some fun with book club and sexting, then go our merry way. But it sounds like he's serious about exploring more, which seems so far-fetched.

Plus, I'm already talking to Owen, and I don't know if I'm willing to throw that away for something on the brink of impossible. Would Braden expect me to? I'm too inexperienced with this stuff to know. And I can't ask Cici for advice since it's about Braden. That would be weird, considering her husband is friends with him, but I could probably have Matt weigh in.

I'm so deep in thought that I'm startled when he reaches for my hand. "What are you thinking about?"

The appetizer only bought so much time.

"I guess I'm confused. I thought we were keeping it casual, but now you're… wanting to date me?" The need for clarification seems crucial.

"Honestly, I don't exactly know what I'm asking for, but I'd like to see what happens."

Well, at least I'm not the only unsure one.

With a glass of champagne in our systems, the conversation starts to flow more freely, and soon, we're deep into discussing our families. Learning about his childhood, I understand why he's so driven in life. It's impressive how far he's come after starting with nothing.

His resistance to relationships makes more sense after hearing what happened with his parents, not to mention his career choice. With each bit of information, I'm beginning to piece together who he is and why.

Had this Braden been the one I met on the plane, we may have gotten here sooner. But then, would we have done the *other* stuff? Because that's the part I'm most glad we did. So Cici's motto could be spot-on, and everything does happen for a reason.

"What now?" I ask once the check is paid, which he insisted on taking care of.

"So…" He turns his body to face me and lowers to kiss my hand.

The feel of his lips on my skin instantly causes a pulse of desire.

He sits up straight, looking pensive, almost afraid to continue. "I didn't want to be presumptuous, but I have a room in town and was hoping you'd spend the weekend with me."

My jaw drops at the declaration, unsure if I'm excited at the prospect or horrified.

"We have fantastic chemistry, and I haven't stopped thinking about you."

I bite my lip, contemplating. I'm supposed to talk with Owen tonight and am already feeling guilty for considering this. Plus, do I want to end up in his bed again? Because that's obviously where this is headed.

"Look," he continues before I say no. Not that I was going to. "It doesn't have to be sexual. We can just hang out."

I raise my brows and look at him sarcastically. "You don't actually expect me to believe that, do you?"

He throws his hands up in surrender. "Really. We can read a book in person together, play board games, watch TV… whatever you want." When I still don't respond, he adds, "I'm serious."

"I'm sure you are. But you're smarter than that. Do you honestly think we could stay in a hotel room overnight without… you know…"

"Fucking like rabbits?" He smirks while wagging his brows.

I can't help but laugh at the familiar flirty behavior.

He keeps going, trying to convince me. "Like I said, there's no denying we're fire in the bedroom, but that's not why I'm here. If anything happens, it'll be because you want it to. Otherwise, my goal is just to be with you."

My brows scrunch doubtingly. "To what end?"

Braden

It's a fair question and one I don't have an answer for. But what can I say to convince her? I'm dying for her to spend the night with me because, quite frankly, I'm desperate for this woman. And not just her body, which I wouldn't say no to, but—I'm simply desperate for *her*.

I'm not sure where this desire is coming from or why now, but I've spent enough time trying to analyze it with no clear answers. So rather than continuing to overthink, I've decided to go with my gut for now and deal with the consequences later.

I move closer and wrap an arm around her like I've wanted to do all night. "How about we take it one night at a time? You don't have to commit to the whole weekend." I'm practically begging at this point, but I don't care. I'm willing to do a lot more than that for this woman.

I'm disappointed at the torment on her face. Is she conflicted because she's supposed to talk to Owen tonight? Maybe she feels guilty for dating both of us at the same time. Good. Hopefully, she'll be wracked with so much guilt that she'll *stop* talking to him and solve my problem for me.

"Did you have other plans?" Shit, I didn't consider she could be seeing someone else. Fuck. I haven't completely thought this through.

"No. I mean, yes, but that's not why I'm hesitating. It's just hard to wrap my head around..." She motions between us with her hand. "You and me. I'm not oblivious to our chemistry, and as much as

I'd like to give in, the rational part of me knows it's a bad idea. I still don't understand how this can go anywhere, and I'm not the type of person who can have meaningless sex… long-term."

"That's not what I'm asking for. Why don't we take it one day at a time and not overthink it? Can you do that for now?"

She doesn't answer immediately but sips her champagne instead. I'm not sure when I became so invested, but the thought of her turning me down makes my gut clench. After what seems like forever, she finally nods her acquiescence, and my lungs release the breath I was holding.

With the knowledge of being her first, I want nothing more than to have a chance to show her a gentler version of me, which, in all fairness, doesn't come naturally, but I'm willing to give it my best effort. Only if the night takes us in that direction, though, because for once, I'm letting her lead… with a little nudge here and there.

With that settled, I discovered the interesting fact that Poppy keeps an overnight bag in her car for just-in-case situations after I offered to stop at her house on the way to our next destination. Part of my surprise is the ultimate date she described to Owen, bringing her to different places for each course. We'll end the night with dessert in my favorite location—the bedroom.

I found out she's familiar with the restaurant I chose, Gallatin River Lodge, which, as the name implies, conveniently has on-site rooms.

We enjoy an amazing dinner in front of large glass doors with a view of the pond and meadow. Once I settle the bill, it's obvious her nerves are creeping in. So instead of going straight to the room, I have a better idea since the sun is about to set.

I gently hold her arm to stop her before reaching the exit. "Hey, how about we grab our coats and one more glass of wine to enjoy while we watch the sunset outside before we grab your bag. We can sit in the pavilion or walk around the pond. Whichever you want."

She beams at the suggestion. "That's a good idea. Let's do it."

I keep my hand on her elbow and lead us back to the bar. It's not long until we each have a drink in hand and make our way out.

"Why don't we sit first, and then take a walk after if we feel like it," she suggests.

"Sounds like a plan." My hand naturally goes to her waist as we meander to the wooden structure. It overlooks the water and large meadow beyond. On our way, I spot two deer.

"Look." I point in the direction where they're grazing in the meadow.

"Oh, pretty. I forgot how cool this place is. It's been years since I was here. My parents used to bring Grayson and me when we were little. We'd have fishing lessons on the pond while Mom and Dad would relax on the patio. We had such a good time running around and playing." She has a nostalgic look about her as we sit down.

"That sounds fun. Did you and your brother get along well then?"

"I'd say so. We had our moments, for sure. But with the four-year age gap, we didn't bother each other too much. The most annoying thing about him was that all my friends ended up crushing on him."

"I bet he loved that," I say sarcastically, chuckling. "What about now? Are you close?"

Her eyes light up. "We are. At least as close as we can be, considering he left for the military after graduation and hasn't been around. He's a Navy SEAL and made a career out of it but he's moving back right before Christmas. I'm so excited." She beams.

"I'm glad. You think he'll still be lecturing you away from men when he's home?" That would certainly work out in my favor.

"Hey, how do you know he did that?"

Oh shit. I'm not the one she said that to; it was Owen. *Fuck, fuck, fuck.* "He's your big brother, so I figured that's standard. Besides, why else haven't you been scooped up yet?" I'm internally crossing my fingers that it holds up.

She smirks. "Cheesy. But yeah, he might've had something to

do with it. Luckily, I'm too old to be told what to do, otherwise, I'm sure he'd have plenty to say about this."

I don't like that she thinks he'd disapprove of me. But more importantly, I dodged a bullet with that slip-up.

Which leads me to the conclusion that I need to figure out this Owen thing and put it to rest once and for all. Speaking of, I wonder how she'll handle canceling her talk with Owen tonight. Usually, I'm the one to text first, but unless she wants an interruption later, she'll have to let him know her plans have changed before that.

"Now that's a sunset," I say, relieved at my narrow escape and ready to move on.

Her head turns to take in the view, and she smiles. "Oh wow. It's beautiful."

"You're beautiful." I tuck a strand of hair behind her ear as she blushes.

"Thank you. I'm glad we came out here."

I reach for her hand and caress it as I answer, "I am too."

She's so tempting that I can't resist leaning over, slowly bringing my mouth toward hers. But before I close the distance, I pause. This is her night, her choice, and if we kiss, it'll be because she wants to.

A second later, I'm rewarded with her plump lips on mine. She's tentative and shy in her approach, and I refrain from taking over right away, giving her time to explore and have the freedom to control the tempo.

She pulls back and draws her brows together. "What are you doing?"

"What do you mean?"

"Why are you being… gentle?"

Her question and scrunched face make me chuckle before answering. "Because I want to show you another side of me."

"What if that's not what I want?"

"What do you want, then?"

"I don't want gentle."

"Tell me what you *do* want, Mouse. Don't be shy." I'm giving her the power this time. We have the whole weekend to explore the many ways we can enjoy each other. In the meantime, I'm happy to satisfy her however she chooses.

"Can you just be like you've been the other times? You don't usually take things slow. And I like when you…" She clams up and bites her lip in embarrassment.

"When I…?"

"Ugh." She huffs out in frustration, her face going red, before she mumbles her answer, "When you… take charge."

"Well, in that case, Mouse, let's get your bag and go to the room." Standing, I reach for her hand, leading us to the lodge to return the glasses.

I've been curious about something, and as we walk to the parking lot, I can't help but ask, "So tell me, what kind of situation calls for keeping an overnight bag in your car?"

She laughs. "I'm surprised it took you this long to ask. I figured that would've been the first question after I told you that." She shakes her head and continues, "Sometimes when I go to my parents' house for dinner, I end up staying over rather than driving home."

The answer fills me with relief. "I'm happy to know it's not because of all the one-night stands you're having now that I've corrupted you. You know, by making it so good that you want it all the time." I bring the hand I'm holding to my lips and kiss the back of it.

She laughs. "I'm not that easy to corrupt. I still have the same thoughts on the matter, but since we've already been together…" She shrugs, leaving the sentence unfinished as she digs for her keys.

When she reaches for the bag, I immediately take it from her while pushing the button to close the trunk. "Now I see why you gave in so easily. You're just using me for sex," I tease, causing her to laugh again.

I'm becoming addicted to the sound. I've never tried this hard to make a woman happy before, outside of the bedroom, that is. But

I must say, I'm enjoying it. I'm also loving the blushes I earn. I'd say the current one is probably because I'm not far from the truth.

"That's not true. I haven't given in to anything yet." She darts a glare in my direction.

"*Yet*, being the operative word." I wink, swinging the bag over my shoulder and grabbing her hand again to lead us toward the room.

Despite her confession that she likes it when I take charge, the plan is still to let her set the pace initially. I don't want another instance of coercing her into doing something she's not ready for—not that that happened, according to her description to Owen, but I'm not taking the chance.

Once we enter the room, Poppy walks around to check it out while I put everything down. I made sure to reserve the best, because why not when it's on the company's dime?

It's what you'd expect for a Montana lodge, with a rustic interior and large beams in the ceiling. A small kitchenette is on one side and a seating area on the other with sliding doors leading onto the deck. As we venture into the room, a king-size bed takes the stage, but my favorite part is the jacuzzi tub, big enough for two and looking out over the pond.

"Wow. This is beautiful. In all the times I've been here, I've never been inside a room," she says in awe.

As she looks around, I only have eyes for her.

"What made you choose this place? I figured you'd be the type to stay at one of the posh hotels downtown."

"That's usually more my style, but I thought this would offer a little more privacy. The restaurant had great reviews, which were warranted, and the location was convenient if I needed to drive to Big Sky."

"Hm. Well, I'm glad you did. It's perfect."

"Do you know what makes it perfect?" I ask, coming up behind her and wrapping my arms around her waist. I dip my head and kiss the top of hers.

"What?"

"You being here with me."

"Okay, who are you and what have you done with Braden?" She laughs timidly while staring out the window.

That's the second person to ask me that in a week—third, if I count myself.

"Hey." I turn her to face me and bring my hands to her neck with my thumbs framing her jaw. "I mean it. Thank you for staying." I kiss her softly but pull away without deepening it.

She bites her lip nervously.

I take pity and save her from responding. "What would you like to do? We can watch TV, play board games, or, my personal favorite, fill that gigantic tub and take a bath."

Pink tinges her cheeks again, beckoning me to lean forward and kiss each one. "It's okay, Mouse. Tell me what you want. You call the shots, remember?"

"But I thought you were going to be in charge."

"I will…" I kiss the tip of her nose. "When it's time. For now, you decide what happens."

She bites her lip again and takes a deep breath. "I think a bath sounds nice."

"Good choice." My lips can't get enough, and I chastely kiss hers before releasing her. "Why don't you use the robe hanging in the bathroom and get ready while I fill it? Take your time… but not too much." I slap her ass as she walks away and am rewarded with a squeal as she scurries in, closing the door behind her.

16

THE BEST FOR LAST

Poppy

SHIT. *SHIT. SHIT.* I'M SUPPOSED TO TALK TO OWEN TONIGHT, but that's obviously not happening. The problem is, I don't know what to say. It doesn't feel right to make something up, but I can't exactly tell him why I'm canceling. Ugh, the guilt is killing me. All I can do is give it my best shot, so here goes.

> Poppy: Hey, so a friend from out of town surprised me with a visit this weekend. Can we reschedule for Sunday night?
>
> Owen: Sure thing, beautiful.
>
> Poppy: Thanks, and sorry.
>
> Owen: No need to be sorry. Have fun with your friend.
>
> Poppy: Thank you.

Well, that was way easier than I thought, but he's so dang nice that I feel worse than before. I can't believe we only have one more conversation until we can finally see each other. Unless that short one counts? How cool would it be if we could exchange pictures next time we talk? The only problem is if this thing with Braden ends up turning into more than just sex.

But come on. That's so unlikely. So much is against us that it would take an act of God to make it happen. A, he's a player and certainly not looking for anything serious, least of all starting a family. B, he lives in San Diego. And C, he'd get bored with me in no time. Mouse, as an endearment or not, *was* his first impression and not entirely off base.

So for now, I won't think past the mind-blowing orgasms coming my way. Thank God I keep a razor in my overnight emergency bag, because the hair on my legs is definitely an emergency, given the bath we'll be sharing. Sitting on the edge of the small tub, I lightly run the water and take care of the problem before standing to touch up another area he'll be eyeing tonight. When I'm finally ready, I'm about as nervous to bare myself for the third time in my life as I was the first.

Opening the door, I slowly leave the bathroom to Braden, already submerged in the water. *Cheater.*

"There she is," he says when I emerge.

"Here I am…"

"Get your sexy ass over here and enjoy this bath with me. The view's incredible, although you'll give it a run for its money as soon as that robe comes off."

My cheeks heat at his words, and when I stop three feet away, my arms instinctively cross over my waist in hesitation.

"Don't go shy on me again. Show me what I've been missing these last few weeks." He jerks his head in encouragement.

"Seriously, you're like a completely different person than I originally met." My words emerge as I shake my head and remove the last layer of defense, exposing myself completely. After laying it on the back of the chair, I quickly climb in to hide under the water, facing him on the opposite side of the tub.

"Now that's a sight I'd love to see every day, right along with that red blooming on your cheeks to match your hair."

"Stop it. You're embarrassing me."

"You should never be embarrassed. You're fucking gorgeous. And Poppy?"

"Yeah?"

"I'm no different from the man you met, but because of you, I'm doing my damndest to become a better one."

I shake my head in bewilderment. I'm so screwed. He's literally unraveling me. I'm walking straight into his trap with each sweet thing he says. Add in the dirty things that come from his mouth, and I'm running toward it. If I'm not careful, I'll need some serious therapy after this weekend—*if* I stay, which, at this point, I'm not sure I have the willpower to resist.

"Come here, Poppy." He motions me over with a tweak of his hand.

I awkwardly maneuver and scoot back as he pulls me against his chest.

"Lay your head on me, Mouse. Just relax." He keeps his arms around my waist, simply holding me.

I take a deep breath, exhaling all the discomfort with it.

"That's it. Just enjoy the moment."

We sit in silence, and my eyes close, listening to our combined breathing in tune with the sounds of the night outside. Both windows next to the tub are cracked, and the sound is soothing. My body melts into his as all my unease slowly fades away.

His hands move to my shoulders and begin massaging, causing me to moan.

"You like that, I take it?" He chuckles.

"God, yes. Don't stop."

"Your wish is my command."

If I thought I was relaxed before, at this point, I've dissolved into a puddle of pure bliss. My moans of pleasure continue unbidden. He's way too good at this. A minute later, he wanders to my chest. Not to my breasts, but close enough to make me *want* him to touch them. Each graze of his fingers builds the anticipation along with frustration.

"You can…" I start to say without thought, but catch myself.

"I can what?"

"Go lower."

He moves down my arms.

"Here?"

"No," I pout. "You know where."

"Words, Mouse. Tell me where you want my hands," he purrs into my ear.

Surrendering my pride, I huff out the response he's waiting for. "You can touch my breasts."

Finally, he makes his way to where I want him, but instead of kneading them and playing with my nipples, he teases me, gently skimming the edge, which is the direction my patience is heading.

"Like this?"

"Braden, pleeease. This is when I want you to take control. You're sooo good at it." Yes, I'm whining, but if that doesn't work, I'm not sure what will. Luckily, it does the trick.

"That's right, Poppy. Don't forget it—stop trying to convince yourself that you don't need this—that you don't need me." He squeezes both breasts, ending with a pinch to each nipple, eliciting the most wanton sound to escape.

"Is this all you wanted, Mouse? Or are you ready for more?" His hand dips lower before retreating.

"More," I whine.

He chuckles again. "Fuck, you feel incredible. I'll touch anywhere you want as long as I can keep my hands on you."

"Yes," I say as he grazes the top of my mound. I'm hoping he takes it from here without further direction, because I'm practically dying over here.

"You didn't give me nearly enough time to look at this sexy body earlier. I'm not sure you deserve it," he says while teasing my clit with the tip of his finger.

"Braden, seriously, you're killing me." I thrust my pelvis shamelessly.

"Be careful, Mouse. We don't want to make a mess. And if you keep rubbing up against my dick, I can't guarantee I won't do something stupid and fuck you right here. Can you stay still for me?"

"Yes, anything, just touch me, please."

One hand grips the front of my belly, holding me in place, which ends up being useful, because when his fingers finally plunge inside, my hips try bucking to no avail.

"Oh, God. That feels so good."

"I know, baby, but you can't move or the water will spill over the sides. If you hold still, I'll make you come. Can you be a good girl?"

Damn, could I be any hotter for this man?

"Yes."

"Promise?"

"Yes, yes, I promise."

Satisfied with my answer, he pushes in farther and finds the spot that drives me wild, flicking and rubbing it aggressively, making my body come alive. My back arches against him as my head falls back in ecstasy onto his shoulder.

"You're so fucking sexy," he whispers into my ear.

He takes the opportunity to lick and kiss my neck, sending me even further toward release. My mewls become moans, and I'm a writhing mess, chasing my climax.

"Come for me, Mouse. Let me feel your pussy squeeze my fingers the way it'll be squeezing my dick later. It's been too long, baby. Need to see you fall apart."

His dirty words always put me over the edge, and this time is no different. The pressure builds, and my core clenches, tighter and tighter, before the dam suddenly breaks, and the first wave of absolute pleasure hits me. I go to cry out, but he's quicker as his hand covers my mouth.

"That's it, baby, ride it out. Fuck, just like that." His groin pushes into me, and the feel of his cock between my ass cheeks adds to the sensation.

Between that, his fingers working their magic and his lips on my neck, my climax goes on forever. When the pulses finally lessen, he removes the hand from my mouth, causing an enormous sigh to escape as my body sags in utter contentment.

"That's what I like to hear." He pulls out of me, eliciting another pulse as he retreats. "Damn, you're fucking magnificent when you come. I practically orgasmed from watching."

"How are you so good at that?" As soon as I say the words, I regret them. What a stupid question. He's been with countless women—bad timing for a reminder.

Braden smiles and nuzzles my neck. "Lucky for you, I've had lots of practice. Lucky for me, I saved the best for last."

What the heck? I'm sure he just means I'm the last one he's with for now. Because he couldn't have meant what it sounded like. Braden isn't a one-woman kind of man, and I'd better keep reminding myself of that.

Braden

What. The. Fuck? Did that seriously come out of my own two lips? What is it about this girl that makes me lose all reason? She practically undoes me. Bringing her to climax in my arms was out of this world. It reminds me of the first time I pleasured her in the hot tub all those weeks ago.

She's so damn responsive, and it's fucking sexy as hell. Her body comes alive whenever I'm with her, like she was made for my touch. Now that I think about it.... Just because she hadn't had sex before doesn't mean she hadn't done other things, and now I'm curious.

"Have you not had luck with other men making you feel that good?" The thought of another man touching her causes my gut to clench, which I won't overanalyze at the moment.

"I, uh, guess they've been less talented."

That wasn't an answer, nor did it tell me what I really want to know. I'll have to be specific to pull it from her. "Have you had anyone give you an orgasm that way?"

"No," she whispers.

"I'm honored, and sorry you had to wait so long for me." I kiss her temple. "That means you've had to fake it all these years?"

I wonder if she'll come clean with me if I continue peppering her with questions. She didn't have any problem telling Owen. I should definitely keep him around and find out more about her sexual history, because she certainly doesn't want to share it with me.

"I'm not like you. I haven't had many boyfriends, and if I had to guess, none of them were very experienced. It's only been a couple of times, and I didn't fake anything, I just didn't have… that reaction."

Well, shit, at least no one stuck their dick in her. But will she confess that to me?

"And how about the sex? Has that been lackluster as well?"

"I'd say that sums it up."

Damn, she's clever with her replies. While I love knowing her pussy is mine and that I own each and every one of her climaxes, I'd love it even more if she'd admit it. For now, the knowledge will have to suffice.

"How about this, Mouse? I'll give you enough orgasms to make up for all those losers before me. Sound good?"

She giggles. "I think that's a great idea."

I jerk my hips slightly, pushing my cock into her ass. He's been ignored but not forgotten.

"We'd better get started then. Let's dry off and move this to the bed." I nuzzle her neck before standing, causing her to giggle some more. The sound is music to my ears.

After wrapping a towel around my waist, I grab another and hold it out wide so she can stand without feeling like she's on full display. As soon as she's up and out of the tub, I wrap it around her and lean forward to take advantage of her restrained arms.

I've never enjoyed kissing a woman this much. It's like I'm sixteen again, and this is the only thing I know how to do. My cock is at full mast when I finally come up for air.

"All right, if I keep this up, we won't make it to the bed. You'd better go."

She manages to maneuver her arms out so that she can hold the towel in place. I'll give her the modesty for now, since she'll be naked and under me shortly.

Now that the sun has set and it's dark outside, I close the windows and blinds as she walks over, but turn around in time to watch her climb in. Her red hair cascading down her alabaster back is a sight to behold, and so is the quick glimpse of her ass I'm finally awarded.

"Now what?" she asks innocently once she settles and catches me staring.

"You relax while I grab our dessert and a glass of wine. See if there's anything good on." I go to hand her the remote, unable to resist leaning down to taste her once more.

When I stand, she's eye level with my cock, sticking straight out under the towel. "Uh, don't you need…" She points at it and circles her finger to indicate her meaning.

"Don't worry, Mouse. He'll survive a little longer. He's had more practice, remember?" I deliver the jab with a wink before walking away.

Serves her right, since she won't tell me the truth about *her* experience, or lack thereof. Probably not the most mature response, but hell, I'm still a man, so it comes with the territory.

Minutes later, we're both settled on the bed, naked and sipping wine while she flips through channels. Something tugs at me that I haven't experienced in ages, but I'm not ready to label it. I will admit this is comfortable, though. For the first time I can remember, I'm content and not even close to being done. In fact, I don't want this to come to an end.

The evidence comes when she lands on the Hallmark channel, and I don't hesitate when she asks if I mind.

"Are you sure? I can look for something else if you want," she says sincerely.

"Only if you scoot your ass over here and snuggle into me like you're supposed to do during a sappy Christmas movie. And you have to let me feed you dessert."

She smiles as she moves over. My arm naturally wraps around her as she leans into me and burrows in. I could get used to this. It's been ages since I was with Layla, and oddly enough, I don't remember ever feeling this content. We were college sweethearts, young, naive, and convinced the world was our oyster. I'd say I was the foolish one who thought she was it for me.

Fresh out of law school and establishing ourselves, we were equally driven and excited to embark on our careers. After landing top positions at the firms we'd been interning at and becoming settled, it was finally time to take the next step. We'd already been apartment hunting, and I figured this was the natural path in life. Having the ring picked out for months, I was weeks away from proposing.

That was, until I came home for lunch one day to change after spilling coffee on my suit that morning. Boy, was I surprised to hear Layla's moans coming from my roommate's bedroom instead of mine. Three years, and suddenly I wondered how long they'd been lusting over each other, or more importantly, when they'd first given in?

That was when I decided once and for all that marriage was bullshit. First my dad, then Layla, not to mention all the countless dumbasses who fucked up by straying that I saw daily. It was no wonder staying single was an obsession. Sex and sayonara. That was my new philosophy and became my permanent life motto.

Until now, when this girl right here—the one in my arms who's making me rethink everything—has me wanting more. I'm not sure how she thawed my frozen heart after only a couple of months, but somehow, she did. I suspect if this keeps up, she'll soon have it melted completely.

I'm lost in thought when I suddenly feel wetness on my chest and look down to see Poppy silently crying. Shit, I've been so stuck in my head, I haven't even been paying attention to the movie. The wine is long gone, and apparently, it's wrapping up with the happily ever after.

The problem with these movies is that they set women's

expectations way too fucking high. We're not all princes, we're not all from perfect families, and we're not all goddamn pussies. But the tears in my girl's eyes make me wish I were every damn one of those things—for her and her alone.

I take her glass, placing it next to the empty dessert plate before lifting her into my lap to straddle me.

"Come here, baby. Let me dry your tears." I wipe under each eye and then pull her lips to mine. It doesn't take long for the innocent kiss to turn into something not so innocent. Within seconds, my dick is hard again, so close to where he knows he belongs.

She's grinding into me, filling me with lust, and from the sound of her wetness, she feels the same.

"Dammit. I want you, Poppy. You're dripping for me. I need you wrapped around my cock."

Without breaking our connection, I reach down as she raises her hips by a couple of inches and guide my tip to her entrance.

"Go on, Mouse. Sit on me. Let me feel you take me in." She starts to sink slowly, her snug channel barely stretching to accommodate me. "Fuck, yeah. That's it, baby. Goddamn, you're so fucking tight."

"Oh, God. It's… a lot." She pauses and retracts slightly before trying to lower again.

"Don't stop now, baby. Keep going." She sinks a little more. "Good girl. Take it all."

She lowers down fully, and fuck if it's not the best feeling in the world. There's nothing like the initial breach—no thrust afterward compares. Her pussy is squeezing me so tight it's like it's never been penetrated. Only I know it has. But not enough to be used to it, and the tension in Poppy's shoulders reminds me she's still new to this.

"Shhh. Relax." I reach up to brush the hair from her face. "You've got this. It only gets better from here. Are you ready to ride me?"

"I'm not sure. I'm scared to move."

"Don't be. I promise you'll like this. Scoot back and forth. Feel how deep I am." I'm dying to take control, but I want her to be comfortable first. She'll see how good it is in no time. I grab her and gently move her forward and back to demonstrate.

She gasps.

"You like that, baby? My cock's all yours. Use it, Poppy. Fuck me however you want."

She gives her hips a slight rock, testing out the movement, and her pussy clenches around me.

"Fuuuck. Your pussy is heaven. It's like you were made for me."

Her head is buried in my neck, but the urge to kiss her is overwhelming, so I lift her up and bring her mouth to mine, heightening our desire. Only seconds pass until we're devouring each other, and she's moving vigorously in sync with our mouths.

I'm groaning into the kiss, the sensation of her fucking me, out of this world. She speeds up, then lifts into a sitting position and braces herself on my chest. Her hands grab onto my pecs while she uses her grip to move back and forth. It's fucking phenomenal. She's a natural.

"You look so good riding my cock."

I can tell she's close, so I take it upon myself to bring her home, because the quicker she's coming, the quicker I can unleash myself toward my own release. If my dick doesn't coat her insides with cum soon, he'll revolt. Finding her clit with my thumb, I slowly circle it, applying just the right amount of pressure.

"Come on, baby. Give in to it and soak me."

My other hand reaches for her breast, and when I tweak her nipple, pure ecstasy lights up her face, and her pace quickens frantically as she chases her orgasm. Two seconds later, she squeezes my dick so hard, I'd have blown if I wasn't so concentrated on her pleasure.

"Oh, God. Oh, God. Oh, my God. Braden. It feels so good. Don't stop." She screams the rest of her climax before crashing to my chest in a heap.

"You okay, Mouse?"

"Holy shit. More than okay."

"Good, because I'm taking over. You ready?"

"Uh, for what?"

"You'll see." I grab her hips firmly to hold her in place and pummel into her from below, hammering in and out at a frantic pace while I keep her still.

"Fuck, I love this pussy. You take my cock so well, Mouse."

I continue rutting into her from below, hitting that spot deep inside that feels like I'm breaking through some secondary barrier, and in my imagination, it opens only for me.

"I own this pussy, don't I? Say it, Poppy. Tell me I own this pussy."

Nothing comes out other than sounds of pleasure.

I spank her ass. "Tell me who owns this pussy. Now."

"You," she yells.

"I what? Let me hear it, Poppy."

"You own my pussy."

"Ah, fuuuck." With her submission and hearing those words come out of her mouth, I fucking lose it. My balls seize to the most epic orgasm of all orgasms as I fill her with cum.

I thrust deep as I ride it out, eventually holding still as it overtakes me, shooting more into her with each throb of my cock, until the last pulse finishes me off.

"Fuck, Poppy. That was… so… fucking… good."

"That was… something else. I just…" Her head shakes into the crook of my neck.

I give her a minute to formulate words, but she doesn't finish.

"You just what?"

"Is it always like this?" she blurts. "Is this normal, or is it because I'm not as *seasoned* as everyone else?"

I lean back into the bed at the same time I lift her chest to look at her. "Hey, listen to me. No. It's not always like this. And it has nothing to do with your experience. Whatever this is between us… it's something more. It's just as good for me—better than it's ever been, in fact." I rub my thumb along her jaw. "And we're only getting started."

17

MORE

Poppy

HOW CAN ONE WEEKEND HAVE ME REEVALUATING EVERYTHING I thought I knew about Braden? I was sad to say goodbye this morning. I'm not sure how it happened, but he's nudged his way into my world.

We did end up fucking like rabbits, but we also talked, laughed, took walks, played board games of all things, and read together while snuggling in bed. It's exactly what I want in a real relationship.

His comments show he wants something more, but he hasn't been specific. He said this wasn't just a booty call, but I'm not sure exactly what that means, and am more confused than ever.

I've started to fall for Owen, and now I'm in the same boat with Braden, if not further. The difference is that Owen is someone who's looking for long-term and lives here, while there's no way of knowing if Braden is capable of a relationship or if we can overcome the distance issue. He's a partner at his law firm, and I couldn't move away from Bozeman. Could I?

If I did, I'd be leaving my parents, but Grayson will be home soon, so they would have him. I'm doing well in real estate but could do that anywhere. Plus, Cici's in San Diego, and I could absolutely fit in with her friends.

Whoa, whoa, whoa. I'm way ahead of myself. This is why I shouldn't do casual sex. Look at me, I'm practically planning a move across the country for a guy I've slept with on three separate occasions and known for four months, while disliking him for two of those.

All day, I've been ruminating over the situation, analyzing every little detail from the weekend, to what Braden said or did to our good-bye. I've been trying to decide whether he seemed relieved to go or reluctant.

After tidying up and attempting to distract myself by reading, I'm startled by a ping from my phone. It's Braden, and I'm immediately giddy as a smile takes over.

> Braden: I'm home and missing you already.

> Poppy: Glad you made it safe. Thank you for a great weekend. I finished the three chapters. Did you?

He misses me. That means something, right? I don't know that I'm prepared to say it back, though. It's too vulnerable, and I'm not sure I completely trust his motives. I want to... but I'm not ready yet.

> Braden: Yes, and you can't go further without me. Do you want to read for an hour every night?

> Poppy: Yeah, but let's start tomorrow?

> Braden: Why? Do you have a hot date?

> Poppy: Something like that ;)

> Braden: You better not...

> Poppy: ...

My phone rings as I'm trying to figure out how to respond. "Hello?"

"Tell me it's not a date," Braden says with a mixture of anger and uncertainty.

"What does it matter?"

"Seriously? We just spent the weekend fucking, and it's not supposed to bother me if you're going out with another guy?"

"Oh, so you've never slept with a woman and then a different one the following night?"

I hear him breathe deeply before he responds with a level of control he's obviously struggling to maintain. "Never with someone I cared about."

"Then what are you really asking?" I need to know for sure where he's at in his head. I can't keep guessing his intentions. If he wants us to be more, it's time to spit it out and quit beating around the bush.

"Are you seeing anyone else?"

"No, but I'm talking to someone and might meet him this week."

The low growl to come from his throat is palpable through the phone. But honesty is important since I'm asking for it in return. Although, if I *am* being honest, I'm not looking forward to meeting Owen as much as I was.

"How can you still be interested in him after our time together? Did it mean nothing to you?"

It's like he read my mind. But I can't put all my cards on the table too soon.

"It did. But I'm confused. I'd already started talking to this guy, and dammit, you came out of nowhere. You weren't even on the radar, and just because you waltz in here and give me the best weekend I've ever had, doesn't mean I can drop everything else on the hope this goes somewhere. I'm not ready for that. *We're* not ready for that." I take a deep breath after using all my air in one go.

There. I said it, and if it blows up in my face, so be it. At least I'll know it was the right decision if he's willing to walk away so easily.

He's silent for what seems like forever before finally responding. "Fuck. I'm sorry, I don't know what's wrong with me." I can picture him running his hand through his hair, making me smile. I do miss him, but I won't tell him that.

"It's okay." I throw him a bone for his apology, which probably isn't easy for him.

"No. It isn't. I'm crazy about you, Poppy, and I'm not sure what to do about it. I'm aware that it's not fair to barge into your life and demand exclusivity, but dammit, that's what I want."

"Normally, I'd be all for it, but it's complicated. We're too far apart, and I want more than you can give me."

"You don't know that."

"Really, Braden? So you'll move here tomorrow, live with me, get engaged, and start making babies?"

He laughs. "I like the sound of the last part. Do we have to do it in that order?"

I can't help but laugh along with him. "I'm serious."

"So am I."

"Braden," I chastise.

"All right, here's the deal. I like you—a lot. I'll admit the distance is a problem for now. If you lived here, I'd be open to the moving-in part, but fuck, Poppy, I don't know how to make this work, but I sure as hell want to try. Are you at least with me on that?"

"I'd like to be, but it's bad timing. I'm not willing to throw away the start of something else on a mere possibility. I need more than that. Can we keep things the way they are and see how it goes? I'm not *opposed* to more, but I'm not ready to go in blind."

"You mean without a crystal ball?" he asks sarcastically.

"That's not fair."

"Dammit, I know. I'm just frustrated. You're right, though. I can't ask you to be exclusive when I can't give you what you want. As long as you don't count us out, I can handle that for now."

"I'm sorry I can't commit to more."

"I'm sorry too… for not being what you need."

I giggle. "Did we just have our first fight?"

He scoffs. "I think we did. You know what that means, don't you?"

"What?" I ask, with a sneaking suspicion of what the answer is.

"Makeup sex."

"You're terrible," I scold, even though my body automatically responds to the suggestion.

"I bet you just clenched your thighs and are already wet for me."

"Don't you dare tease me when you can't do anything about it."

"Fine. We'll make up properly tomorrow, so plan some extra time for me. Okay?"

"Okay, bossy."

"Don't pretend you aren't excited."

I giggle in acknowledgment. "Not at all. I'm looking forward to it."

I'm grinning ear to ear as we end the call. When did he turn into the man who makes me smile instead of scowl? Or maybe he's always been that man, and I was too hung up on my sexual conservativeness to notice. Either way, I like how he is—a little sweet and a whole lot filthy.

Noticing the time, I rush to the kitchen to pour a glass of wine before curling up on the couch for my chat with Owen. I'm anxious to see if it's all in my head or if I'm as into him as I remember. I'm also excited to exchange pictures tonight and hopefully set up an actual date. We need to move on to the next step so I can figure out if I'm interested in the real deal or just the idea of Owen.

My phone pings on the dot with a notification from the dating app. We're still communicating through that since it's required. We found out early on that we weren't allowed to enter numbers into the chat. Their algorithm even looks for numbers spelled out and blocks the text if it detects you're circumventing the system. We're supposed to receive approval after our fifth qualified exchange, and I'm more anxious each time we talk, counting down conversations.

Owen: Hey, beautiful. Is this a good time?

Shoot. I'm immediately disappointed when no message pops up telling us we can send pictures. I'd like to know whether we're physically compatible, because like it or not, it's important. But I shake my frustration off for now, not wanting the sour mood.

> Poppy: It is. Chilling on the couch with a glass of wine. How about you?
>
> Owen: I'm enjoying my wine in bed. Would you like to join me?
>
> Poppy: Sure. You can tell me about your weekend while I get comfortable.

Crap. I shouldn't have suggested that. Now he'll ask how mine was. That was stupid. I go to the bedroom and am almost situated when I hear his reply chime in.

> Owen: You inspired me to catch up with a friend. How did your visit go?
>
> Poppy: It was good. Really good, actually. I was sad when it came to an end.
>
> Owen: Same. I'm glad you enjoyed yourself. Are you excited for your brother to come home?

That was easier than I thought, and even led to a topic I don't have to shy away from. It's weird, but I'm not as enthusiastic as I usually am when we chat, and it most definitely has something to do with another man I'd like to be talking to.

> Poppy: Yes! I can't believe he'll be here to stay. It's the best present ever. What are you doing for the holidays?
>
> Owen: I always go visit my mom.
>
> Poppy: Where does she live?
>
> Owen: Florida
>
> Poppy: I bet you're glad to escape the snow then. I'm jealous.
>
> Owen: Don't be. I'd rather be where you are.

That's a weird statement. He couldn't have meant he'd rather be with me. He probably means that he'd rather stay in Bozeman. His profile shows he lives within a certain distance, so he must be near here.

Poppy: Well, we're even then, because I'd choose the heat.

Owen: If you prefer the heat so much, do you think you'll ever move somewhere warmer?

Poppy: Funny, I was just thinking about that today. I would love to, but I don't think I could leave my family.

Owen: Didn't you say your best friend moved? What about where she is?

Wow. It's incredible how he remembers things we talk about. He really does pay attention, which shows he cares about this. He couldn't *be* any more perfect, unless he needs some major dental work or something. Shoot, they should put that question in the profiles. *'Do you have all your teeth and are they healthy?'* Or maybe, *'On a scale of 1-10, how would you rate your teeth?'*

Poppy: She's in San Diego, and that's where I was thinking about. But it was just a fleeting thought, nothing serious.

Owen: It's a nice place. Sun, salt, and sand. Is there anything better?

Poppy: Normally, people from Montana don't feel that way. I take it you've been?

Owen: Plenty of times. It's great.

Poppy: What about you? Would you ever move?

Owen: Well, I wouldn't choose Florida, I can tell you that. I hate the humidity. As for moving? Only time will tell, I guess.

Just then, a notification pops up. *'Congratulations! You and your match now qualify to level up. Your account will allow for numbers in the text and attachment capability with a qualifying membership. Upon payment, this match will be unlocked. Should you choose to forgo the membership, you are welcome to continue chatting at no additional charge. Happy dating!'*

What the heck? I didn't know you had to sign up for a membership. This is total crap.

> Owen: You saw the notification?
>
> Poppy: Yeah. What do you think?
>
> Owen: I think I like talking to you.
>
> Poppy: What does that mean? Do you want to exchange pictures? Or we could just pick a place to meet. Then it won't be flagged, and we could skip the membership. I didn't know about that.
>
> Owen: I didn't either, but maybe it's a sign we should leave things as is. I feel like we've gotten to know each other on a deeper level, and that might not have happened in person. What if we keep it like this for another week and reevaluate?

To say I'm disappointed would be an understatement of huge proportions. What if he's hesitating because he's four hundred pounds and can't get up? But then again, maybe he's right, and we're feeling this way *because* of this process.

Ugh. This sucks. I'm not sure if I should force the issue or give in and wait. The thing is, I can't move forward with Braden until I've let this go, and a few more days won't make a difference. I also don't want to push Owen away by putting my foot down since I like him so much.

> Poppy: We can do that. But after the week, I'd like to take the next step if we want to keep dating ;)
>
> Owen: Deal.

Sleep after our conversation was fitful at best, and this morning at work is about the worst Monday imaginable. The inner turmoil over this new thing with Braden, while letting things play out with Owen, is weighing on my mind.

When Matt walks into my office, he stops dead in his tracks.

"What's wrong?"

"Huh?" I glance up to gauge his meaning.

He appears concerned, not disgusted, which is what I'd expect given how unput-together I am.

"You look like you haven't slept in days, which means something happened since we last talked."

I plop my elbows down and drop my head into my hands, groaning. The sound of the door shutting brings it back up as Matt sits in one of the two chairs in front of my desk.

"Is this about Braden?"

"Him and Owen, the guy from the app."

"Have you met him in person yet?"

"No, and that's the problem. We got approval to exchange pictures last night, well, with the purchase of a membership, which is total bullshit. But anyway, he doesn't want to meet *or* send photos. He just wants to keep talking."

"He obviously has something to hide."

"That was my first thought, but then he said he feels like we've gotten to know each other more this way. I said I'd give it a week and then we take the next step or I'm out—more or less."

"More or less?"

"Well, I didn't say exactly that, but he got the point and agreed to my terms."

"Well, I told you once, but I'll say again. Be careful with what you tell him. He might have a reason for not wanting to show his face, and the last thing you want is some stalker figuring out who you are."

"He's not like that. It's no different than any other new relationship."

He leans forward, taking a more serious stance. "Except you've never laid eyes on him and have no idea who he is. Like I said, you used your real name, which is unique to begin with. You live in a fairly small town, and because you're a realtor, you're easy to find on the internet."

"Okay, you made your point. I still don't think he's like that." At the look he gives me, I concede. "But, fine, I'll be more careful."

"You said this was about Braden too. Why?"

I'll have to tread lightly since I know he doesn't like him. "He surprised me with a visit this weekend."

Matt's mouth drops open. "Here? To Bozeman? That's why I didn't hear a peep out of you."

"Yeah. He has a client in Big Sky, so he came for a meeting and stayed until yesterday."

"How convenient." His sarcastic tone is annoying.

"Listen, I know you don't like him, but I do. At least I'm starting to. A lot. And that's the problem. He wants more, and I'm not ready to give it to him."

"More as in… what exactly?" he asks suspiciously.

"As in exclusivity. Which means I'd have to cut things off with Owen, but I like him too."

"Fuck Poppy. How did you end up with one guy who's a potential stalker and another who basically is, since he showed up unannounced?"

"You can just go if you're going to be a dick about it."

He sighs in resignation. "I'm sorry. I'm not used to you being so stressed, and I don't like it. What does Cici say about it all?"

"I can't talk to her about it. She sees Braden all the time, and I don't want her to say anything to him. Plus, if she told Eli, it would make its way back to Braden since they're such good friends." I look at him guiltily. "That's why I'm talking to you."

He scoffs. "So I'm your only option, basically."

I nod, and he shakes his head.

"It sounds to me like a week from today you'll have your answer. Either Owen will agree to meet, or you ditch his ass."

"But what if we do and he ends up being perfect?"

"That's easy. He's here, and Braden's not, so that's a no-brainer in my book."

"Ugh." I drop my head in my hands again and groan. This is why I've hardly ever dated. It better be worth it.

My head pops up, realizing how self-absorbed I've been. "Oh my God, speaking of… What's going on with your love life? You were dating a girl named Stacey, right? How's that going?"

"It's over. She turned psycho. Started calling the office when I wouldn't pick up the phone, and after she showed up last week when I was with clients, I told her we were done and had to block her number."

"Geez. That's intense."

"Yeah, you never know someone until you do. But it's fine. I'm so busy with work these days, I don't have time to date. How's business for you?"

"It's not slowing down, that's for sure. But that's good. Make it while you can and save it for when you don't, right?"

"No doubt. Speaking of work, I was coming in to find out if you're listing that house we talked about last week. I may have some clients who are interested."

"Trying to. I'll keep you posted. I'll tell the owners you've got someone, and maybe they'll speed things up. Thanks for thinking of it."

"Of course. Hey, sorry about being a jerk earlier. I just worry about you."

"I know. Thanks, Matt."

After he leaves, my body slumps in defeat. I'm not sure if I feel any better than before, but Matt's right. The bottom line is, I'll have my answer soon.

Hopefully.

Braden

The situation with Owen is more complicated than it's worth, except that I learn so damn much about her when she's talking to him. But after another night of shitty sleep, stressing about it, I'm considering my options.

She basically gave me an ultimatum, so I've got one week left. I might as well use the time I have before ending it. No harm, no foul, and in the meantime, I'll enjoy every extra minute of her.

Speaking of, I'm missing the hell out of my little mouse. Waking up without her in my arms this morning didn't help. Spending the weekend together pretty much did me in. I'm already obsessed with the woman, and if I could have her in my bed every night, I would.

> Braden: Hey, Mouse. How's the day treating you?

> Poppy: Wow, a midday text.

> Braden: Part of that wanting more thing I mentioned.

> Poppy: Riiight. Anyway, today is rough. Super tired.

> Braden: I must have worn you out this weekend ;)

> Poppy: That you did. How about you?

> Braden: Not worn out enough. I missed you last night.

> Poppy: That's not what I meant. How's your day going?

> Braden: It's a Monday for sure. A busy one since I was out Thursday and Friday.

> Poppy: I bet. I should let you go then.

I'd love to keep her talking, but Warren just walked in and is staring at me with raised brows. He can tell I've been off my game, which is unlike me. So, it's probably a good idea to finish the conversation anyway.

> Braden: Looking forward to reading tonight. Hope your day goes better.

> Poppy: Talk to you later.

Warren pounces as soon as I put my phone down.

"Dude, what's up with you? You've been dragging, and we have a lot of shit to get through. Are you seriously letting a woman interfere with work?"

I narrow my eyes at him. "Hardly. I just sent a quick text saying hi. It's not a big deal."

"The big deal is you took two days off last week for the first time in years for this gal. You should be grinding to catch up. Instead, you're sitting here, texting a woman with stars in your eyes."

"It was two minutes. Chill the fuck out. I got shit done from the plane on the way *to a meeting*. I'm fine. Plus, isn't that what I pay you for? Quit your bitching and tell me where we're at on the Waymore case."

We talk shop for a bit before he circles back to my distraction.

"So tell me about this Poppy chick. You've never been this into a woman. Is it serious?"

"I don't know how it can be, considering she lives so damn far away."

"Then what gives? What's your end game?"

"I've been asking myself the same thing. So has she, in fact. Unfortunately, I have no idea, but I know I'm not giving up."

"I wouldn't expect otherwise from Braden the Butcher. You wouldn't move there, would you? You'd lose your partnership and have to start over with another firm."

"I don't think we're anywhere close to that step—regardless of what I'd like. But fuck man." I run my hand through my hair. "I've considered it. That's how fucked in the head I am over this chick. She's got me by the balls, and she doesn't even know it."

"Well, holy fucking shit. Never thought I'd see the day."

"Yeah, you and everyone else."

The afternoon went better after the conversation with Warren, which prompted me to pull my head out of my ass. New rule: focus on the job during the day—Poppy at night. I'll need to practice work-woman balance.

By Wednesday, work is back to normal, and I've had two great nights talking to Poppy, both as Owen and Braden. I feel like I've known her for years by now. We've also had more fun times reading together, meaning my dick is as satisfied as it can be without the real thing.

The only problem is she's all I can think about, and the desire to have her in the flesh again is driving me insane. So much in fact that I'm sitting at my desk booking another ticket to Bozeman.

It's only one day away from the office, and I'll work on the plane and layover to keep up. Warren's overreacting. I'm the best damn divorce attorney they have, and three days off won't change that. I think what's really bothering him is that he lost the other half of his tag team.

Speak of the devil. "Hey, you up for the club on Saturday? I'm hoping if I convince you to join me for a round, you'll come to your senses," Warren says as he plops into a chair.

I sigh exaggeratedly. "You're not getting it, man. I'm trying to be in a relationship."

"You're trying, but is she on board?"

"Sort of. It's complicated…. Anyway, I'm heading back to Bozeman this weekend, so I'll be out Friday. I'll come in for a couple of hours in the morning and have shit laid out for you. I'll meet with Marlow while I'm there, so let me know if you need anything else from him."

"Fuck man. You're seriously into this girl."

"I thought I was clear on that last time we talked about this?"

"Damn. I might be in denial. Sex is going to be so boring now." He shakes his head in indignation, causing me to laugh.

"I'm sure you'll survive. You could always try this new dating app with no pictures I heard about?" *That would cover one of my tracks.*

His face fills with horror. "Hell to the no. First of all, I don't need an app to hook up, and secondly, what the fuck good is it if you can't window shop? Is that some sick bastard's idea of a surprise in the sheets or what?"

It was worth a shot. "Must be. Hey, thanks for your help this week. And every week. I appreciate it."

"Okaaay… I suppose Poppy's responsible for this… nicer version of you. Just be careful not to lose your edge. I'd hate for people to think the Butcher has gone soft."

"Not a chance. Here. Bring this over to Neil's desk. He's taking this one."

"Why are you throwing a case to that buffoon? I can toe the line while you're out."

"I know you can, but the client's an asshole, and he's the one who cheated on his wife. Justin gave me the intel this morning. I'm glad we didn't waste a lot of time on it."

"Ah. I'll drop it off then."

"Thanks."

Warren shuts the door, and I sigh in relief. I hate it when my time is wasted on lying pieces of shit. The irony is, I'm a lying piece of shit at the moment. I just hope my good intentions counter the bad.

My phone pings with an incoming text, followed by three more before I have a chance to grab it. What the hell? Quickly wrapping up the email I'm working on, I reach for it to see what the emergency is.

> Eli: Need a guys' night. Babies are more full-time than my job. Who's in for Saturday?
>
> Sebastian: You're telling me. I'm in.
>
> Jackson: In.
>
> Justin: Count me in.
>
> Braden: I'll be in Bozeman. Catch you next time.
>
> Jackson: I thought that was last weekend…
>
> Braden: It was. I'm going back.
>
> Jackson: Oh fuck, welcome to the club, man.
>
> Braden: What club?
>
> Sebastian: The pussy whipped one.
>
> Eli: Thanks for warning me, fucker. I better not be doing damage control.
>
> Justin: Did you tell her you're coming this time?
>
> Braden: That would ruin the surprise.
>
> Justin: Call me when you're arrested for stalking, and I'll see what I can do to bail you out.
>
> Braden: You're all a bunch of assholes.

Eli: Dinner next week. You can fill us in.

Braden: Decide which day on Saturday and let me know.

That should be a fun dinner—about as fun as a trip to the dentist.

The following two days drag on as I impatiently wait to be with Poppy again. The evenings have been my saving grace when I can talk with her. I've refrained from texting her during the day because once I start, my hand itches to grab my phone the rest of the afternoon, as experienced on Monday.

The plane is rolling into the gate Friday evening when I text her.

Braden: Happy Friday. Any plans tonight?

Poppy: Just dinner with Matt. Probably won't be out too late if you want to read after?

Braden: Are you sure that's what you're asking for, Mouse? Don't be shy.

Poppy: I'm open to suggestions.

Braden: I have plenty. So where are you having dinner? Anywhere I've been?

Poppy: Urban Kitchen, and not unless you have a secret life I'm unaware of.

Braden: I'll have to give it a try.

Poppy: Next time you're in town?

Braden: It's a date. Enjoy your dinner. I'm looking forward to suggesting things later.

Poppy: LOL me too…

That went exactly as planned. The timing is perfect for picking up the rental car and heading that way. I've been wanting to meet this Matt guy anyway. Make sure he's not after my girl while I'm not around. If he isn't, he's an idiot, and if he is? He'll understand she's mine by the end of the night.

18

OLD NEWS

Poppy

"WHAT'S GOOD HERE?" MATT asks as he stares down at the menu.

"Everything. Let's hurry and order. I'm starving."

He laughs, but quickly stops when his gaze moves behind me in confusion. "What the fuck is he doing here?"

I turn to look and am shocked to see Braden striding toward our table, looking like he stepped off the cover of GQ. Damn, the man is gorgeous. Like, serious eye candy. From the suit to the sideburns, to the body underneath, that I'm now familiar with… it doesn't get any better.

"Did you know he was coming?" Matt asks, interrupting my thoughts from going the wrong direction in the presence of company.

"No," I insist, still in disbelief.

When he makes it over and swoops in for a hug, there's no denying he's really here, especially as he cups my cheek and kisses me. That's when it strikes—I'm utterly smitten. Straight up, I'm hooked on this man who came in like a hurricane, turning my world upside down.

I've been falling harder every day, and each night becomes more difficult to deny the pull he has on me. I'm sad when our calls end, immediately anticipating the next one. I kept wishing he'd text me during the day, like on Monday, but he didn't.

When I asked him why, his answer fueled my growing infatuation. He said that once he started, it's all he wanted to do and couldn't focus on work—that it was hard enough concentrating while thinking about me all day.

"Surprise, Mouse," he says as he pulls away and straightens to his full height.

He then turns his attention to my companion. "Matt, I don't think we've been properly introduced. I'm Braden, Poppy's boyfriend."

The choking sound to escape my mouth is unintended and met with a "what the fuck?" look from Matt, along with a smirk from Braden.

Matt quickly recovers and shakes Braden's outstretched hand. "Funny, Poppy forgot to tell me you were official. Congratulations."

"Well… we're testing the waters. It's not—"

"It's a work in progress." Braden cuts me off. "One weekend at a time. Right, Mouse?" He winks at me.

Oh my God. Is this really happening? I'm not sure what to say. Thankfully, he has enough to say for both of us.

"Sorry to barge in on your dinner, but I thought it was a great opportunity to meet one of Poppy's friends, since we didn't have a chance to talk at the wedding. Do you mind if I join you guys?"

"Take a seat. We haven't ordered yet, so you came at the right time. I'll go tell the waiter we have an addition," Matt offers, subtly giving us a moment to ourselves.

When he's out of earshot, I turn to Braden. "What are you doing here? Did you have another meeting?"

"No. I came for you. This week's been hell without you."

"Braden," I warn. I may feel the same, but we shouldn't say things like that.

"Full transparency, Poppy. I'm all-in. I'll be here every weekend until you believe me—until you're the one introducing me as your boyfriend."

My heart flutters at his declaration, and I lose the ability to breathe. I'm ready to jump into his lap and give him anything he asks for.

Luckily, Matt returns before that happens, taking away the opportunity to say something I'm not ready for.

"All right, we're all set. I grabbed another menu," he says, handing it to Braden.

"Thanks. So what's good here?" Braden asks as if it's the most normal thing in the world for him to be here, while I'm teetering on the edge of a breakdown.

"I was just asking Poppy the same thing," Matt states.

They look up to meet my blank stare as I'm still in a stupor.

"Poppy? You okay?" Braden asks gently as he places his hand on mine and squeezes, bringing me back to the present.

With a huff, I reply, "Yeah, sorry. I'm just shocked you're here. Um, everything is good. My favorite is the meatballs."

"Poppy loves her balls."

"Matt!" I screech.

Braden's eyes narrow while Matt laughs.

"What? You do. You order them wherever we go."

"He obviously means meatballs, not balls, balls," I explain to Braden.

"I'd hoped that was the case, considering mine are the only balls you'll be having from now on," Braden says, causing Matt to raise his brows at me.

My elbow hits the table, head falling into my hand, and I groan. "Oh my God."

This is going to be the longest meal in history.

"Have you had enough time to view the menu?" The waiter appears like an angel to save me from a slow and torturous death.

"Yes!" I say enthusiastically, popping my head up. "Thank you, I'll start."

When the orders are placed and the waiter leaves to grab our drinks, I've mainly calmed down, praying the rest of dinner goes less embarrassingly.

"Poppy tells me you have business here. It must be hard to travel so far for work all the time," Matt asks Braden.

"I don't usually. And I'm not here for work this weekend, just Poppy. Although we are having lunch with my client, Jim, tomorrow." Braden tilts his head sheepishly. "If that's okay with you?"

I smile in response. "I'd love to."

He's bringing me to meet one of his clients, which seems like something you'd take your girlfriend to, but… I'm not. Except I'm reconsidering my refusal on the issue. If this is really happening, maybe I'm wasting my time with Owen. If only I could combine the two into one person, I'd have the perfect man.

His face lights up. "I'm glad. I'm excited for you to meet him. Hopefully I'm not interfering with any of your plans for the weekend."

"Nope, just breakfast at my parents on Sunday. You could go with me," I suggest shyly.

"I'd like that." His smile makes the butterflies in my belly go wild.

And suddenly, I'm done holding back. I'm not sure how to handle the distance issue or what to do about Owen, but I'm ready to commit. I want more with Braden and I'm willing to risk a broken heart to give us a chance.

After staring at him for a beat too long, I turn my head, my eyes colliding with Matt, who's looking at me knowingly. No doubt he sees right through me and can already tell what I've been denying for days. But if Matt knows, does that mean Braden does too?

Someone's phone rings, and both Matt and Braden reach for their pockets. Braden's is lit up as he pulls it out, but after glancing at the screen, he silences it, placing it on the table.

"Sorry. That was my mom. I'll call her back later."

"She lives in Florida, huh?" Matt says more as a statement than a question. He nods toward the phone. "I recognized the area code. I grew up there. Is that where you're from?" he asks with interest.

Braden appears stunned. "Uh…" he starts, then clears his throat and quickly collects himself. "No. She moved there after getting married."

Wait a minute… Owen's mom lives in Florida. That's weird. Too weird. What are the chances that both the men I'm… *dating*… have moms that live in Florida? They also both have dads who are out of the picture. Oh fuck. Didn't Owen say he worked in law the second night we talked? Fuck, fuck, fuck. No. I'm spiraling. These are just coincidences, I'm sure.

I take a sip of my wine while the guys talk about Florida. I'm zeroing in on Braden's responses, listening for anything that sounds like Owen. But where Owen said he hates the humidity, Braden doesn't mind it. Shit, Braden's going to his mom's for Christmas… just like Owen.

What does this mean? So they have similarities. Wait… Owen did say he was busy this weekend after we had the most amazing week of conversations. Is that because… Owen is Braden? Is Braden Owen? Am I an idiot for not noticing any red flags until now? This can't be happening. Okay, deep breath. Stay calm. Act cool.

But the more I listen to Matt and Braden speak, the more convinced I become. Things slowly click into place, and the bits and pieces I've learned about each one begin to overlap.

I'm trying to slow my heart rate and focus on breathing when an idea hits me. If Braden is Owen, then he'll have the app, and if I message him, we'll see it come through. Okay, I've got this.

"Sorry, guys. I forgot to respond to a client this afternoon. I'll go take care of it and be right back." I say while grabbing my phone from my purse.

Getting up, I quickly head to the bathroom and text Cici, hoping this works.

> Poppy: Hey, how's life treating you these days? Is Abby still behaving? I'm having dinner with Matt, and he wanted me to tell you hi.

That should prompt a quick response. But I need to be at the table when it comes through.

"I'm back," I pant out aggressively after rushing through the restaurant, relieved I made it before anything came through.

"Did you get it taken care of?" Braden asks as my phone dings, giving me pause from the slight guilt at my deception. But if I'm right, guilt will be the least of my emotions.

I look at my phone while answering. "Shoot. Yeah, but now they have another question. Keep talking, and I'll wrap this up."

I quickly open the dating app, type out a message, and hit send. Taking a deep breath as my heart pounds, I wait for the answer I'm afraid of. Dread fills my chest as soon as Braden's phone pings with a notification.

I feel like the ground has swallowed me whole, and everything I thought I knew comes crashing down.

I was played.

How often was I warned that all men were the same, yet I fell into the trap? I can't believe I was so stupid—that I was ready to tell Braden I wanted to give this a try and be exclusive.

Braden looks down. When he sees the message, his confusion is evident until realization dawns, and shock registers. A second later, his gaze meets mine.

"Poppy, wait—" he starts, as a wave of anger hits me.

"Save it. I don't want to hear anything you have to say."

"Please. Give me a chance to explain."

"Oh, I think you've had plenty of chances. I can't believe you played me like that. What? Were you hoping to learn enough information to stay in my pants?"

"What's going on?" Matt asks, clearly concerned.

"Matt, meet Owen. Because, in case you missed the memo, Braden *is* Owen."

"What the fuck?" The anger radiating from Matt rivals mine.

"My only intention was to get to know each other."

"Is that what we've been doing, or has everything been lies?" I throw my napkin down on the table. "You know what, I don't care. I'm done with this. I'm done with you. You and your alter ego can go fuck yourselves. I'm out of here."

I grab my purse, jump up, and scramble out of the restaurant as fast as humanly possible. From behind, I hear Matt tell Braden not to go after me. Thank God he stopped him. I can't deal with any more bullshit at the moment, and I certainly can't trust a thing he says.

Braden

"It's not what you think," I tell Matt as soon as she's gone. I tried following, but he stopped me, and frankly, I don't blame him.

"Yeah, I'm pretty sure it is. It sounds like you've been playing her, making her believe you're someone you're not, and you got caught."

"I wasn't trying to play her. Everything Owen said is true. I didn't feed her any bullshit. It was all real. I didn't lie to her."

He scoffs. "I'd say posing as a fake person is a lie in itself, wouldn't you agree?"

"Fuck. I didn't want her to find out like this."

"You mean you didn't want her to find out at all."

"It was the only way I could think of to get her to talk to me. I liked her. She couldn't stand me. But then, when she finally started talking to *me*, as in Braden, I didn't know what to do about Owen."

"A decent person would've dropped the charade—you didn't, and now you're paying the price. The best thing you can do from here is leave her alone." Matt stands, throws twenty dollars on the table, and walks away without another word.

How did this night go downhill so fast? I knew it would be an issue when Matt announced my mom was from Florida. I should've confessed right then and there. What was I thinking?

With no reason to be here, I take my meal to go and book the nearest hotel for the weekend. My original plan was to ask Poppy if she wanted me to stay with her, but that's out of the question after this fiasco.

Between lunch tomorrow with Jim and my flight on Sunday, I'm not sure what my next move will be. I don't know where she lives, so I can't knock on her door and beg for forgiveness. I'm certain she won't answer my call or respond to a message, but I have to do something to make her understand.

I barrage her with texts, one after another, reassuring her that nothing I said was a lie, trying to explain that my intention wasn't to deceive her. As expected, I received nothing in return. For all I know, they might not even getting through. She could have me blocked.

I'm devastated, and I have no one to blame but myself. Matt's right, I'm paying the price for my deceitfulness. I'm just like my father. I didn't cheat on her, but I may as well have with how badly I've hurt her. Finally, I give up and go to bed, knowing I can't do anything more tonight. Tomorrow's a new day, and I'll start fresh.

When I wake up the next morning, though, I'm still completely fucked in the head. I have no idea where to go from here. After hitting the hotel gym for a couple of hours, I've still not come up with a solution, and it's time for lunch with Jim. Hopefully, he'll have some advice for me.

"Well, that's the sorriest face I've seen in a while. Since your girl's not with you, I'm assuming it has something to do with that. Take a seat, son. Tell me what happened," Jim says before my butt hits the chair. He was already here and saw me approaching, looking like death warmed over.

For the next half hour, I spill everything. I've puked my whole life story out by the time I'm done. From childhood, to my ex-almost-fiancée, my aversion to relationships, to the shit show of a mess I'm in with Poppy—all of it.

"Braden, if anyone needs a drink right now, it would be you." He raises his hand to signal the waiter and orders two old-fashioneds.

"I don't know what to do. I like this girl—a lot. She came out of nowhere, and I'm ready to tie her to me any way I can. I fucked up."

"You sure did. That's because you're human, and humans fuck up. You're not the first, and you won't be the last. You just need to decide how you're gonna fix it."

"That might not be possible."

"I heard somewhere they call you the Butcher. I would think if a butcher excelled at cutting something up, he could certainly put it back together. So figure out how to do that."

"I got nothing. If you have a suggestion, I'm open to anything."

"Have you tried knocking on her door yet?"

"I don't have her address."

"I know you've got private investigators working for you. Seems like a no-brainer to me."

He has a point, however…

"I'm not sure how much more I should dive into her life after using Owen to find out everything I could about her. Don't you think it would piss her off even more?"

"What about those friends you share? Can't you explain the situation and ask for it?"

I laugh. "I'm betting our mutual friend won't be on my side."

"I'd say if you're sincere and you tell them how you feel, you might be surprised."

I shrug, figuring nothing can make it worse at this point. "I guess it's worth a shot."

"Anything is worth a shot right now, wouldn't you agree?" he says, raising his hand to signal another round.

"Yeah."

"So, you get her address, go to her house, and beg her to listen to you for five minutes."

"You think groveling will be enough?" I ask, hopefulness filling my lungs.

"Nope," he says matter-of-factly.

I deflate.

"But it's a start."

By the time lunch is over, four hours later, I'm two sheets to the wind and not fit to talk to either Eli or Cici. Instead, I go back to the hotel room and pass the fuck out.

The next morning, I have a slight headache as I struggle to remember everything we discussed yesterday afternoon. As I try to recall the evening before, losing count of how many old-fashioneds we drank, at least one thing stands out. Not to be deterred from my goal, I tuck my tail between my legs and dial up Eli.

"Well, look who's calling. Surprised I'm hearing from you while you're with Poppy."

"Yeah… about that. We had a misunderstanding."

"You don't say…. This wouldn't have anything to do with the fact you went onto the same dating app she was on, would it?"

I groan. "Did she already call Cici?"

"No. But it doesn't take a genius to figure it out when I ran into Warren last night. Funny, but when I asked him about it, he said it was the craziest shit he'd ever heard of and that he wouldn't be caught dead on a site like that."

I groan into the phone. That's two for two. I'm crap at this whole deception thing… obviously. Apparently, I'm not like my dad, since he was pretty damn good at it.

"Look, I feel like a broken record, but I wasn't doing it maliciously. I just wanted to get to know her. I like her and she wouldn't give me the time of day, so that was my solution. I didn't mean for it to blow up like this."

"I can't imagine you did. I'm sure we'll hear all about it on Wednesday, so why are you calling now?"

"I was hoping you could help me out. I need to talk to her and explain. I can't just give up."

"Where do I fit in?"

"Can you ask Cici for her address. And her parents' address. I can easily have Justin find it, but I'm trying to go about it the right way."

He chuckles. "Isn't it a little late for that?"

"Listen, I'm beating myself up enough. I don't need it from you too. Are you willing to help me or not? If Cici hasn't heard yet, you might want to do it *before* she hates me."

"You sound like shit, so you're obviously wrecked. I'll at least give it my best effort."

Instead of staring at my phone for the next however long it takes, I decide to jump in the shower. I'm toweling off, stepping out of the bathroom, when I receive a notification from an incoming text. Holy shit—he fucking did it. I'm not sure how he managed to drag the information from Cici, but I'm hella glad he succeeded.

With a clear mission, I dress quickly, with more fervor than I've had since Poppy walked out of the restaurant, ready to make the first attempt at getting her back.

Thirty minutes later, I realize I'm probably making the dumbest move of my life by knocking on her parents' door. This is *not* how I wanted to meet them, but I have no other choice with my flight taking off in a couple of hours.

The door opens to the last person I expected. Matt. What the fuck? I'm out of the picture, and he decides to swoop in to pick up the pieces?

"What are you doing here?" he asks, venom pouring from his mouth.

Anger clouds my vision as I respond. "I could ask you the same thing?"

"I was invited—unlike you. So you can turn right around and leave. Poppy wants nothing to do with you."

"If that's the case, she can tell me herself. I'm not leaving until I see her."

"I don't think you're in any position to make demands. You're old news as far as I'm concerned."

He starts to shut the door in my face, but I stick my foot out to stop it.

"Poppy! It's Braden. Please, just give me five minutes." I'm yelling as Matt shoots daggers.

I open my mouth to shout again when Poppy's voice sounds.

"What is going on?" she hisses, on her way to the door. "How did you know where to find me?"

"Eli gave me the address. Look, just hear me out. I'm begging," I plead.

"You don't have to, Poppy. I'll get rid of him if you want." Matt tells her, making me want to punch him in the face.

"How about you stay out of it. Poppy can handle this herself."

"It's okay, Matt, I'll take it from here. Thanks, though," she says, pulling the door open.

"Okay." He steps back and turns into the house. "Come get me if you need my help," he adds, walking away.

She smiles at him, walks outside, and shuts the door behind her, barely looking me in the eye. "Nothing you can say will change my mind at this point, and I certainly have nothing to say to you."

I back up to give her space. Her body language clearly states she doesn't want me here.

"I have so much to tell you, but I'll start with, I'm sorry. I fucked up, I know that. It was a dick move." I shake my head in frustration. "When I heard you went on a dating app, I went crazy. I wanted more time with you, but your opinion of me was less than stellar, and I thought that was a good way to do it. Obviously, it wasn't. I know that now."

"Yeah." She scoffs. "You mean, now that I'm on to you?"

"No. I knew it needed to stop, but I couldn't figure out how."

"Telling me the truth didn't occur to you?" Her arms cross over her chest while cocking her hip.

My head drops, and I blow the air from my lungs. This isn't going well. "It did. It's just…. Fuck. I'm not doing a good job at explaining."

"It doesn't matter because it's too late for that."

"Can I do anything?"

"You can leave."

She's right, nothing will change her mind at the moment, and the last thing I want to do is make it worse. "Okay, I'll go. For now."

"How about for good. And don't bother texting or calling. We're done. What's interesting is that you're so against cheating and lying, yet you just spent weeks lying your ass off." Her parting words hit their mark before she goes inside and slams the door in my face.

19

MOVING ON

Poppy

" **I** 'M SORRY, POPPY. I DIDN'T HAVE THE WHOLE STORY WHEN ELI asked for your address. I wouldn't have given it to him, I swear," Cici says over the phone after I've filled her in on everything.

"Braden would have found it one way or another, I'm sure."

"True. This sucks. I can't believe he did that."

"Tell me about it. But what's worse? That he did it, or that I was dumb enough to fall for it? I'm so stupid," I whine.

"You are not. How could you have known?"

"There were signs. I should've picked up on the similarities or noticed how they talked the same. Instead, I was oblivious while chatting with them each night. Dammit… I'm just so mad at myself. I can't believe I almost committed to someone who lied so easily."

"You're not the first and won't be the last to be catfished. It's not your fault. He fooled me too. First, he needed your number because he said you left something at his house, then he asked Eli about the dating app. I should've figured out right then that something was up. I'm partly responsible."

"If it's not my fault, then it's definitely not yours, so don't beat yourself up. That's reserved for Braden."

"You're telling me. Next time he's here, I'll give him a piece of my mind."

"Don't waste your breath—it won't make a difference. And anyway, I'm moving on. I just wish I hadn't started liking him so much. It feels like we broke up, but we weren't even together. Ugh, it's so frustrating. I'm all over the place—one minute, I'm pissed, the next minute I'm sad, and every now and then, I want to call him up and forgive him. And that just proves how stupid I am."

"Stop saying that. He was the first guy you were with, which made him special, and you were falling for him."

"I'm pretty sure I fell off the cliff, but rather than soar, I sank straight to the bottom."

"Oh, Poppy, I'm so sorry. You'll get through this, especially with the holidays around the corner and your brother coming home. You'll be fine in no time—just hang in there."

"Thanks, Cici. But let's change the subject. How's Abby doing? And what about Lily and Sami?"

The following twenty minutes fly by as Cici tells me how awesome it's been to have Lily and Sami next door. They're together all the time with their new babies. And while I love hearing how great everything is and how happy they are, it's another reminder I'm back where I started and nowhere closer to finding my Mr. Forever and starting a family. This sucks.

Four days later, I'm in worse shape than before. Probably because of the letter I got today from Braden. He must've figured out I've blocked him and resorted to snail mail. It went straight into my junk drawer. Since my brother's arriving tonight, I can't focus on the Braden situation. I'm already nervous about concealing my crappy mood, and reading that won't help.

He arrives at six after flying for thirty hours, so he'll probably be exhausted, but that won't stop us from celebrating his arrival with dinner at my parents'. He'll stay with them until he figures out where to live permanently, whether he buys something or rents. I would've offered to let him crash at my place, but they have way more room than I do.

"Grayson gets in today, right?" Matt asks as he pops into my office and leans his hip against the desk.

"Yes, I'm so excited." I smile genuinely for the first time in almost a week. "He hasn't been here since last Christmas, and won't be leaving this time. It's weird—in a good way."

"I'm sure it'll be nice to have him back. Not to mention a great distraction. Are you feeling any better?" He crosses his arms, concern written in his features.

"No, not really. I'm so used to talking to them every night. And now, I go home, read a book—something I did with Braden—and realize how alone I am again. It's so stupid since neither of them were even here." I groan. "I need to stop saying *them*. It was only ever Braden. The whole thing sucks. And the worst part is that I miss him."

"That's normal. Feelings don't go away overnight, no matter the circumstances. Don't be so hard on yourself. It'll fade, and having your brother around should make it easier."

"Yeah, I hope so. Speaking of, I was hoping the three of us could go for dinner and drinks this weekend. Are you free?"

"Definitely. I've got to meet this brother I've heard so much about."

My second genuine smile appears as we make a plan before getting back to work.

Leaving a few hours later, I drive to Mom and Dad's house so we can pick up Grayson together. At the airport, I hold a sign that says, "*Welcome home, Grayson... For good*," as he exits the doors. He hugs my parents enthusiastically, then picks me up and swings me around as we embrace.

I expected him to have multiple bags full to the brim from seven years away, but he only has his army-assigned duffel filled with clothes, as if returning from a vacation.

Our family dinner didn't last long. Grayson was exhausted and could barely function due to the flight and time change. So, shortly after we ate, I told him to rest so we could go out on Saturday to catch up, and then quickly took my leave.

Now that we're older and somewhat on the same level, it's a different relationship than when he left. I've matured, and we seem to relate better. I'm excited to become more like friends than siblings *if* he doesn't go crazy on the big brother role by interfering in my dating life. Although I may need some intervention since my intuition seems to be lacking.

As I lay in bed replaying the night, I realize how nice it was to stop thinking about Braden for a few hours. I managed to appear normal instead of the blubbering mess I've been for the past week. From having missed Grayson so much, the excitement of him being home made it easy.

But now that I'm alone again, the distraction is gone. I've started sulking in the evenings around the time I used to text or read with Braden for *"Book Club."* It sucks to realize how much I looked forward to it now that it's gone. And boy, is it hitting me hard.

I've tried to pass the time by calling Cici, but she should only have to endure so much of my misery, so I've been trying not to overdo the whole *woe is me* thing. Her telling me about the guy's night out midweek and what bad shape Braden is in didn't help. Cici thought it would make me feel better to know how miserable he was, but it made it worse to know he's as torn up as I am.

Unfortunately, it's another crying spree that finally lulls me to sleep.

By Saturday night, I'm still a mess after another letter arrived today, tossed in with the first one. Depending on how long he keeps this up, I may have to do something about them, but for now, I do my best to doll myself up and paste a big smile on before walking into the restaurant to meet Grayson and Matt.

"Hey, you. Are you feeling rested yet?" I ask Grayson as I reach the table and lean in for a hug. Matt isn't here yet.

"Yep. Sorry I didn't come by yesterday, but I'm glad I found something." Grayson spent the day car shopping and went to bed right after dinner, still jetlagged.

"No worries. What did you end up with?"

"The biggest truck I could find. I'm used to driving military vehicles, so a car wouldn't cut it."

"Well, I'm happy you got one then. I'm excited for you to meet Matt. I wish Cici was still here so you could meet her too, but you're a few months late."

"Is this Matt guy your boyfriend, or what?" He raises one eyebrow, making me laugh.

"He's just a friend, I swear. Why would I hide it if he *were* my boyfriend? It's not like I require your approval or anything."

He gives me a stern look. "Uh, think again. I'm still your older and wiser brother."

I roll my eyes. "In case you forgot, I'm an adult who dated plenty while you were gone." No need to tell him how I screwed that up.

"If any of them were serious, I'd have known and checked them out."

"Oh geez, you can't protect me forever."

"Says who?"

"Me."

It's his turn to roll his eyes, but before he makes a retort, Matt joins us.

"Hey," Matt says, approaching the table.

"Yay, you're here." I smile and rise to hug him.

Grayson also stands, and I introduce them while they shake hands. Matt welcomes him home as we take our seats. The waiter comes for our drink orders and then leaves us to visit.

"So is it true you and my sister are just friends?"

"Grayson!" I chastise.

Matt laughs and answers, "Yes. I did try to date Cici once, but Poppy and I were fast friends."

Grayson nods in acceptance.

"So you'll take his word for it but not mine," I admonish Grayson.

"Just making sure I'm not missing anything."

I roll my eyes for the second time tonight. "You're annoying."

He laughs. "And you're glad to have me back." He winks at me, then turns to Matt. "Poppy told me you two work together. How long have you been in real estate?"

"A little over a year now. The timing was right, and the market was in my favor, so it worked out. I'm loving it. How about you? What are your plans now that you're home?" Matt's a natural at conversing with people. It's one of the reasons he's so successful.

"I'm still throwing around a few ideas. Thankfully, I'm not in a rush. My first priority is to find someplace to live."

"Well, I know a realtor if you need one," Matt says conspiratorially.

I butt in. "Hey. Nice try—he's my brother." After scolding Matt teasingly, I turn to Grayson. "Are you looking to purchase or rent a house? You could always stay at Mom and Dad's until you figure out what you want to do. I'm sure they wouldn't mind."

Grayson scoffs. "I'd mind. I love being home, but not living at home. I'm too old for that. I'm ready to put some roots down."

"Can you afford to buy something?" I ask, surprised.

The waiter arrives with our drinks and takes our orders before Grayson answers.

"Poppy, I've been in the military for twelve years with no expenses whatsoever, no family, and no time to waste money on stupid shit. The only thing I've done with it is learn how to invest it and make more of it." Grayson smirks and swigs his beer.

"Oh, well, that's good," I say, stunned at the revelation that he's done so well for himself. I wasn't expecting him to have anything to his name after the military, but I obviously didn't give it much thought. "Let me know what you're thinking, and I'll see what's out there. Don't be surprised if it takes longer than it took to find your truck, though." I smirk back at him.

The rest of dinner goes better than expected. Matt and Grayson hit it off remarkably, almost making me feel like a third wheel. Grayson tells us about wanting to start a business with a few of his SEAL buddies, but he's not sure exactly what yet. He's got some great ideas, though, and the three of us have fun brainstorming.

All in all, dinner is a perfect distraction—until it isn't.

When I walk in my front door at the end of the night, I'm right back where I started the day he left. It may be the couple of drinks I had or just the long week, but either way, as soon as my head hits the pillow, the tears flow heavily.

Braden

It's been a long week, and I'm a fucking wreck. It feels like I'm trapped in an endless pursuit. I've texted, called, sent two letters, and I'm no closer to getting her back than the day I left. Short of stalking and showing up on her doorstep, I'm out of options. I feel like shit, I look like shit, and if it weren't for the fact that it's Monday, I'd smell like shit.

As it is, I'm freshly showered, shaved, and styled. I'm on autopilot these days, and the motions come naturally. My mind, however, is constantly fixated on the one thing I've managed to screw up completely. Never in my life have I fucked up this bad. And usually when I do, I can fix it.

It's one of those rare situations where I have no solution, and I've exhausted my brain trying to find one. It must show because as I walk toward my office, Warren glances up before following me inside and shutting the door.

He flops down in front of my desk. "I was hoping you'd be somewhat coherent after the weekend, but it's obviously intervention time. What's it gonna take to have you pull your head out of your ass and focus? You may have earned your partner status, but if you keep this up, you'll lose it just as fast."

"It's almost Christmas. Everyone's too busy preparing for the holidays to notice. I'll be fine." I wave my hand in the air, brushing him off. My job is the last thing I'm worried about right now.

"Well, you're not fine now, and we've got a lot of shit to do before you leave next week."

The trip to Florida for the holidays with my mom and stepfamily is weighing me down. It's the last thing I want to do while the situation with Poppy is unresolved, but I've already committed and can't cancel the one time of year I visit.

"Yeah, I know. I'll pull my shit together."

"You better, or I'll return your Christmas present," he says straight-faced.

I laugh, which feels foreign since it's been so long.

"I'm serious." He chuckles and makes his way to the door. "You love presents, so do what it takes to get back on track," he calls over his shoulder on the way out.

The minute the door shuts, an idea comes to mind, and I open Amazon to look when the sequel to the first book Poppy and I read together on the plane is due to be released. Dammit, not until mid-January. Well, it's better than months from now, and there's a chance she still won't be talking to me by then, which means it's worth a shot.

I looked up the author's website to contact her, and after sending an email that hopefully doesn't end up being discarded, I'm feeling more optimistic than I have in days. If I don't hear back within a week, I'll have Justin track her down. While this new strategy doesn't guarantee forgiveness, it might bring a smile to Poppy's face. That's the least I can do at this point.

With a plan in place, I was finally able to concentrate on work and make sure everything was in order for Warren while away. I sent two more letters to Poppy before flying to my mom's and another from her house. With a Florida postmark, I was worried it might stir the pot, but if I'm working on transparency, it is what it is.

Luckily, the author responded enthusiastically, and the wheels are set in motion for a special delivery in a couple more weeks. I'd love it to be sooner, but beggars can't be choosers. I'm just glad she had a soft spot for me and was willing to fulfill my request.

The holiday at my mom's went well and ended with promises to visit more. But with the distance and both of us settled in our own lives, the chances aren't likely. She hasn't come here since she remarried, and although I'm thrilled she's being taken care of, I'm not altogether fond of her husband.

Hence, I'm relieved to be back home, and about to meet up with the group for New Year's Eve. The only thing missing is Poppy, who hasn't left my mind for weeks now. It pains me to think she's spending New Year's with someone else, a date perhaps, which tears me apart to consider.

Every day, I wonder if she's read my letters while deep down knowing she hasn't. My plan is to send two more per week until my peace offering arrives and then decide what to do from there—most likely another trip to Bozeman. I've given her space, but she'll have to face me eventually.

Walking into the luxurious party at Sebastian and Eli's club, I'm ushered to the VIP area. The gang's all here, and I'm greeted with a glass of champagne from Jackson.

"Hey, buddy. Happy New Year. No date?" he asks, handing it over.

"Nope. The only woman I want is a thousand miles away."

"Still going, huh? I was wondering if you'd stick this out or if it was fleeting," Eli comments.

"It's not. I'll win her back somehow."

"You should sign up for a dating app under a fake profile and talk to her that way. Oh wait, that's what got you into this mess." Cici butts in, her words slightly slurred.

"Sorry. You let this girl loose for one night, and she goes crazy." Eli swings his arm over her shoulders and pulls her into his side.

Apparently, Cici's parents are watching Abby for the night. It's the first time the new mom has been out, and she won't last long by the looks of it. Lily and Sebastian stayed home, not ready to leave their newborn behind.

"Hey, I'm not the crazy one, he is." Cici points to me. "He's the one who bamboozled my friend into falling in love with him."

"What?" I ask her, shocked at the use of the word love. That wasn't even on the radar as far as I knew. It was hard enough trying to convince her to be exclusive.

"You heard me. You bamboozled her," Cici slurs again.

"You said she was falling in love with me. Did she say that?"

"What do you care?"

"Because dammit, I'm already *in love* with her, and I need to know if she might feel the same way."

Eyes go wide all around. "You love her?" Cici asks, tearing up.

"Oh boy, I think it's time to call it a night," Eli says.

Jackson and Mia chuckle, watching from the side.

"Nooo. It's not even midnight," she whines, not answering my question.

"How about you switch to water for a while then?" Eli suggests.

"Fine. Mia, let's go hunt down some water." Cici grabs Mia's arm and drags her away as Mia gives Eli a thumbs-up and a smile over her shoulder.

"What the hell, man, why haven't you said anything?" Jackson asks right away.

"Fuck… I didn't know until you did," I respond, dumbfounded.

The moment Cici said the word, the light came on, and I recognized it. It's an intense, desperate feeling like I can't breathe without her. I've been miserable since we split, simply going through the motions. But with this newfound clarity, I have a renewed sense of purpose. If it's possible she feels a sliver of what I do, then I won't stop until she's mine.

Eli looks at me sympathetically. "Well, shit. Have you tried anything after going to her parents' that day?"

"I've written her letters."

"That's it? You haven't sent her flowers?" Jackson asks, astonished.

"Or gifts?" adds Eli.

"No. I thought the letters would mean more. She hasn't let me explain yet," I say in defense, before hanging my head in shame. I should have sent flowers, dammit.

Jackson rests his hand on my shoulder, speaking plainly. "Braden, let's be honest, man. What's to explain? You fucked up. The best you can do is ask forgiveness for being a complete idiot."

I shrug his hand off. "Thanks for the vote of confidence, buddy. And you wonder why I haven't said anything."

Jackson goes to respond, but Eli interjects. "We feel for you, man, but you got yourself into this mess, and you'll dig yourself out. But you'd better do more than a few letters. What's your next move?"

I tell them my plan and add, "You're probably right about the flowers, though, I'll add some to the mix. I'm hoping she'll talk to me after the books arrive."

"Sounds weak, dude. Maybe another trip to Bozeman is in order," Jackson suggests.

"Yeah, I've thought of that. I think it's too soon. I'll gauge her reaction and then go."

"You sure it's wise to wait that long? It's already been a month, and the longer it goes, the harder it'll be to get her back. Jackson and I are proof of that," Eli chuckles, along with Jackson uttering, "No shit."

"Then you'll both understand that when I say I'll get her back, I will—no matter how hard or long it takes. But I need to do it right and then pray to God it isn't too late."

20

LAST CHANCE

Poppy

IT'S NEW YEAR'S DAY—TIME FOR RESOLUTIONS. I HAD FUN WITH Matt and Grayson, and I'm not even hungover, which is a great way to start.

The first thing I do is call Cici. I tried wishing her Happy New Year right after midnight, but she was three sheets to the wind and impossible to talk to. It sounded like she kept asking if I loved Braden, but with all the background noise, it was hard to tell, and it seemed too out of character for that to be the case.

Which means I'm projecting, hearing what I want instead of what's actually being said. I'm still despondent from the whole thing, and even last night, Braden was never far from my mind.

"Happy New Year!" I shout as soon as she picks up.

"Oh my God. Not so loud," she groans, making me laugh.

"Did someone have a little too much fun last night?"

"Definitely too much to drink. Not sure about the fun part. It's a little foggy."

I laugh some more. "Well, I'm glad you let loose. You haven't gone out since Abby was born. It probably felt good."

"At first it did, now it feels like shit."

"Well, buck up, buttercup, because we're doing resolutions. You with me?"

"Oh geez, let me suck down my coffee for this. You're way too peppy this morning. I'll just call you Peppy Poppy."

"Better than Pouty Poppy, which is what I've been."

"That's true. But you sound good all of a sudden. What's changed?"

"Nothing, but it's time to *make* changes by starting over. We're wiping the slate clean and pretending the past five months never happened. I'm creating a new dating profile."

She groans. "Oh, God no. You're making my hangover worse with those words alone. The pictureless thing sucks. Look where it got you—a broken heart."

"Yeah, still not talking about that. But you're right, it does suck, so I'm signing up for one with pictures. I'll just weed through the jerks looking for hookups."

"Well, that's a relief. Listen, I know you didn't want to, but have you read the letters yet?"

"No, and I'm not going to. Nothing can change the fact that he did what he did, so why indulge in the fantasy that he's someone he's not?"

"Maybe he's trying to be a better someone for you."

"Uh… where is this coming from? You've been anti-Braden from the start. You can't just turn on me."

"I'm not. But I love you, and you've been miserable. I'd hate for you to give up without giving it a chance."

"The last time I decided to give us a chance was when it blew up in my face, so I'm done with chances. He had plenty of opportunities to tell me the truth, but kept lying instead. Ugh. Obviously, I'm still upset over it, but the best way to move on is with someone else."

"Let's make a deal. If you don't find anyone you're interested in after three dates, you have to read the letters."

"Why are you suddenly pushing this?"

"Because maybe there's more to Braden than I originally gave him credit for."

"You definitely drank too much last night. It's fucking with your head."

"That, I won't deny."

After hanging up, I spent the afternoon creating my dating profile on the site we picked out together. I'm going in with eyes wide open, so I'm not as nervous this time. I'm actually feeling hopeful.

Well, except for the tiny problem that the man I want isn't on this app. I already found him on the last one, and I'm not sure anyone else will do.

The following week and one date later, I'm sitting in my office when Matt walks in carrying flowers.

"Another delivery for Poppy Whitaker. Where do you want it?"

I groan. "Put them on the bookshelf. Did a letter come with this one?"

"Yep. Here." He hands it to me after setting the flowers down. "Still haven't read any of them?"

"No," I answer, putting it in my purse to add to the others at home.

"And you have two more dates until you have to, right?"

Cici hasn't let me forget the condition I finally agreed to, which I made the mistake of telling Matt, who also likes to remind me. They've been conspiring together and driving me nuts.

"Yeah. The next is this weekend."

I'm crossing my fingers that this will be the one that changes everything, but my hope is fading after the first one turned out awful. I kept comparing him to Braden the entire time. Unfortunately, he didn't measure up.

"Good. I'd wish you luck, but I don't need to. It'll happen if it's meant to. I'll support you no matter what."

He's referring to whether I give Braden another chance. Matt was Braden's primary critic until Cici somehow swayed him. I'm still not sure what got *her* to cave, but something changed after New Year's.

"Thanks. We'll see, I guess."

I'm home from my second lackluster date on Friday night and let out a huge sigh of frustration as I close the front door. I'll search for the last one tomorrow, too tired to do it tonight, and cross my fingers it'll hit the mark.

Crawling into bed, I grab my Kindle as the familiar pang of sadness sets in. I miss reading with Braden and talking to him about the books—playing around during the spicy scenes. In fact, reading hasn't been enjoyable since. I'm frustrated that he's affected me so much, but despite common sense, the heart wants what it wants. Good thing the mind is stronger and winning the battle… barely.

The next day, the doorbell rings as I'm scrolling through prospects for my final date. It's Saturday, and for a moment, I panic, wondering if I forgot about plans with my brother or Matt, but quickly shake it off. I'm contemplating who it could be when Braden comes to mind. Suddenly, my heart is racing, but it plummets the second I open the door.

A delivery guy is here with a package.

"Poppy Whitaker?"

"That's me," I say with a sad smile.

"Sign here, please."

I do, and he hands me the box.

"Thank you, ma'am. Have a nice day."

"You, too," I say before shutting the door.

That's odd, it doesn't show who it's from. I open it and find two books inside, *First King To Fall* and *Last King Standing*, along with a notecard.

Poppy,

Enjoy these signed copies of books one and two of the Kings and Queens series. You're on my list for the next two releases. I don't know the whole story, but it sounds like you have a King begging you to be his Queen. I hope it works out the way it's meant to.

Best of Luck xoxo

I open the first book, *First King To Fall*, when it hits me—this is what Braden and I read on the plane when we met, and the other is the sequel he was so mad about having to wait for. Holy shit, it must've just come out.

I'm about to close it to look at the other one, when I notice an inscription on the inside flap:

I fell for you, and I'm on my knees begging for another chance.
Yours truly, Braden

My heart thunders as I open the sequel, *Last King Standing*, to another inscription.

You showed me how to stand… to go for what I want… and what I want is you.
Truly yours, Braden

Braden

The author sent an email today to say the books were delivered and to wish me luck, so why haven't I heard from Poppy? I expected a text at the very least. Has she truly written me off, or is this when I should fly there?

I'm losing my mind trying to decide my next move when a message from Cici shows up.

> Cici: Hey, if you're really in love with Poppy… then I have an idea. Come over for dinner at six, and if you can convince me, I'll help you out.

Well, I'll be damned. Ambiguous but promising. Six o'clock can't come soon enough.

"All right, Romeo, lay it on me. I want to hear your side from beginning to end, and don't leave anything out. If I'm going to do this, you have to prove you're sincere," Cici says from the couch across from me, her legs curled under her, while Eli sits on the floor with Abby.

When I arrived, Eli answered the door with Abby in his arms, handed me a drink, and said I'll need it if I'm joining forces with Cici. Man, was he right. She told me Poppy called her about the books, which prompted her to intervene. She said someone had to step in and help the two idiots sort this out.

I spend the next thirty minutes recounting everything, fessing up to why Poppy couldn't stand me at first, to when my feelings changed, to how I got myself into this mess. She shakes her head and sighs when I'm finished.

"You really screwed up."

I raise my beer in a mock toast. "Tell me something I don't know." Then I take a large swig.

"She signed up for another dating app."

I'm barely able to swallow without spitting all over their carpet. "WHAT? When?"

"New Year's Day. It was her solution to put this behind her, which happened to be her resolution. And before you go ballistic, she hasn't had any luck." Then, with raised brows, a tilt of her head, and crossed arms, she adds, "And you can thank *me* for making a deal with her that if she had no success after three dates, she'd have to read your letters."

A smile forms in response. "I could kiss you right now."

"Let's not," she deadpans.

"I second that," Eli pipes in.

"So has she?" I ask eagerly.

"No, she's insisting on her third date first."

"Seriously? She's still going on another, even after she got the books?"

"Hence, my intervention. So are you ready to hear my plan?"

"I'm all ears since nothing *I've* done has worked."

"You should set up a profile on her new dating app."

This time, I do spit my beer out. "You've got to be fucking kidding me."

She cracks up as Eli shakes his head.

"I told you you'd need that drink," he says.

She can't stop laughing as she speaks, "That's… the crazy… thing. I'm… not… kidding," she finishes while trying to catch her breath.

I can't even crack a smile at the suggestion after the hell I've gone through. I can't imagine where she's going with this.

"Start explaining then," I demand.

After she finally calms down, she tells me her insane idea. "What better way to fix the situation than the same way you fucked it up in the first place? Only this time, you'll make the profile as yourself and fill it out for real. With pictures, mind you. The key is that all your answers will point to Poppy specifically when it asks what you're looking for."

"I like where you're going with this, but how do we know she'll see it?"

"Leave that to me. I'll figure it out. I've already talked her into taking the day off from searching."

"Oh shit, you really are serious."

"Well, somebody needs to fix this craptastic mess, since you two knuckleheads can't. Are you ready?"

"What? You want me to do it now?"

"Duh. I need to make sure you do it right. Plus, it needs to be in the system by tomorrow."

I shake my head and sigh. When Cici puts her mind to something, there's no getting out of it. This I've learned well over the years.

Forty-five minutes later, after completing the about information and uploading a photo, we reach the question section.

Cici bounces on the couch and claps her hands excitedly. "Yay. We're finally to the good part. Hand me your phone."

"Why?"

"So I can ask you the questions and input your answers. It's more fun this way." She smiles.

As I hand it over, Eli laughs and rises from the floor. "Time for another beer?"

"Apparently." I chuckle, then add, "Since my hands are free."

"Okay, first question, oooh, this is good. What are you looking for in a relationship?"

"Faithfulness—"

"No, this is where you make it all about Poppy specifically. So, your answer would go like this: Marriage and babies."

"Seriously?"

She cocks her head to the side. "Do you want this to work or not?"

"Sure. Go for it." I say exasperated, ready to move on.

Eli hands me a beer while chuckling. "Sucks to be you, man."

I give him the finger.

"Okay, what does a successful relationship mean to you?"

"One where my girlfriend's name is Poppy."

"Perfect. You're learning."

I respond by chugging half my beer, wondering if I'm wasting my time or if this harebrained idea has a chance.

"How important is honesty and communication to you in a re-lationship? That's a tough one, considering." She cocks a brow.

"Thanks," I say sarcastically, then hum in concentration. "How about, much more than a month ago?"

"We can just skip this one."

"Wait. How about… Honesty is very important, and putting Bozeman in my profile is the last lie I'll tell."

"Yeah, let's skip it. Next. How important is physical attraction to you? This is where you can put her specific traits that stand out."

"My tastes are particular. I'm attracted to red-haired, freckled, slim girls about five-foot-four with perfect pouty lips and an ass to die for."

"I'm leaving the ass part out." She beams cynically. "How important is it to find someone who shares your hobbies?"

"It's a must. I want someone to read romance novels with, have book discussions, and act out certain scenes with."

"Okay, TMI. I'm cutting you off."

I laugh and down the rest of my beer. I'm having fun for the first time since I left Bozeman. I never expected Cici to be the one to help me get Poppy back, but with her in my corner, I'm more hopeful than I've been in weeks.

"Three more. How do you feel about long-distance relationships?"

"Love them. Five states away is ideal, somewhere on the western side of the country."

She laughs as she types.

"What are your dealbreakers regarding online communication when first contacting someone?"

"If they're unwilling to FaceTime to verify they match their profile."

"Oh boy, we'll see how she takes that one. Ooh, ooh, the last one is perfect. What are your intentions for being on a dating site?"

"To win my girlfriend Poppy back by any means necessary. Groveling until she can't resist me any longer."

Cici squeals in delight as she finishes entering it.

"So, do you think this will work? Because if it backfires, this very well may be my last chance." Until I think of something else, anyway.

"I know it will. We just need her to find your profile—the rest will take care of itself. You might want to fly to Bozeman for that date, though. Eli, do we have a plane he could borrow?" She smirks at her husband, who rolls his eyes.

21

FINAL MATCH

Poppy

S LEEP DIDN'T COME EASILY LAST NIGHT AS I REPLAYED Braden's words. I'd memorized each inscription after staring at them for hours. It was overwhelming to say the least. It was so tempting to call and forgive him. But then I thought about what he had done and ended up right where I started—angry and hurt.

Yes, I'm being stubborn, but I'm allowed to be, dammit. He really messed up. He can't just say a few sweet words and make everything better. He pulled the wool over my eyes. What if he's doing it again?

Deep down, I recognize the excuse it is, because let's be real, he wouldn't put that much effort in if he wasn't serious. I'm miles away, and he could probably have any woman he wants within a twenty-mile radius.

After the books came yesterday, I bawled my eyes out for five minutes, then called Cici. She talked me down from the ledge and convinced me to sit on it for a day before searching for the last date, which I insisted on to see the process through. I'm stubborn when I make a decision.

We said three dates, and it's only been two, so I'll go on one more and *then* decide what to do. So now it's time to search for my final match. I open the app and start scrolling. If I can find someone today, I could schedule for tonight and have it over with sooner rather than later. And as they say, the third time's a charm, so this could be the one.

Even though I come across a few possibilities, I want to go through everyone since this is my last try. I'm almost done looking at all the new prospects when my eyes bug out at the next profile. I bring it closer to make sure I'm not hallucinating.

Nope. That's definitely Braden. What the hell? He can't be serious. This is insane. He has some nerve. Did he not learn his lesson the first time around? I'm skimming through it, about to throw my phone across the room, when the pictures he used stop me in my tracks.

The first one is from Cici's wedding, but the crazy thing is that I'm in it with him. The next is from the weekend he visited, with me as well. Oh my God, I'm in all of them. Wait. I scroll up to actually read his profile this time. Oh. My. God. I'm laughing out loud and partly crying as I go through his answers.

He did this for me. He wanted me to find it. When did he do it, and what if I hadn't come across it? Wait a minute. How did he even know I was on here?

I dial Cici, who picks up on the first ring. "Yessss?"

"Did you tell Braden I was on another dating site?"

"Now why would I do that?" she asks sarcastically.

"Cici. He couldn't have found out unless you told him. You knew about this, didn't you?"

"Okay, it may have slipped. Aaand I might have helped him with his account."

"What the heck?"

"Ugh. You wouldn't read his letters or even give in after you got those books, which, by the way, is the sweetest thing I've ever heard of. I had to do something, and I figured this would speed up the inevitable."

"You little brat. Why didn't you just tell me that?"

"Because this was way more fun. Also, need I remind you how stubborn you are?"

I groan.

"So what are you gonna do?" she asks.

"Open the letters? Or should I call him?"

"Hmmm." She doesn't answer, instead giving me a minute to think out loud.

"I'm so frustrated."

Why did I let this go on so long? We've both been miserable. What he did was wrong, but it might have been my pride that kept me from forgiving him.

"I felt so stupid being duped. And yeah, I sort of understand why he did it in the first place, but he should've stopped when we actually started talking."

She remains quiet.

"Maybe I'll read them. It might help me get past it."

"I think that's a good idea. Decide what to do after that."

"Okay."

"Hey, follow your heart, whichever direction it takes you."

"Thanks, Cici."

I'm a puddle of tears over the next thirty minutes reading through the six letters. He really did grovel, just like his profile said. His sincerity is evident, and I can see how things progressed before it got out of hand. After the first letter explained everything, the rest became more like love letters.

He wrote them as if we were long-distance lovers keeping in touch through the mail. He told me how much he missed me and would fill me in on his daily life. He talked about his past and the relationship that broke him—the woman who cheated on him, which I learned about originally from Owen.

It was Braden the entire time, split into two people. The letters combined both personalities and blended them into one. I'm weeping as I lay the last page down, trying to decide what to do. When I pick up my phone to look at the pictures on his profile again, an idea comes to mind.

Braden

Private jets are the way to go. I arrived by ten this morning and am sitting in a coffee shop near Poppy's house waiting for… well, I'm not exactly sure what for, but I hope whatever it is, that it happens soon. I've been anxious since Cici told me that Poppy found my profile.

Poppy's reading the letters as we speak, according to Cici, and I'm a bundle of nerves, wondering if they'll have the intended effect or backfire. Bringing up the entire situation after she may have been ready to forgive me might not be the best idea, but how can you go forward without putting the past to rest?

After weeks without her, my patience has run out, and if I don't hear something soon, I'll end up at her door, regardless of whether it's a dumb move or not. I can't stay away any longer. I need to hold her, tell her how I feel, beg for forgiveness, and a chance to make it right.

I'm staring into space, eyes fixed on the sidewalk outside, when my phone pings. Hoping it's Cici with an update, I'm surprised to see a message notification from the dating app. A woman would have to be psycho if they saw that profile and still reached out, but I guess some people can't resist a good chase.

Oh, the irony.

When I open it up, though, it's not some psycho woman, it's my woman. I'm out of my seat in a flash, practically running as I type my response.

> Poppy: It says you like to read. What's your favorite book?

> Braden: Whatever my girlfriend is reading.

> Poppy: If you have a girlfriend, why are you on a dating site?

> Braden: To get her back.

> Poppy: What happens if you do?

Braden: Then I make it up to her in the best way possible.

Poppy: Such as?

Braden: Me, on my knees, willing to do whatever it takes.

Poppy: What if you're too far away for that?

Braden: We could always FaceTime.

Poppy: What if she won't? It says that's a deal-breaker for you.

Braden: What's your deal-breaker?

I need to keep her talking until I'm at her door.

Poppy: Someone who poses as someone they're not.

Braden: So are you up for a FaceTime to prove we're who we say we are?

Poppy: We probably should.

Braden: Give me a few seconds to ring through.

I stand in place and hold my phone up to dial.

She picks up after three rings, and I'm instantly relieved at the sight of her face with a shy smile to go with it.

"Hi," she says quietly.

"Hey, beautiful. I've missed you."

"I've missed you too."

Those are the best words I could ever hope to hear, and my heart grows ten sizes.

"Then let me in."

"Wait. What?" She squints into the screen, bringing it closer to her face. "Is that… Are you?"

I can tell she's getting up by the movement on the screen, and a few seconds later, her front door is thrown open.

"You're here!"

Her gorgeous smile tells me all I need to know, and without

hesitation, I plow into her, enveloping her in my arms, kicking the door shut behind me.

"God, how I've missed you," I say into her neck.

She laughs. "I can't believe you're here. How did you do this? You just… oh my God, you just… came."

I lean back and cradle her face in my hands. "I'll visit as often as it takes, just give us a chance. I want you in my life. I want everything with you. I *only*. Want. You. I'll do anything to make you believe that because I love you, Poppy."

I don't allow her to respond in case she feels obligated to say it back. Instead, my lips crash to hers, taking their fill and luxuriating in what they've been denied for too long. The passion is returned wholeheartedly as she matches me with each stroke of our tongues.

Before we're out of hand, I need to clear the air, so I pull away. Her disappointed whine causes me to chuckle.

"We'll get back to that, I promise. But first, I'm so sorry, Poppy. I mean it. I don't ever want to hurt you or lie to you again. Please believe me when I tell you how truly sorry I am for deceiving you. I don't regret what I did because it brought us together, but I am sorry I kept it going."

I kiss her chastely before continuing, "I want this to work. I want a relationship with you. I don't know how that looks, but I'll do whatever it takes if you give us a chance."

I finally stop talking to let her respond, still afraid that what she says won't be what I want to hear, but I can't prolong the inevitable. Besides, even if she doesn't want this, that doesn't mean I'm giving up.

"Anything?" she asks coyly.

"Anything."

"You'd move to Bozeman, get married, and start making babies right away?"

My eyes widen, and I'm about to say yes, when she puts her finger over my mouth and giggles. "I'm kidding."

"You had me at making babies."

She giggles again.

"I love you, too, you horndog. Now pick me up and take me to bed so you can make up properly."

I pause for a moment, soaking in the three most important words that just made everything right in the world.

"Yes, ma'am," I say, scooping her into my arms.

Epilogue

LAST QUEEN STANDING

Braden and Poppy
One Year Later

POPPY ADDS THE FINISHING TOUCHES TO HER MAKEUP WHILE getting ready for dinner with Braden. She's nervous since it's their one-year anniversary. They've talked about marrying, but she's trying not to get her hopes up that he'll propose tonight. She's already done that and learned her lesson the hard way.

If it happens, it happens. If it doesn't—she's sure he'll ask her eventually. But the clock *is* ticking. Mia's pregnant and Cici and Lily are hoping to be soon. She'd love to be alongside them, starting her own family.

The last twelve months have been quite the roller-coaster. After Braden won her back, they continued their long-distance relationship for six months while taking turns visiting each other. Soon, Poppy found herself wanting to be in San Diego, instead of the other way around so she could see her friends there.

Though she loved having Grayson home and will always be close with Matt, the minute those two became buddies, she often felt like the third wheel. Talk about wingmen—they must have gone through every woman in Bozeman by now.

So, when Braden suggested they take the next step and move in together, there was no question where Poppy's heart was and where she wanted to be. It's been six months of true bliss, and the only thing that would complete the picture is a ring on her finger. Well, and a bun in the oven. But first things first.

Braden stops dead in his tracks when she turns the corner. On nights out like this, he still pauses to appreciate her in all her glory. She's always beautiful in his eyes of course, but when she does herself up, she's a sight to behold.

The long, fitted dress accentuates her curves in all the right places, and her gorgeous red locks pinned up on one side allows for the perfect view of her delicious neck he loves to devour.

"You look incredible, Mouse. I swear, I'm the luckiest guy alive."

"You're not too shabby yourself, *Suits*." She still likes to tease him with the nickname she gave him when spotting him for the first time, while *he* secretly thinks those characters don't do him justice. She would agree.

They're dressed to the nines for their one-year celebration, although Braden has kept the evening a secret. After helping her into a light jacket, Braden grabs their overnight bag and leads her outside to the car waiting at the curb.

Once they're settled, Poppy can't help but ask, "So, where are we headed?"

"Nice try, Mouse. You'll see soon enough. But we should make use of the time on the way," he says cheekily as he squeezes her exposed thigh from the slit at her leg.

"Don't you dare. I'm not messing up this dress. I'm sure we'll have plenty of that later."

Poppy knows there will be, because that's the part she has her own special surprise for, and another reason he'll have to wait.

"You're denying me? Since when does that happen?" he asks incredulously.

"Since you won't tell me where we're going. Fair is fair."

"How does one have to do with the other?"

"So how is your new case going?" She ignores the question, changing the subject instead.

She's well acquainted with Braden's tactics, and it wouldn't surprise her if he were able to persuade her to do something on the way. She's also aware that it wouldn't take much to convince her. Better to play it safe.

"We've almost nailed down where the money's been siphoned, so we can retrieve her share of the assets. Hopefully, she'll end up with more now that we have proof of his indiscretions."

She shakes her head. "I can't believe the amount of cheating and money laundering that goes on with that level of wealth. It's crazy to me."

Braden shrugs. "It's not just the rich—it's everyone. People in all walks of life are dirtbags, but the wealthy are the ones who can afford to prove it, so that's what we hear about."

She nods her head, silently contemplating. She's proud of Braden and his high morals regarding whom he takes on as a client. It's something she's always admired about him. It's no wonder he's taking so long to propose, seeing broken marriages and unfaithful spouses day in and day out.

Braden understands more than anyone how marriage can end badly, but witnessing his friends find their wives and how happy they are has helped him realize it's possible. He wants that with Poppy—has for a while now—but he was waiting for the ideal moment. After months of planning, Braden's excited to unveil a special proposal for Poppy tonight.

When the car pulls up to the Hotel del Coronado, Poppy turns to Braden, beaming. "Oh my gosh, this was such a good idea. I can't believe I didn't think of it myself."

"This is where it all began, so it seemed fitting that we celebrate our one-year anniversary here."

Could he be any more perfect? She muses, thinking how lucky she is.

After checking in and sending the bags to the room, they leisurely stroll to the restaurant hand in hand. Poppy can't help the butterflies in her stomach in anticipation of what might be coming.

Although the evening is romantic and the meal is terrific, her excitement vanishes by the time Braden pays the check, and her hope has deflated. She tries not to let it show, but Braden can tell she's disappointed and smiles to himself.

He stands and reaches for her hand. "Hey, since it's such a beautiful night, and I have a gorgeous woman on my arm, what do you think about walking down Orange Avenue and grabbing some ice cream before we turn in?"

"Ooh, I like that idea. Let's do it." She smiles, her missed proposal all but forgotten.

He can always win her over with ice cream, which will distract her until the next part of the evening.

They each get a scoop and continue their walk, looking at all the shops. Coronado might not be far, but it seems like a different world from where they live, making them feel like they're on vacation.

Two blocks down, the ice cream has been devoured, and Braden pauses outside a bookstore. "Hey, they're open for another five minutes. Let's pop in and look for a book," he suggests while casually sending a text.

"Okay," Poppy happily responds, always up for perusing a bookstore, since it's one of her favorite things to do. They've made a tradition of buying two copies of whatever book they choose and reading side by side every night. Braden's favorite part is acting out the spicy scenes, and Poppy secretly agrees.

He pulls her toward the back of the empty store. "I'm in the mood for a romantasy. What do you think?"

"Sure. You know me, I'm up for anything."

Braden looks at her with raised brows, prompting her to roll her eyes.

Poppy laughs. "You know what I mean."

They never brought anyone else into bed with them again and decided they were happy that way. They don't regret their one-time threesome but don't have any desire to do it again.

While Poppy's busy browsing, Braden nudges her toward a display next to the shelf. "Hey, isn't that the fourth book in our series?" Meaning the one they began that first fateful day, three thousand miles in the air.

"Oh my God, it is. I didn't even know it was out yet." Poppy snatches *Last Queen Standing* from the table and flips it over to look. Meanwhile, Braden picks up the other.

"Should we buy these? It looks like they only have two copies," he says.

"But she'll be sending them to us. Shouldn't we wait for hers?" she asks, referring to the author who didn't forget the couple who used her books to reconcile their relationship.

"Nah. Then we'd have to wait to read it, and I'm too anxious to hear how the story ends."

She shrugs. "Okay, we can always pass them on when we're finished."

"Let's look at what her dedication says. Maybe she mentioned us," Braden suggests teasingly.

"Yeah, right, I don't think we're that important." Poppy scoffs but opens it anyway.

As soon as she reaches the page, her head pops up in shock, and tears begin to form.

"Read it," Braden tells her.

Poppy can barely see the words; her eyes are so watery. However, she does notice Braden lower to his knee beside her while reaching into his pocket. Her heart starts thumping.

"Read it out loud," he instructs softly, returning her focus to the book. He's excited for this part after working directly with the author to have two books specially printed with his personal inscription inside and then getting the bookstore to set them out prior to arriving.

"Oh my God. Okay. *You stand before me as the love of my life, but will you stand beside me as my queen? Forever yours, Braden.*" Her tears are falling freely now as she sniffles and wipes her eyes.

She starts to ask, "Did you—"

"Marry me, Poppy. Make me feel like a king by saying yes to becoming my queen."

She lowers to her knees as she utters the word "yes" repeatedly, completely ignoring the ring he's holding. Their kiss is passionate, full of love and promises.

Braden is the first to pull back. "Hey, are you ready for your ring now?"

Poppy laughs, happiness radiating from every cell in her body. "Yes." She looks down at his hand and gasps. "Holy shit, Braden, it's huge."

"Well, you're used to big things. I had to make sure it was up to par." He wags his brows.

She shoves his shoulder. "Stop it."

"Give me your hand. Let's make this official."

Seconds later, the ring is in place as they rise from the floor.

"You know what this means, don't you?" Braden asks Poppy inconspicuously.

"What?"

"It's baby-making time." Braden's brows go up and down again, causing Poppy to laugh.

"Well, you can practice, but it doesn't happen overnight. I need to be off birth control first."

"Oh, don't worry, I plan on practicing a lot, Mouse. In fact, let's go get started."

She giggles as he ushers her toward the door.

They can't seem to go fast enough. With their books safely wrapped and in a shopping bag, their steps become quicker and quicker, eager for what comes next.

Poppy still can't believe how perfect the night turned out and almost forgets about the surprise she has underneath until they rush into the bedroom.

"Wait… wait," she pants out between the frantic kisses Braden bestows while leading her to the bed.

He pulls back abruptly in concern. "Why? What's wrong? I thought you were just as eager to consummate our engagement."

"Consummation is for the wedding," she corrects with a giggle. "This would be celebrating. But first, I have a present for you."

"Can you give it to me after we're done celebrating?" He frowns, causing her to smile.

"Nope. Turn around so I can go grab it."

He growls in frustration but does as instructed. No isn't in his vocabulary when it comes to Poppy. "You're killing me, Mouse. My cock is so ready that he might hold this against you."

"We'll see what he thinks after the surprise." She goes to the closet to act as if she's getting something so he won't hear her remove the dress, which she hurries to do, leaving her shoes on.

She's excited for the big reveal but also self-conscious as she stares at herself in the mirror. She's never worn sexy lingerie before and isn't sure if she can pull it off. She feels like an imposter trying to be someone she's not.

With a final calming breath, she exits and clears her throat. "You can turn around now."

The instant he does, his lungs quit working. Is this the woman he just proposed to moments ago, or has she been replaced with a siren? There's no way this is his mouse—the shy girl who blushes every time he spanks her ass cheek or uses the word pussy.

She's not sure what to make of his silence, whether he's trying to hold back from laughing or if he likes it. If he doesn't say anything soon, she's going back to the closet and stripping out of her humiliating attempt to be sexy.

She should have known better. This isn't her. She's… boring and nothing like what he was used to having before her. Poppy doesn't usually let Braden's past reputation bother her, but at a time like this, it's impossible not to wonder if she's not enough.

"It's ridiculous, isn't it? I'll take it off." She begins to turn around but quickly freezes at his command.

"Don't you dare move. That is the sexiest damn thing I've ever laid eyes on, and I just need a moment to soak it in."

He's never seen her in anything like that. The netted full-body catsuit and high heels have his dick leaking in appreciation. He reaches down to adjust his cock, which is suddenly rock-hard and painfully constricted.

Poppy notices and, feeling a little braver now that he appears to appreciate her purchase, cocks her hip and offers to help. "Would you like a hand with that?"

"I've got a better idea." He unbuckles his belt. "Let's start with your mouth." His cock bounces free as he lowers his pants, then strokes himself as he tells her what to do. "I want you to walk to the end of the bed, so I can enjoy the view, then stop and crawl to me on your hands and knees."

He was so turned on from the moment he laid eyes on her that he couldn't help but become a beast. He also knows Poppy secretly likes a little degradation, and with that outfit, that's precisely what he'll give her.

He continues jerking his cock in anticipation as she lowers to the ground and crawls toward him. She moves slowly to prolong the show, making his balls bluer by the second. By the time she's nearly to him with her sexy ass in the air, wiggling side to side, he almost changes course and plunges into her from behind, but the image of her servicing him while in that getup has him holding out.

When she stops before him, she looks up, awaiting instruction. Poppy prefers when he takes control and tells her exactly what to do. It's her favorite way to play and always has her panting for more.

"Up on your knees, hands behind your back," he orders.

She's practically dizzy from desire, his dominance causing her to pant in lust.

"Open up, Little Mouse. Show me that tongue."

Poppy does as instructed, eager to please.

"Thatta girl." He taps his cock against her outstretched tongue a few times before moving in and out by only an inch. Poppy starts to close her mouth. "Keep it open until I say."

Bringing his hand up, he spits into it and coats his cock in saliva. "Now wrap those pretty lips around it and suck."

She eagerly obeys, thankful for the slick surface, as she watches his face for signs of pleasure. She's rewarded the minute she closes around it with a lustful groan from Braden as she slides down his member.

"Goddamn, Poppy, you're so fucking sexy. I'll never tire of seeing you on your knees. You're such a good girl, following directions."

He lets her set the pace at first, enjoying the show while allowing her to get comfortable. A few minutes into it, though, he's done holding back. "All right, beautiful, time's up. You're going to take what I give you now."

Braden fists her hair and grabs her chin. "Hold still, sweet thing," he says right before he starts thrusting, head thrown back in ecstasy. "Fuck, Poppy. Your mouth is incredible. I could come so easily, but there's only one place my cum is going from now on, and that's inside your fertile pussy."

His words cause her to clench with need. She wishes more than anything she'd already stopped birth control, but she was holding off until he proposed. Now, they'll have to wait for the shot to wear off.

He pulls out abruptly. "Fuck, that was close."

She stares up at him as she catches her breath, waiting for instruction as her pussy aches for relief.

"Come here, Mouse." He helps her stand before asking, "Is it your turn?"

"Yes, please."

"What would you like?"

"Will you finger me?"

"I will, but first, why don't you lie down and take care of yourself.

Let me enjoy the view a little longer. I promise I'll make it worth your while."

"Okay." Poppy loves when he has her do this. It always results in the best orgasm, and she likes to watch Braden stare at her with lust-filled eyes as she does.

She crawls onto the bed, lying her head on top of the pillows with her pussy facing Braden as he removes his clothing.

"Spread those legs nice and wide for me. Show me everything."

Luckily, the netted full-body suit is crotchless for this reason exactly.

As Poppy touches herself, she realizes she doesn't need any lubrication since she's already soaking, dipping her fingers into her core, and bringing the moisture up to where she needs it.

Braden strokes himself as he stares between her legs, and as she watches, the feeling she's chasing skyrockets to put her right at the edge.

"Braden, oh God, don't stop, I'm about to..."

"Let me see it, Poppy. I'll finger fuck you so good as soon as you come."

His words, in addition to the sight of him rubbing his cock, have her crashing into her climax, moaning in ecstasy. But when his fingers plunge inside and he laps at her folds, her moans turn into screams, bringing her to the next level.

"Fuck, baby, that's it. Damn, you're sexy as fuck when you come." He loves when she falls apart, her pussy pulsing as her orgasm takes over, and watching her face as she loses control—there's nothing quite like it.

"Oh my God, Braden. That was…"

"A wonderful appetizer." He moves up to kiss her passionately, fondling her breast.

A second later, the head of his cock finds her entrance, and without hesitation, he plunges to the hilt. Poppy cries out in pleasure.

"God, your pussy feels so good."

"Yes, Braden. Please, more."

"You need me to fuck you hard, baby?"

"Yes. Oh, God, yes." She loves when he gives her everything he's got and doesn't hold back.

"Then turn over for me."

He pulls out and helps her flip over. He never tires of this view. Her back curved, waiting for his touch. He caresses her butt while pushing her upper body to the bed, then brings his hand down in a loud slap.

"That's it, baby. Stick that ass out so I can give you what you need."

He lines up and rubs the head up and down her slit. "You ready, Mouse? I'm gonna fuck you so hard. Gonna fill you with cum until you're dripping."

"Please…"

"Please, what?"

"Fuck me. Hard."

Without another word, he bottoms out in one thrust, grunting with force and offering no pause before repeating the movement again and again. He pushes so deep her pussy opens fully, drinking him in each time.

Braden fucks her relentlessly, with no reprieve until his climax approaches. He grabs a fistful of her hair and hauls her torso up as he sits back on his haunches.

"Is this what you wanted?"

"Yes," Poppy pants out.

"Good. Now give me one more orgasm. I need to feel you squeeze my cock. I want you milking every drop of cum until you're full of me."

His hand slides down, circling his fingers over her clit while kissing her neck and continuing to fuck her. Less than a minute later, she reaches her peak, bringing Braden with her.

Her pussy contracts around his cock, milking him exactly as he wanted. He folds over, forcing her to the bed again as he releases deep inside.

"Fuck, fuck, fuck," he chants in tune to his thrusts as his orgasm takes over. "That's it. I'm filling you up. I'll fuck you every night until you're pregnant with our child."

Their combined cries of pleasure continue as he rides out his climax. After the last pulse, they tumble to the side, Braden holding her close.

"Wow. Just wow." Poppy says a minute later, after they've caught their breath and her heart has slowed.

"No kidding. We'll have to do this every night, you know. Babies don't make themselves."

Poppy giggles. "We pretty much already do. But regardless, I can't even get pregnant until my birth control wears off."

"We'll have to keep practicing then."

"Don't you think we should be more concerned about planning a wedding first?" Poppy doesn't have any qualms about doing things backwards, but she doesn't necessarily want to be pregnant in her wedding dress.

"No way. Baby-making can definitely happen alongside that part. When I first met you, I distinctly remember you saying you were way behind in that regard—no time like the present." He kisses her head right before she flips around to face him.

"So you're ready to marry me next month?"

"Baby, I would've married you last year. I was just waiting for those damn books to come out so I could propose."

She smiles. "That was the sweetest proposal ever, by the way. I can't believe you arranged all that. You're amazing."

"Tell me something I don't know." Braden smirks as Poppy shoves his shoulder.

"But seriously, even if I got pregnant right when my shot wears off, I wouldn't show yet for another three months, so maybe we could plan a June wedding. And by then the weather will be warmer."

"And by warm weather, you mean back home?"

They've had conversations about where to get married. Poppy

chose Bozeman since she grew up there and it's where her parents and brother are.

"Is that okay still?"

"I'm good with whatever it takes to make you mine. But the short answer is, yes, anything for my future queen. A Montana wedding it is."

She squeals in delight as he cups her cheeks and brings her in for another passionate kiss. June can't arrive soon enough.

Acknowledgments

I hope you enjoyed Braden's story as much as I enjoyed writing it. These two characters were fun to imagine. From book one, I always thought there was more to Braden than the jerk he was portrayed as, and I'm glad we were finally able to see what made him tick.

This group of friends has come a long way, and I'm sad that they are nearing the end of their story. The good news is I have one left, dying to be told. Matt will see his happily ever after in the sixth and final book in The Pursuit Series.

I still can't believe I've made it to book five. Five books! When the idea came to me to write Pursuit of Innocence, I never imagined I'd continue writing or that I'd end up with six books in two years. But when readers kept asking about other characters and what happens to them, I couldn't resist telling their stories.

As for getting better in the process of publishing, that's a work in progress. This one is going the smoothest, by far, so I must be getting the hang of it. I want to roll back the clock, though, and thank someone from way back in the beginning who I've thought about a lot lately and have realized how much she helped me when I needed it the most.

Polly from My Word Publishing was a godsend when I was green and didn't know a thing about getting my book out in the world. She walked me through, step by step, how to market and publish for the first time, and to this day, I'm still referring to the advice and lessons she gave.

Another person who has been with me from day one is my graphic design artist, Jolene, who consistently creates the masterpieces that grace my covers. She's also the first one who filled my head with the idea of more—more Jackson, more Eli, more Cici, and so on. I can't thank her enough for her support and friendship. I'm lucky to have her in my life.

Since I'm on the theme of people from the beginning, Cassie, my daughter, who also serves as my PA, PR specialist, promotions manager, and event coordinator, is my MVP. She truly does everything except write and publish the book, so essentially, none of you would know who I am or have discovered this series without her. So thank you, Cassie.

A big thanks goes out to Abby, another daughter, who is one of the best alpha readers I know. I'm so grateful for an honest source to critique my stories and give me ideas for improvement, along with the encouragement I need to keep going when I feel like I have no idea what I'm doing.

My sister-in-law, Kaley, is another alpha reader whom I can make the identical statement as above, so I will. Thank you so much for your honest and encouraging feedback. I honestly couldn't do this without it.

A big thank you to my beta team, who were hand-picked through my ARC readers, along with the last-minute addition of my niece, Bri. Christie, Mary, Stephanie, and Sarah—you all provided excellent critiques, and each of your perspectives was more helpful than you can imagine.

A local writing group has become dear to me, comprised of fellow authors, both new and established. Christina, Terra, Melissa, Laurynn, and Halie: you have kept me writing when my days are filled with procrastination. I'm so grateful for this wonderful group of ladies that has become a staple in my life.

A couple of staples that I must mention are Hot Tree Editing, for their impeccable system and quick turnaround times. Champagne Formatting took over around book two, and I've been loving my beautiful interiors ever since. Thank you, Stacey, for accommodating me despite my late scheduling and all the corrections you've put up with, turning them out in record time. I do believe this is the first book that I won't have any. Knock on wood.

And last but not least, the love of my life, John. Your encouragement and praise are by far the greatest of anyone. I'll forgive you for not reading a word of my books because you blindly tell me how wonderful I am at writing them, regardless.

Read Cici and Eli's story in *Pursuit of Love*, book four in
The Pursuit Series.

**They say if you love something, let it go… but what if letting
go is the very thing that breaks you? How far will love take you
when the road keeps twisting?**

Loving Cici was easy. Keeping her was the hard part.

I thought if I let her go, she'd come back when she was ready. I
didn't expect her to take my heart with her.
Being gifted a second chance was the prayer I'd been hoping for.
Until it all fell apart again when a question she wasn't ready for, met
an answer I didn't want to hear.
Now she's gone.
And I'm engaged to someone else for all the wrong reasons.

Loving Eli was easy. Staying was the hard part.

If only my heart and head weren't at war. But now he's in a coma,
and the secret I carry is becoming impossible to hide.
He's trying to remember what we were—what we are, and
why he ever let me go. But the silence between us says more
than the truth ever could.
Because love doesn't always wait for clarity. And sometimes,
remembering isn't the hard part—choosing what to do with it is.

It all began with Sebastian and Lily's story in
Pursuit of Innocence, book one in
The Pursuit Series

"I'm done waiting around. You're mine. No more games or pining over someone else when it's me you want. You won't remember his name after I get through with you."

Lily knows exactly what she wants in life. To graduate, land a high-paying job, and forge her own way. Nothing will distract her. Until the ultimate playboy, billionaire Sebastian Dubree, barges in. Not to be overlooked, Lily's longtime crush, Jackson, decides she's worth the fight.

Reluctant to succumb to either, she quickly becomes a challenge to conquer. Lily must decide between the familiarity of her childhood longing or the newly discovered passion ignited by the dominant CEO. But can she surrender without losing herself in the process, or will someone take matters into his own hands?

Boundaries blur between desire and resistance in this gripping coming-of-age romance, leaving readers yearning for more.

Visit bethanyrosa.com or scan below for a link to explore other books in *The Pursuit Series*

Ready for a fun, holiday novella in The Pursuit Series?
Check out Lucy and Justin's story in *Holidate Pursuit*.

**Do I have a sign on my back that says, 'Love her and leave her'?
Because that's what it feels like these days.**

I thought I'd never see Justin again when he ghosted me after the best night of my life. But guess who shows up at the company Christmas party months later wanting to talk? I don't think so Mr. Burns. Burn me once, shame on you. Burn me twice, shame on me. That's sober Lucy talking. Drunk Lucy has a different idea—she asks him to stand in as my fake fiancé this Christmas. Thank God he's smart enough to say no… or is he?

One week. One bed. How could I resist?

I had my reasons for disappearing on Lucy, and I've regretted it ever since. So, when the opportunity presents itself, I can't refuse my shot at redemption. Just as it starts to feel like a second chance, the tree comes crashing down.

Filled with humor, heart, and holiday magic, Holidate Pursuit is a fun, steamy romance about second chances and choosing love over all else.

To purchase this or other books in the extremely hot Pursuit Series,
visit www.bethanyrosa.com
or simply scan the barcode below.

Did you miss Jackson and Mia in *Dangerous Pursuit,*
book three in *The Pursuit Series?*

Mia Nightingale Marcos is more nightmare than nightingale.

I'm handed the reins to the family business along with an
inexperienced assistant barely out of high school. Not to mention,
she's distractingly beautiful and completely off-limits. I plan to be
so unbearable she'll quit, but she's tougher than she looks. Now
she appears to be hiding something and the deeper I dig, the more
invested I become, causing my world to spin.

Just when I think I've got her figured out, she vanishes,
leaving a trail of unanswered questions, sending me on
a dangerous pursuit.

Jackson Soloman is the boss from hell.

But I can handle him. Balancing work by day and poker by
night was a breeze until Jackson stepped in. It was easier
when he was making my life hell, not trying to play hero.
Now, I can't shake him off, and with the growing attraction
between us, I'm not sure I want to.

Just when I think I've hit the jackpot, I'm forced to fold, leaving
everything behind for a chance at salvation.

Will Mia and Jackson survive the trials of deceit and danger that lie ahead? In a heart-wrenching climax that tests their love and commitment, every decision could be their last bet.

Visit bethanyrosa.com or scan below to explore book three, *Dangerous Pursuit,* in the unbelievably hot *Pursuit Series.*

If you'd like to learn more about author Bethany Rosa or keep up on recent releases, visit www.BethanyRosa.com

Or scan below: